MW01505751

Praise for
New York Times and USA Today Bestselling Author

Diane Capri

"Full of thrills and tension, but smart and human, too."
*Lee Child, #1 New York Times Bestselling Author of Jack
Reacher Thrillers*

"[A] welcome surprise....[W]orks from the first page to 'The
End'."
Larry King

"Swift pacing and ongoing suspense are always
present...[L]ikable protagonist who uses her political
connections for a good cause...Readers should eagerly anticipate
the next [book]."
Top Pick, Romantic Times

"...offers tense legal drama with courtroom overtones, twisty
plot, and loads of Florida atmosphere. Recommended."
Library Journal

"[A] fast-paced legal thriller...energetic prose...an appealing
heroine...clever and capable supporting cast...[that will] keep
readers waiting for the next [book]."
Publishers Weekly

"Expertise shines on every page."
*Margaret Maron, Edgar, Anthony, Agatha and Macavity Award
Winning MWA Past President*

SECRET JUSTICE

by *DIANE CAPRI*

Published by: AugustBooks
http://www.AugustBooks.com

ISBN: 978-1-940768-37-3

Original cover design by Michelle Preast
Interior layout by Author E.M.S.

Secret Justice (formerly titled *Harper's Hell*) is a work of fiction, revised from the previously released novel by M. Diane Vogt, *Gasparilla Gold*. Names, characters, places, and incidents either are the product of the author's imagination or are used fictitiously, and any resemblance to actual persons, living or dead, business establishments, events, or locales is entirely coincidental.

Published in the United States of America.

Visit the author website:
http://www.DianeCapri.com

ALSO BY DIANE CAPRI

CAST OF PRIMARY CHARACTERS

Judge Wilhelmina Carson

James Harper
Suzanne Harper

Margaret Wheaton
Ronald Wheaton

Armstrong Otter
Dr. Marilee Aymes

Gilbert Kelley
Sandra Kelley

Chief Ben Hathaway
State Attorney Michael Drake
Chief Ozgood Livingston Richardson (Oz or CJ)
Larry Davis

George Carson

For Ophie

SECRET
JUSTICE

Tampa, Florida
Sunday, 3:00 a.m.
February 18, 2001

MIGUEL STRUGGLED TO TURN the corner at Seventh Avenue and Sixteenth Street. He grunted with effort as he pushed a heavy plastic trash barrel on wheels, piled high with garbage. The cleaning crew had been working on the streets in Tampa's Ybor City since the parade ended and the crowd finally dispersed about one a.m. Miguel had a lot of cleanup to do before the small businesses along the brick-paved streets opened.

Who would believe these rich Americans could be such pigs? Miguel thought. In his country where people were poor, maybe, but not in Florida, "land of flowers." In his country, people weren't tidy like they were here, he'd noticed. Tampa was a clean place. Nice. Miguel wanted to stay here, with his father's family. He liked Tampa.

Miguel bent his head to his task, left hand bracing the garbage towering perilously higher than the five-foot barrel should hold. He felt stretched to his limit. He couldn't see the ground in front of the small wheels that seemed to catch on every crack in the old sidewalk

A beer can clattered as it hit the ground. Miguel stooped to pick it up, along with a few candy wrappers that fell off the pile when the barrel stopped rolling. "Pigs," he spat again, as he leaned his weight into the barrel and got it moving again.

Watching the ground as he walked, Miguel tried to stay close to the buildings because the sidewalk sloped toward the street and he couldn't control the trash barrel if the small wheels started downhill.

He wasn't in any mood for delay. He had been picking up beer cans, beads, condoms, half-eaten candy and other human trash from the old urine-stenched streets for the past three hours. Miguel was cold and tired. His eyelids felt heavy, scratchy, when he allowed them to close for a few seconds. He wanted to finish his work as quickly as possible and go home. Miguel gave the barrel a mighty shove and smiled to himself as it began to move more quickly.

Suddenly, the left front wheel of the can struck something on the sidewalk. The force and speed of Miguel's efforts pushed the barrel toward the building on the right. It bumped into the building and bounced back. The rebound blow caught Miguel off guard and nearly knocked him down. Several beer bottles fell to the ground with a loud crash, brown and green glass shards flying everywhere. One sharp edge caught Miguel's cheek and he felt the burning scratch as the piece of glass sailed past.

Wiping the blood off his face with a grimy work glove, Miguel cursed himself for not paying attention. Impatiently, he pushed the heavy barrel, trying to straighten its path again and avoid the problem in the sidewalk. He would clean up the broken glass on the way back, he thought, his anxiety mounting.

Miguel had been on his way to the large dumpster in back of Maria's restaurant so that he could dump the barrel and start again. His boss had yelled at him twice already. Miguel didn't have time to fool around. This was his first week on the job and he was on probation. He couldn't make his boss angry. He needed this job if he was to stay in this country.

Miguel put both hands on the middle of the plastic barrel, braced himself with one foot against the building, and pushed harder.

The trash barrel pivoted on its left wheel. It turned slightly and the right side rolled downhill on the sloped sidewalk. And stopped. Now both front wheels seemed to be stuck by a block of some kind. Miguel wailed in frustration, but the barrel didn't move.

Miguel wanted to make as few of these trips to the dumpster as possible, to finish quickly, make his supervisor proud. But he'd piled the barrel too full. A stupid mistake, he realized too late.

The barrel was close to the building and seemed wedged into a hole or something now. Miguel couldn't back up. Nor could he see in front of the barrel to try to go around the blockage.

Miguel shoved the barrel with all of his strength. Instead of rolling over whatever was blocking its path, the barrel tilted wildly and fell forward, spilling its contents across the sidewalk and into the street.

Shouting a loud stream of Spanish curses, Miguel jumped back as every foul liquid left over from the parade splashed all over his clothes. He swiped ineffectively at the stinky, gooey mess that now covered his overalls. He was drenched through to his tee-shirt and jeans. He could feel the cold as his shirt stuck to his narrow chest.

Still cursing, Miguel walked around to the side, righted the barrel and moved it off the pile of garbage that now covered everything within a two-foot radius. Miguel found the shovel that was knocked off the hook on the side of the barrel when it fell and began to toss the garbage back into the trash can, cursing with every stroke.

On the fourth scoop, his shovel hit something solid on the ground, under the slop the barrel had spewed. The stroke of his shovel against the solid lump jarred his arms sending a sharp pain up to his shoulders. Miguel let out a new and more heartfelt stream of outraged curses.

He bent down from the waist, trying to see what was causing him such a problem without actually touching the disgusting pile. In the vague light from the street lamps, the big lump looked like another pile of garbage. But Miguel thought not. He could see something bright and colorful on the ground. And this pile, even though his trash barrel had been too full, was too high.

Miguel had run across two previous drunken revelers on his route tonight. Now, he could see that this lump on the ground was a third pirate. Causing him so much trouble, making him late. His boss would be very angry. "Americanos!" Miguel spat, giving the lump a sharp, rough nudge with the toe of his heavy work boot. The lump didn't move.

Miguel removed his glove, reached into his pocket for his flashlight. Re-gloved, he stooped down and swept the garbage off the pirate, pushing aside the slop. When Miguel saw the man's costume, his impatience and anger returned. These Americanos seemed to have nothing better to do than to party themselves into a stupor while hard-working Latinos cleaned up after them, he complained under his breath.

"Wake up, señor. Wake up," Miguel said, shaking the man as roughly as he could, given the disparity in their sizes. The drunk didn't stir. Miguel almost left him there then, to sleep it off, but something about the man didn't look right. Miguel bent toward him and shook the pirate again, imploring him to wake up and move along. Just then, the angry supervisor came around the corner.

"Miguel, where the hell are you? We need that can over here, now!" the supervisor shouted in Spanish. He walked toward Miguel, moving quickly. He stopped just before he tripped over the mound on the sidewalk. The supervisor looked down. "What the—?"

"He won't wake up," Miguel said, a sorrowful expression on his face.

"The hell he won't," the supervisor responded. The supervisor had cleaned up after sixteen parades and he knew how to deal with these drunks. He didn't care who they were in real life. On his watch, they were a menace.

The supervisor pushed the pirate hard with his boot. The man's head lolled over loosely, revealing a grey-blonde ponytail bound at the base of his skull with a limp, wet ribbon. Even in the weak ambient light, they could both see the bloody depression in the man's skull where it had been resting on the heavy piece of concrete jutting up out of the sidewalk.

"Miguel, this man is dead," the supervisor shouted. "Who is this guy?"

Frightened now, Miguel shook his head and lifted both hands, palms up. "I don't know. I found him here. I don't know."

When the police officers got to the scene, they checked for identification on the body and found none. Miguel, the supervisor and the rest of the crew were interviewed, but they had no more information to disclose. There had been outrageous revelry that night, but these workers hadn't been part of it. None of them recognized the dead man.

The police labeled him "John Doe" and sent him off to the morgue.

CHAPTER ONE

Tampa, Florida
Friday 7:30 p.m.
January 26, 2001

WHEN I OPENED THE front door of our flat Friday night, Jim Harper stood in the hallway with a smile on his face big enough to light up the Grand Canyon. He said, "This is my daughter, Willa Carson, and her husband, George," introducing us to her.

Then, quickly, before I had time to pretend that my father's unannounced appearance at our home with a woman of any kind wasn't as astounding as, say, the arrival of green men from Mars with ray guns, and as if he was presenting the Queen of England, he bowed slightly at the waist and extended his left arm toward George and me, palm out.

Dad's voice held reverence and awe when he dropped his bombshell. "This is my precious one. Meet Suzanne Harper. My new wife."

An involuntary gasp sprang to my lips and my hand gripped George's arm so tightly my fingers left bruises.

A less sturdy daughter than I, one whose features were unused to strict non-responsiveness, would have collapsed in a dead faint. I've lived thirty-nine years, practiced law for about fifteen of them, and I'm now a United States District Court judge. I have the same full range of emotions as other humans, but my job demands that I refrain from displaying them.

So instead of shouting, "Are you out of your mind?" I smiled and exclaimed and hugged them both. And managed not to vomit.

I was proud of the way I'd behaved because I hadn't embarrassed anyone, especially myself.

Still, the scene's images, and the rest of the awkward evening that followed, intruded into the silent darkness of Friday night as if replaying in a continuous loop.

"My wife, my wife, my wife," I heard as I tossed about on our king-sized bed and raised weary eyelids to glance at the clock every hour while George slept like a hibernating bear.

Both of our ninety-plus-pound Labradors had jumped up on the bed about four o'clock. Harry lay draped over my left leg at the bottom of the bed and my struggles to move him were futile. Meanwhile, Bess lay between George and me, her head on my pillow, blowing disgusting dog-breath into my face with every exhale.

Just as I eventually settled into an uneasy sleep during Saturday morning's wee hours, the sound machine that functioned as my alarm began its violent roaring, a noise more like Big Sur than the gentle lapping of our own Tampa Bay. The racket jarred me back rudely, into events I'd been trying to escape. But I was literally and figuratively trapped. The dogs didn't wiggle so much as an eyebrow.

I opened one bleary eye, saw it was only six o'clock and groaned out loud.

Gasparilla's Parade of Pirates, Tampa's much smaller version of Mardi Gras, would begin in less than two hours. George's restaurant, which is located on the first floor of our home, would be filled with several hundred guests. No mere hurricane in my private life would stop the party.

I punched the off button and dragged my leg out from under a comatose Labrador, rose to a sitting position and allowed my sleepy head to drop onto my chest while I waited for the sharp pains of Labrador-crushed muscles to leave my calf.

"Cheer up," George mumbled, his back to me as he moved slowly to sit on the edge of his side of the bed. "Maybe a pirate will steal you away from all of this."

Had I the energy, I'd have thrown a pillow at him.

The aroma of fresh coffee sidled into the bedroom then like the scent of a hot meal finding the nose of a starving hobo. A divine bouquet strong enough to lift me to my feet.

I shuffled into the kitchen, belting my robe, then rubbing sleep from my heavy, tired eyes. It was impossible not to notice her—Suzanne Harper. My father's new wife. I'm pretty sure I groaned out loud.

"Morning, Willa," she chirped, in her sweet, high-pitched voice. She prattled on, barely stopping to breathe. "Fresh coffee in the pot. I found eggs and cheese in your refrigerator, so we should have a baked omelet in a few minutes. I hope you don't mind that I brought in the paper. I'm so excited about my first Gasparilla parade! I couldn't sleep! This is all just so fabulous!"

The last exclamation point was too much, too early, too nice.

My mind clicked off and refused to register her chatter after that.

I reached into the cabinet for my favorite "I hate mornings" mug and filled it with black coffee. Sitting at the end of the kitchen table, I watched Suzanne as she babbled on, her stream of words tumbling over my sullen resistance, wearing me down like water on a stone.

Incredibly, Suzanne was as beautiful this morning as she had been last night. Her long, artfully streaked blonde hair was softly curled. It fell attractively around narrow shoulders wrapped in a lavender warm-up suit sporting a designer logo on the breast pocket. The white tee-shirt under her silk jacket had the same logo in the center, and molded to her slender but full-breasted frame. She wore lavender sneakers to match. Her eyes fairly sparkled with a level of excitement usually exhibited by children under the age of six.

I, on the other hand, sat with my short auburn hair matted to my head and green eyes barely open, feeling older and even less attractive than I surely appeared.

My negative comparisons didn't stop there.

I barely had my skin on at this outrageous hour, while Suzanne's makeup was perfectly applied to her flawless complexion. Except for the glossy lavender lipstick inside the deep purple lip liner on her full mouth. There should be a law against such foolish lipstick being worn by a grown woman.

That was the problem, I realized again, as soon as the uncharitable thought entered my mind. She was twenty-three years old, but in no other way did she remotely resemble a grown woman.

No, Suzanne was a sweet, engaging, loveable, childlike waif. Did that make my situation better? Or was it worse? Definitely worse, I decided immediately.

If only I could've hated her on the spot.

I dropped my head back into my hands.

My father, Jim Harper, was a cliché. He'd married a woman

less than half his age. Hell, she wasn't much more than half *my* age.

Everything about her screamed trophy wife.

The prospect of introducing the two of them to all of our friends today made me nauseous again. My inner adolescent was alive and well, wailing, "How could you do this to me?" while my adult self had the grace to be ashamed of such thoughts. I was on edge and exhausted. The very idea of the long celebration ahead felt overwhelming.

George entered the kitchen then, followed by both dogs. He grinned crookedly in response to Suzanne's incessant drivel. When he sat down next to me with his coffee, he nodded in my direction and I flashed him a weak smile in return.

Dad came in shortly afterward and kissed me on the cheek. "Morning, Jim," George said, his nose buried in the newspaper, when Dad clapped him on the shoulder before approaching Suzanne.

Dad's precious one managed to silence her lips to receive his long and soulful kiss, a kiss that seemed to go on forever. The sight of their total immersion in the greeting caused my hands to shake as I drew the coffee cup to my mouth and looked away.

Beads of sweat broke out on my brow. Our tiny kitchen became so crowded all of a sudden that I struggled to stand, mumbled a lame excuse and escaped, confident that no one noticed my departure.

Gasparilla month, continued downhill from there.

CHAPTER TWO

Tampa, Florida
Saturday 9:30 a.m.
January 27, 2001

AN HOUR LATER, I'D forced myself downstairs to George's restaurant, not quite ready to join the party in progress. I knew the day would be a lengthy one, but I was physically and emotionally drained by my father's unexpected appearance, with a new child-bride, no less. As I went about the business of playing hostess, I didn't fully comprehend the import of what seemed to be mundane, unrelated events.

My gaze roamed the crowd. Members and guests of the social and service club George had founded, called "Minaret Krewe," were gathered everywhere, practically standing on top of each other.

Minaret Krewe is one of the more than thirty social clubs, or "krewes," that participate in Gasparilla month events. Older krewes, with membership rosters as diverse as the Tampa population, had been doing so for a hundred years. At least two krewes consist entirely of women members while others celebrate the area's Latin history or its African-American traditions. Because of Tampa's connection to President Teddy Roosevelt, there's even a krewe of Rough Riders.

Minaret Krewe is one of the newer ones. They named themselves after our historic home, called Minaret because of the large, steel onion dome on the top. Today, several hundred members and their guests would filter through the restaurant, beginning with breakfast and continuing until after midnight snacks.

Professional makeup artists, hired by the Krewe to transform its members into ferocious sea robbers and tawdry wenches for today's parade, were hard at work near the staircase.

A few guests had already begun the day's heavy drinking with mimosas, bloody Marys and several varieties of frozen coladas. Long before midnight, our home and all of Tampa would be filled with drunken revelers. There was nothing to be done except to join them.

With weary resignation, I bowed my head and asked quickly for an event way too busy for quiet chats with my father or his new bride. And for a while, my entreaty was granted.

Mid-morning, about seven hundred members of Ye Mystic Krewe stacked onto their barge made over to look like a pirate ship. *José Gasparilla* landed at the Tampa Convention Center and took over the city while the party at our house continued unabated. I managed to avoid Dad and Suzanne, although I caught a glimpse of them from time to time and they seemed to be enjoying themselves.

George provided traditional Gasparilla fare, nonstop food and refreshments appeared throughout the day. Cuban sandwiches and Ybor Gold beer, brewed locally in Ybor City, were available. For those seeking a full meal, there were black beans and yellow rice, George's version of the famous *1905 Salad*, and several other Cuban dishes.

Café con leche, the rich, Cuban coffee heavily laced with heated milk, flowed as freely as the beer. My caffeine of choice, I'd had a cup of that coffee in my hand the entire morning.

I glimpsed only portions of the Parade of Pirates on the television in the Sunset Bar. Parade floats populated by pirates, wenches, beauty queens, Rotary, Lions and Kiwanis members, politicians and sports figures passed slowly by the television camera. High school marching bands filled the gaps between the krewes.

The local news anchor had dressed like a crusty buccaneer and joined the parade. From time to time, he interviewed a few of the half-million or so spectators lining the sidewalks along Bayshore Boulevard.

Most parade watchers were dressed in heavy coats, hats and gloves. Mother Nature, apparently out of sorts, had decided the high today would be forty-three degrees. What warmth the sun provided was overcome by the gusty, cold wind. I shivered in sympathy, hands folded at the elbows, providing my own warmth and glad to be inside.

When I turned away from the television, two of my favorite people in the world were standing next to me. "I'm so glad you could come," I said to Margaret Wheaton as I hugged first her and then her husband. "I haven't seen you in weeks, Ron. How are you feeling?"

Margaret, my secretary and good friend, looked tired and older than her sixty-something years. She is a kind person, always helping, never asking much for herself. At work, Margaret seemed to be handling her husband's terminal illness with compassion and very little fuss. Only someone who knew her as well as I did would have noticed the toll on her.

"As well as can be expected," Ron replied to my question. He held my hand, with little strength. "Thank you for inviting us today. I don't go to many parties." He said this without self-pity, but it made me sad just the same. "Who knows how many Gasparillas I have left?" Anyone could see the answer to that question was "not many."

Ron was dying of Amyotrophic Lateral Sclerosis, abbreviated ALS. Often called Lou Gehrig's disease, ALS is a progressive wasting away of certain nerve cells of the brain and spinal column called motor neurons. The motor neurons control the voluntary muscles, which are the muscles that control movement.

The disease would eventually kill Ron when the muscles that allowed him to breathe ceased to function. In the meantime, since Ron continued to be fully aware of himself and his condition, Margaret had told me his mental depression was overwhelming them both. I could barely force myself to think about Ron's illness, and I wasn't living the nightmare twenty-four hours a day like the Wheatons were. Had I been in Ron Wheaton's shoes, I'd have been investigating euthanasia.

"He's doing much better lately, thank you," Margaret put in. "If he gets his rest, he can still square dance with the best of them." I saw the grief she tried to conceal behind the false cheer as Margaret put her arm through her husband's and he patted her hand.

Ron was a tall man, once robust but now thin and frail. Leaning against a bar stool for support, he smiled down on his diminutive wife with a deep level of love that was almost painful to watch.

"Sure, honey, as long as I do it in my chair." He nodded to a wheelchair sitting in a corner not far from where we stood. "I get tired quickly," he said to me, by way of explanation.

My sorrow for him and for Margaret coursed through my body and caused me to shiver involuntarily. There was nothing I could do for Ron. Nothing anyone could do. I felt every bit as helpless as I really was.

We talked a few minutes longer, until another guest demanded my attention and I was forced to return to my hostess role, when I'd have preferred to stay with Ron and Margaret. I made a silent vow to spend more time with them both as I made my way over to help another elderly guest find a comfortable chair. But I never got the chance.

Later, I stopped into the Sunset Bar and glanced up to see the television reporter interviewing Gil Kelley, the current King of the Minaret Krewe, outside on the street along the parade route.

"What do you think of our parade, King Kelley?" the reporter asked him. Gil's answer was drowned out by an upsurge of laughter inside the Sunset Bar.

Gil's makeup, created here this morning, was particularly good. He had a wicked-looking slash wound down the left side of his face with fake blood oozing from it, and one of his front teeth was blacked out, giving him a snaggle-toothed appearance. Gil's black hat, colorful yellow silk blouse, tight black pants and long sword were realistic enough. His all-too-real shaggy grey hair and paunch completed the expensive, if stylized, version of pirate wear. In his costume, he looked nothing like the president and majority shareholder of Tampa Bay Bank, which he actually was.

"Isn't he dashing?" his wife, Sandra Kelley, said when she saw me watching Gil on television. Sandra herself was dressed in the twenty-first century version of a promiscuous wench's costume, an off-the-shoulder red blouse and a full yellow skirt that matched her husband's blouse. She wore several strands of cheap red and purple and green Gasparilla beads around her neck.

"Yes," I smiled down at her, "he certainly does." I nodded emphatically. "Or were you talking about Gil?" We both laughed.

"You and George are so good to have the Krewe here," she said.

The comment seemed genuinely pleasant and thus unlike Sandra Kelly. "Are you having a good time?"

Sandra frowned daintily, a slight downward bend to her plucked black eyebrows over the bridge of her pert nose. The snide Sandra we all knew well resurfaced. "I was. Until *he* came in." She inclined her head toward a man I didn't recognize talking with Ron Wheaton, who seemed more exhausted. He was leaning against a wall and appeared to need the support.

"Who is that?" I asked Sandra.

"It's Armstrong Otter. The one and only." The disdainful tone conveyed her opinion precisely. There were two famous jewelers from the small beach community of Pass-a-Grille across the bay. One was the highly regarded Evander Preston. Armstrong Otter was the other.

Not wanting to encourage Sandra Kelly's brand of vicious gossip, I said, "I don't know Mr. Otter."

"So much the better," she snapped. "If Otter crawled back under whatever rock he slithered out from, all of Tampa would be better off."

Sandra's ire encouraged me to examine Otter more closely. He and Ron Wheaton appeared to be engaged in a serious conversation, although I couldn't hear what they were saying. Of course, Ron was one of the kindest souls on the planet. He would have been pleasant to Jack the Ripper.

The same could not be said of Sandra Kelley. At least, no one who knew her said so. I'd never liked Sandra and every time I saw her, she reinforced by initial distrust. I took her venom with a side order of antidote as I excused myself to attend to our other guests.

Or so I told Sandra Kelley. What I really did was to escape in the opposite direction when I saw my newly-minted stepmother headed my way. The absurdity of having a stepmother more than ten years younger than me struck me again.

The onslaught of guests, my lack of sleep and exercise today, and the stress of seeing Dad cozying up to Suzanne finally overcame me. It was only early afternoon but I was exhausted. I figured no one would notice if I ducked out, so I trudged up the stairs to our flat, dodging people seated and standing everywhere, until I reached our bedroom. Thankfully, even though there is a television in our room, no one had camped out there. I locked the door and collapsed on top of the damask comforter, in the mistaken certainty that nothing more serious than my father's new wife could possibly happen for the rest of the day.

CHAPTER THREE

Tampa, Florida
Saturday 7:00 p.m.
January 27, 2001

WHEN I RETURNED TO the noisy party, the sky was dark and no one had missed me. I saw as many people in all the gathering places of our flat and the restaurant as had been there hours before. Maybe the faces had changed, but with all the makeup, it was hard to say.

The parade was long over, but the thousands of people who had come to watch it were slowly finding their way from Hyde Park to downtown Tampa, where the after-parade festivities would reverberate into the early morning. An arts and crafts show, fireworks and the festival, featuring live stage shows would fill the downtown Tampa streets. This day wouldn't end for hours yet.

As I descended the stairs from our flat and into the lobby of George's restaurant, I saw Gil Kelley sitting with my new stepmother, openly flirting with her. Whether Suzanne was flirting back or not was hard to tell. Her head tilted toward Gil and he laughed at something she said as if he was totally captivated by her. A few feet away, Dad bent his head to hear Gil's wife, Sandra. Poor Dad, I thought. Sandra Kelley was certainly no substitute for Suzanne Harper

Steering clear of them all, I moved in the opposite direction. I finally found George sitting at our favorite table in the Sunset Bar with Armstrong Otter. Because the television was now turned off, it was marginally quieter in here.

Up close, Otter was good-looking for his age, which I guessed to be between sixty and seventy. He appeared fit, lean and quick. He had a full head of grey-blonde hair, brushed straight back and worn in a silly pony tail tied at the base of his skull with a ribbon that made him look like an aging rock star. His eyes were an unremarkable cloudy blue. Whatever it was about Otter that incited Sandra Kelley's anger, it wasn't obvious to me.

I snagged a cup of *café con leche* and headed toward my husband. George stood when I approached, as he always does when a woman joins his table. One of the things I love about George is that he treats me at least as nicely as he does everyone else, usually better.

Otter was well back in the booth and made no effort to rise.

"Willa, do you know Armstrong?" George asked, as I slipped into the booth across from Otter. I bumped his foot on the way in, but he didn't move it.

"No, I don't think we've met," I said, holding out my hand, which he took softly, as if he wasn't used to shaking hands with women. He had manicured fingers, oddly flat at the tips, like little spatulas. And I noticed a small diamond stud earring in his left earlobe.

After I was settled, a few moments of uncomfortable silence followed, until George smoothly rescued the situation.

"Armstrong was telling me about the new work he's entered in the Gasparilla Festival of the Arts competition. He hopes to win the grand prize."

"Really?" I said, looking at Otter with renewed interest. The art festival was my favorite part of Gasparilla month, partly because it was the end of the festivities.

"The piece is a pin. I call it Gasparilla Gold." He pulled a picture out of the pocket of his rumpled tweed jacket and described the pin to me as if dictating copy for a catalogue, holding his cocktail straw in those flat fingertips and using it as a pointer. "It's quite large, about eight inches long. The pin is meant to be worn on the shoulder of a coat, on the outside of the lapel." He gestured to a spot on his own shoulder just below the seam in his jacket, above where you'd lay your palm to say the pledge of allegiance.

"The platinum dagger has semi-precious stones set in the handle, and a gold chain connects the scabbard to the knife." He glanced up at me and I nodded my understanding. "The dagger sits on top of the open treasure chest filled with gold nuggets." He handed the picture to me for closer examination.

I'm not an avid jewelry hound, but even I was impressed. "Can I see it sometime?"

"Sure. The piece is on display at my studio. It'll be there until a few days before the art festival. Come over anytime," Otter said, in haughty tone. His manner was off-putting and I began to have a little more sympathy for Sandra Kelly's view of him.

I handed the picture to George, who was about to say something when Dad walked up, peeked at the photo over

George's shoulder, and folded his lanky frame into the booth next to Otter. Dad, ever the salesman, whistled then asked, without a trace of embarrassment, "How much does something like that cost?"

George looked down at the table and I glanced away, too, so as not to show our amusement at Dad's trademark lack of decorum.

Otter, though, was thoroughly offended. "Well, it's not for sale, actually," he said, with even more arrogance. "The point is to win the competition, and then I'll return it to display in my store."

Dad wasn't so easily deflected, though. "No, I mean, really. If you were going to sell it. How much?"

With no graceful way out, Otter said, "Oh, probably about one-hundred-seventy-five thousand dollars, particularly if it wins." He inched toward Dad trying to get out of the booth. "Would you excuse me, please? I need to speak with Gil Kelley for a few minutes."

As he was standing to let Otter out of the booth, Dad said, "Somebody would pay one-hundred-seventy-five thousand dollars for that thing? Why, that would feed several entire families for more than a year!"

Dad's feigned awe was humorous, since he wasn't half the rube he was pretending, for the moment, to be. Dad knows that people are frivolous with money, even if he's not. Dad has always made good money and managed it wisely. Over the years, he'd accumulated a sizeable net worth.

Before Suzanne, Dad preferred the simple life. Yet, I'd noticed all the status symbols she wore and the fashion show she'd given us since she arrived. Suzanne would change Dad's comfortable modesty. Nor would his quiet living be the only change. I worried anew Dad had no idea what he'd gotten himself involved with when he married his precious one.

While Dad continued his tongue-in-cheek marveling at the price of jewelry, I glanced over and noticed Armstrong Otter and Gil Kelley arguing in the corner. I couldn't hear their words, but I saw Otter poke Kelley in the chest several times with his index finger. Kelley's face suffused with angry color. I nudged George and whispered that he might call one of the on-site paramedics, just in case Kelley stroked out or something.

Just as I said it, Kelly gestured with his arm in a wide arc and his hand knocked several glasses off the bar. The glasses flew onto the floor and shattered in a cacophony of noise that stopped all conversation in the room.

George rose to break up the argument, but before he covered half the distance to the pair, Kelley stomped off into the dining room and Armstrong Otter stalked out in the other direction.

Guests glanced at each other, embarrassed, and then turned back to their conversations. George organized the cleanup and in a short while, the noise level in the room returned to the same low hum I'd heard before the incident.

I turned back to Dad. We were alone in the booth. It was our first private moment since I'd met Suzanne. I searched my mind's "social graces" database for something acceptable to say in the circumstances, and could think of absolutely nothing. Everything I wanted to say was simply not appropriate.

Finally, Dad broke the ice. "How about those Bucs?" he asked, and tension relieved, we both laughed. We'd heard the question fifty times today, or more. That's been the standard greeting around Tampa since our football team won the Super Bowl. A few moments of uncomfortable silence followed our laughter, and then, for half an hour, we discussed the Bucs, a safe topic that kept us from talking about his marriage or our own uneasy relationship.

Fatigue and the easy talk relaxed me. I dropped my guard too soon.

I gulped the last of my coffee in one large mouthful just as Gil Kelley walked over, punched Dad in the shoulder and boomed loudly into one of those awkward silences that sometimes happen in a crowd, "Congratulations, Jim! Suzanne tells me you two are expecting! Didn't know you still had it in you, you old dog!"

The surprise propelled the coffee right out of my mouth. I spit caramel colored liquid all over me and began to cough uncontrollably. Which was fine because it gave me the opportunity to excuse myself from the now impossible situation.

I hurried away and tried to hide out in a corner of the dining room. My attention was focused on blotting the coffee off the front of my blouse, allowing Margaret Wheaton to approach me as she came out of the ladies' room, a happy smile on her face.

Giving up on the coffee stain, I studied her as she navigated the crowd. My concerns over Suzanne, my father and now, unbelievably, a new sibling on the way, were trivial by comparison to Margaret's situation with Ron. I tried to focus on Margaret as a way to avoid my own impossible situation.

Since Ron Wheaton had been diagnosed with ALS about a year ago, his illness had progressed too quickly. I'd watched Margaret become more and more exhausted, which I'd attributed to the stress of dealing with Ron.

In the past few months, Ron had become weaker and less mobile. He was confined to his wheelchair much of the time and they rarely went out. Ron would soon require twenty-four hour care.

Yet, on the few occasions when I spoke to him on the telephone, he sounded as strong as he had ever been. I could only imagine the horror of knowing you would one day be unable to breathe and would actually suffocate. The thought brought instant tears to my eyes again. Ron and Margaret Wheaton deserved better treatment from life. It seemed at the moment that the Sandra Kelleys of the world succeeded despite their meanness while Ron Wheaton suffered so unfairly.

When Margaret eventually reached me, I gave her a hug, partly to hide my glassy eyes. She felt small and frail to me and I marveled at how heavy a burden those small shoulders could carry.

"Can you believe this madness?" I asked her.

She smiled and her face lit up a little more than usual lately as she nodded. "I love it, though. I've lived in Tampa my whole life and I never get tired of Gasparilla. When I was a little girl, the Gasparilla parade used to be held downtown and it was the same time as the State Fair. The parade was actually my very first date with Ron." She sighed here, giving my hands a quick squeeze. "Gasparilla holds many good memories for us."

Before I could reply, we heard several screams, as if a thousand marauding pirates had landed at Minaret. Alarmed, I moved as quickly as possible through the crowds toward the noise, with Margaret close at my side. Several other guests joined us en route.

When we got to the veranda, I could see Ron Wheaton slumped over in his wheelchair, not moving, while Suzanne Harper, my stepmother, stood near him. Suzanne's mouth was wide open, head thrown back, resembling the heroine of a horror movie as she screamed repeatedly at full volume.

But not loud enough to wake the dead.

CHAPTER FOUR

Tampa, Florida
Saturday 8:00 p.m.
January 27, 2001

IGNORING THE NOISE OF Suzanne's screaming, Margaret turned her face into my shoulder as someone rushed to Ron Wheaton and began to administer CPR, shouting, "Call nine one one! Call nine one one!" I held her close to me and tried to shelter her from the elbows and stares of the gawkers.

Above the heads of the small crowd of people pushing too close to Ron's wheelchair, I saw George working his way through, trying to calm everyone down. The paramedics George had hired to be on the scene today could not get through the throng.

Tampa's Police Chief Ben Hathaway, dressed in full pirate regalia as a member of the Minaret Krewe, came forward. "Step back, people. Please step back," he said, pushing gently to move the spectators aside.

Too quickly, it seemed, I heard sirens coming up the

driveway. Soon, more paramedics, these in official uniforms, went out to the veranda, asked questions and tried to revive Ron, but even the uninitiated among us could see that their efforts would be fruitless.

"Is he dead?" Margaret asked me.

"I can't really see much," I lied, unsuccessfully trying to shelter her from the truth. Having failed, I looked into her wide eyes and said, "I'm so sorry."

Margaret blinked a couple of times, then "Don't be. It's a blessing," she told me. Turning her head away, she continued crying softly and moaning against my shoulder. The morbid thoughts I'd had earlier about Ron's suffocating to death could be abandoned. But as I'd feared, he was not able to say a final goodbye to his beloved wife.

I motioned to Chief Hathaway that Margaret and I were moving into the smaller dining room where we could sit down. I realized that Margaret's happy memories of Gasparilla would be forever changed, now, and felt even sorrier for her than I had just a short while ago.

She said nothing more about her husband's death as we sat together, waiting. Margaret didn't deserve unhappiness in her life, yet sorrow seemed to follow her like a black cloud these past few months. We sat in silence, for I could think of nothing comforting to say and Margaret seemed to be lost in her own reverie.

Ron Wheaton was eventually taken away by an ambulance crew in no hurry to reach Tampa General Hospital, and Chief Hathaway took charge of the scene. He asked everyone not to leave because the police would soon arrive to take witness statements.

"Why do you need to take statements now?" George asked

him. "Hasn't everyone been through enough already?" His glance took in Margaret's small form and her tear-streaked face. As well as he knew me, George could see my fatigue. I was sick at heart, too.

"Death in a public place? During an event filled with unknown spectators?" Chief Hathaway said, as if George's question was two strokes short of imbecilic.

I saw George clench his fists at his sides. The last thing we needed was George to assault the police chief. I jumped in quickly, as if I was explaining to Margaret, "The police need to record witness statements now, just in case."

She blinked a couple of times and then said, "Of course."

Chief Hathaway approached the spectators and began to collect their contact information.

Turning to my husband, who was still breathing a little too hard, I asked, "How does it look out there, George?" I tried to get Margaret to drink a little water.

"In the front of the restaurant, people haven't even noticed that anything's happened," he told me. "It's just nine-thirty. There's still a pretty big crowd out there and we've had sirens all day. I think there will be people who leave here tonight not even knowing that Ron died," he looked at Margaret as he said, "if that's how you want it."

Margaret nodded in response. She wanted to protect her privacy, which was so like her. Margaret had led a closed life. There was no reason to believe she'd want to change that now, even though her husband had just died a very public death.

"I'm going to take Margaret upstairs and put her in a guest room. Ben Hathaway can talk to her in the morning," I told George, as I got Margaret to her feet. We made our way deliberately up the stairs to our flat. She came along meekly, allowing me to take her hand and lead her without complaint.

I don't know if she was in shock or just exhausted and emotionally drained, but when Margaret entered our guest room, she lay down on the extra bed and fell into rhythmic breathing almost immediately. In sleep, her small face relaxed and she seemed years younger.

Would her life be better now? I wondered. Without a terminally ill husband to care for, I hoped so. At the moment, she needed rest. I closed the door softly as I left her in deep slumber. When she awakened, Margaret's world would be completely changed. How would she deal with that?

When I returned to our living room, Dad and Suzanne were seated together on the couch and Chief Hathaway sat across from them. "Just tell me what happened, in your own words," Hathaway said to her, in a tone of voice that he probably used to talk suicidal teens down from the highest peak of the Sunshine Skyway Bridge.

For her part, Suzanne seemed more upset than Margaret had been. I poured yet another cup of coffee and stood in the doorway to listen. Between bouts of tears, Suzanne described finding Ron Wheaton on the veranda, while Dad held her and patted her shoulder, looking concerned. He obviously cared for her and showed as much. It was the most caretaking I'd ever seen him do and I was more than a little astonished that he knew how to comfort someone in distress. He'd certainly never demonstrated that skill with me. I tamped down the green-eyed monster inside my heart and paid attention.

"I wanted to go out for some air," Suzanne told the chief. "I'm pregnant, you see, and I had gotten a little light-headed in there with all those people. I didn't know where Jimmy was…" She looked at Dad, the grown man everyone calls "Jim."

"I'm so sorry, honey," Dad consoled her, as if not being by her side every minute was a capital crime. My heart pounded a little harder in my chest as I watched him through the eyes of the neglected child I still felt myself to be at the moment.

"That's okay. You couldn't have known," she smiled, a little shaky. The purple lipstick had long since been chewed from her mouth and black mascara streaked from her raccoon eyes. She looked far less beautiful and much more vulnerable than she had at six o'clock this morning. Which made it that much more difficult to hate her.

Hathaway got them back on track. "About what time was that?" he asked, as he wrote in the notebook balanced on his beefy thigh. We only had one chair big enough to accommodate Ben Hathaway. Whenever he comes to our flat, he always sits there.

"I don't know. About nine o'clock, I guess. I'm not wearing a watch," Suzanne sniffled into one of George's linen handkerchiefs.

Traitor, I thought silently when I saw his monogram. Of course, he'd given it to her. Chivalry personified, that was my husband.

"And then what happened?" Hathaway asked her. Clearly, she needed prodding.

"I had trouble getting through the crowd, but I did make it to the veranda." A few more dainty sniffles followed.

Hathaway's patience seemed to be wearing a little thin. "Were the doors closed or open?"

"Closed. It was pretty cold outside," she said, shivering as her body remembered that thirty-degree night out there. Dad pulled her shawl closer around her shoulders, over her wench's blouse. She offered him a wobbly smile.

The whole tableau could have been an amateur theater production, I thought uncharitably. The contrast between Suzanne's hysterical reaction and Margaret's stoic one—when it was Margaret whose husband had died, after all—would have been comical in other circumstances.

"Then what did you do?" Hathaway prodded again.

Suzanne gulped and wiped fresh tears. "There wasn't anyone outside, because of the cold, I guess." She hiccupped and her breath caught a little. A wobbly smile followed. "Anyway, I went out and it was sort of quiet, which I thought was great. It was so noisy inside the restaurant and I had started to get a headache," she almost whined, and Dad patted her again while she laid her head on his shoulder and calmed.

"What happened next?" Hathaway displayed a little of the impatience I felt now, himself. He didn't normally question witnesses. He did so now as a personal favor to me and George. If Hathaway hadn't been here for the party, this job would have fallen to a detective or patrolman, most likely.

Hathaway's discretion was touching, and I appreciated it, even if I thought he was a little overzealous. He had no way of knowing how long he could find Suzanne Harper here in Tampa. But I felt this could have been done another time. Ron Wheaton died tonight of natural causes, after all. And Suzanne was planning to continue her visit for several weeks, unfortunately.

"I turned toward my right and I saw a man in a wheelchair," Suzanne continued. "It startled me at first because I hadn't noticed him when I went out." She hiccupped again and took another deep breath. In a rush of words, she said, "So, I talked to him."

I stifled a guffaw. Not because what she said was particularly funny, but because Suzanne hadn't stopped talking since I met her. She would have talked to Ron Wheaton—responsive or not, dead or alive.

Suzanne started to tear up again. Dad took the thoroughly soaked handkerchief from her gently and replaced it with a fresh tissue. "And he didn't say anything." She began crying hard now, but continued her story. "So I walked closer and spoke louder. I thought he just didn't hear me." She gave me a look that I took to be a reproach. As if to say that she'd noticed I had been ignoring her this morning in just the same way a dead man had tonight.

"But he still didn't say anything. I thought he might be sick or something, so I went around in front of him and I saw…" At this point, she broke down completely and we all had to wait a few minutes for her sobs to pass.

When she'd returned to silent sniveling, "What did you see, Mrs. Harper?" Hathaway asked.

The question jolted me again. Sweat popped out on my forehead and my stomach began to churn. I leaned more solidly into the doorway to keep from falling down on suddenly wobbly legs.

That was the first time I'd heard Suzanne referred to by my beloved mother's name. "Mrs. Harper." How could Grace Harper's name be owned by this young woman? Would the vicious surprises never stop?

My attention was drawn back to Suzanne when she answered. "I saw he was blue. I just knew he was dead. And—I don't know what came over me," she took a deep breath and finished her sentence, "but I just started to scream and scream and scream…" Her voice trailed away as Suzanne looked at Dad with her sorrowful expression. Finally, she whispered, "I couldn't stop."

After a few quiet beats, Hathaway asked her, "Did you see anyone else outside, near Mr. Wheaton's wheelchair?"

She shook her head and the tears rolled down her cheeks again. She made no move to wipe them away, but the tears continued. Hathaway let her go then, saying he'd talk to her more later if he needed to do so.

Suzanne and Dad stood. They walked down the hallway toward their room, Suzanne still crying while Dad held her and crooned, "It's okay, honey. It's okay," over and over.

I watched them go as tears sprang to my own eyes, out of the watchful gaze of Ben Hathaway or anyone else. For I realized that Dad loved Suzanne, in a way that defied logic. He loved her.

The knowledge was like a steel dagger, piercing my heart.

CHAPTER FIVE

Tampa, Florida
Saturday 11:00 p.m.
January 27, 2001

I'VE NEVER DISCOVERED A dead person, myself, and Suzanne was probably more upset than I would have been due to the raging hormones of pregnancy. Yet, when I saw Ron Wheaton out on the veranda, he had looked peaceful. Not frightening in the least.

But then, I had known he was going to die soon and Suzanne probably had not. Although her distress was real enough, Suzanne was more emotional than the situation called for, if indeed anyone had told her about Ron's condition and his prognosis. Like Margaret, I felt it was a blessing that he'd gone now, and gone quickly.

"I'm glad Margaret wasn't alone at home with her husband when he died," I told Ben Hathaway when we sat in the more sturdy chairs around our kitchen table and discussed his interview notes a while later. "What a horrible experience that would have been."

He looked at me quizzically until I told him about Ron's ALS.

Hathaway had been treating Ron's death like a crime scene, in part because he hadn't known about Ron's medical condition and in part because he knew the urgency of getting the names of witnesses who were probably tourists and would soon be on their way back to wherever they had come from.

"If I had to guess, I'd say Ron Wheaton died of a heart attack. He had all the signs," Hathaway told us now. "But we won't know for sure until the autopsy comes back."

"Why do an autopsy at all?" George asked

"We're required to perform an autopsy when someone dies away from a hospital or under suspicious circumstances," Hathaway explained. "It's just routine." Then, he added with a little too much enthusiasm for my taste, "And, it's always possible that the man was murdered."

My mouth dropped open. I couldn't have been more astounded. Maybe Hathaway really did need more work to do since Tampa's crime rate was down.

George said what I'd been thinking. "You're making a mountain out of less than a molehill, don't you think, Ben?"

Before Ben could deny it, I asked him, "Who would murder Ron Wheaton? He was going to die soon anyway. What would be the point?"

Hathaway stirred more sugar into his already sweetened coffee while he considered his answer. "We don't have a lot of information right now, so I can't tell you whether or not Ron Wheaton was killed, let alone what the killer's motive might have been." His face assumed a contemplative pose and his tone became thoughtful. "I'd say there's the usual possibilities: profit, revenge, jealousy, to conceal a crime, to avoid humiliation or disgrace." Then, he looked at me and actually smiled. "Or my personal favorite, homicidal mania. That's usually an easier one to solve."

The question, and the tone, got my back up. "Is this cop humor or something?" I snapped, more than a little angry and ill-tempered with him, I admit. "Murder a man who soon wouldn't even be able to feed himself?" The very idea was insulting to our guests, people we'd invited into our home. Why, the thought was outrageous. "What kind of a monster would do that?"

Hathaway gazed at me as sympathetically as he could arrange the features of his pugnacious face. "Maybe someone who loved him very much and didn't want to see him suffer anymore. Did you ever think of that?"

He stopped a minute to let his words sink in. I felt my eyes widen as the implications of his suggestion traveled to my tired brain and registered somewhere around my gut.

Then he said, "Maybe you're not aware of it, but we have way too many mercy killings here in Tampa, Willa."

"Come on, Ben," George said, having reached the same conclusions I had about what Hathaway was about to say.

Hathaway was not deterred. Once he got rolling, there was no stopping him. "Too often, it seems like the only way out of a terrible terminal illness is to end the elderly patient's life."

He might just as well have slapped me. My anger flared anew and my words came out in a rush of outrage. I jumped to my feet. "What? You can't even consider the possibility that Margaret could have murdered Ron, if that's what you're suggesting. Margaret loved Ron. They've been a devoted couple for more than thirty years. Even if she were capable of murder, Margaret wouldn't have killed Ron. He was the only family she had. She cherished every day he had left. We've discussed it

many, many times. No. That is just not a possibility. Not at all!"
I finished with all the sternness I could muster, which is
considerable.

Hathaway craned his neck and looked me over as I stood
towering above his head. Calmly, he said, "There's no point in
arguing about it until we find out the cause of death, anyway."
He stood and picked up his notebook, putting it back into the
pocket of his now frivolous looking costume. Making it clear
that he was not persuaded by my outraged defense of Margaret,
he said, "Let's just wait and see."

SUNDAY MORNING, I AWAKENED to the aroma of freshly
brewed coffee again, but it didn't wield the same power over me
as it had yesterday.

After everything that had happened during the past forty-
eight hours, I had neither the physical, emotional, nor mental
stamina to deal with Suzanne again now. I was supposed to be in
training for the Gasparilla Distance Classic in three weeks. I
virtuously decided to get my morning run finished first.

I dressed quickly and let the dogs out ahead of me. Then, I
crept down the back stairs, sneaking away like a mischievous
child. I threw sticks in the water for Harry and Bess to chase,
hoping to tire them out a little, as I stretched my achy muscles.

We live on an island named Plant Key, after Henry Plant, the
railroad tycoon who built our home and the island in the late
eighteen-nineties. The island is eight miles around its
circumference and I would do two laps today. For training
purposes. But also to avoid my father, his child bride, and her
child-to-be.

I'm not a fast runner. It would take me about two hours to

complete the sixteen miles. By the time I finished, Suzanne could be off somewhere, to the playground or something. One could only hope.

I threw two sticks quickly westward and after Harry and Bess took off to fetch them, I started jogging eastward, toward the rising sun. If I get a head start I can sometimes stay in front of them for ninety seconds or so. Today, it took them only about sixty seconds to reach me, shake water all over me, and then leave me freezing in their wake as they bounded ahead.

While I ran, heavily and slowly, trudging along the hard, packed sand of our beach, I dodged the cans, bottles and other trash left by yesterday's party crowds. We'd need to clean up out here later.

Too quickly, I realized I wasn't dressed warmly enough. A cold wind blew in from the north, chilling me to the bone. I cursed my decision to sneak out of the house before I was properly prepared. The cursing didn't make me any warmer.

January and February are iffy months in Tampa. Sometimes the weather is perfect—sunny, clear, highs in the 80s—for weeks on end. Other times, it's cold, windy, rainy and generally miserable. Which beats the Detroit snow, ice, and slush I moved away from, but miserable weather in the winter is a problem here.

The first quarter of the year is a big tourist time all over Florida. Gasparilla preparations begin here in January and the whole month of February is one big celebration. Most events are held outside. So if the weather sucks, well, it spoils the party.

Hundreds of thousands of tourists flock to Tampa for the Gasparilla Parade of Pirates and Pirate Fest. Dates vary based on criteria I've never learned. Celebrations continue for several weeks. Among other festivities, we participate in the Illuminated

Knight Parade in Ybor City, the Distance Classic run for charity and, the Festival of the Arts on the last Saturday.

Because we live on Plant Key, right in Hillsborough Bay, we have no choice but to join in all of the Gasparilla festivities for the entire month. That's why the weather matters. We can't just turn on the fire, curl up with a good book, a bottle of wine, and unplug the phone.

Instead, our home is flooded with diners at George's five-star restaurant.

Tourists are forever coming over the Plant Key Bridge, thinking that they can just use our beach, stroll around the grounds, and make a complete nuisance of themselves. South Tampa residents know better, I thought, as I kicked the cans out of my path and farther onto the grass to keep them out of the bay. No point in polluting the water even further with this mess. We could always pick it up off the island later. The bending over would do me good.

During Gasparilla month, we post a guard at the entrance to Plant Key and only allow guests with reservations, which are booked months in advance. For the invasion and parade, we have to hire private security because boaters pull up to our shores, beach their boats and invite themselves to our celebrations.

Just one guard at the driveway isn't enough. Most people who live along Bayshore Boulevard, Tampa's long and winding waterside drive, stay home in self-defense since it's impossible to go anywhere, anyway.

And, to be fair, February is usually George's best revenue month, so we need to keep the doors open. Gasparilla month alone accounts for a third of George's annual receipts.

Having company in the house, as we did this year, makes matters even more complicated under the best of circumstances.

But when old friends call and say they're coming, there's not much we can do. Hotels are booked to overflowing, so our guest rooms are their only option.

Allowing my thoughts to wander shortened the run considerably, and I was back to the house after the first lap in what seemed like a few minutes. My feet wanted desperately to turn into the walkway and go upstairs for warmth, but I forced myself to keep running until I was so far from the house that it was better to continue than to turn back.

Which was a mistake, because then my thoughts returned to Dad and Suzanne. Suzanne pregnant. Dad, father to an infant. Unbelievable. Jim Harper, as much as I have come to love him and accept his failings, hadn't been a great father to me. While Mom was alive he tried to be a good dad. But he was just not comfortable around kids at all and certainly not around a little girl.

Jim Harper is really my stepfather. He married my mother when I was five. She was a widow at the time, so he's the only father I have ever really known. Not that I know him all that well.

He traveled a lot, brought me gifts and listened to my reading, but he wasn't like any of the television dads I saw. I never doubted that he loved me, although he didn't say so often. He was not demonstrative, not a "Mr. Mom" type at all.

Eleven years after they married, when I was sixteen, my mother died. Jim was so overwhelmed by grief and absolutely unable to cope that he gratefully sent me to live with my mother's best friend and her three children.

That was twenty-three years ago, in which time we had forged an uneasy truce. I tried to understand how he could possibly have left me when I was already so bereft; he tried to comprehend how I could fault him for the way he dealt with his own grief. We both failed in our efforts.

During our infrequent visits and phone calls, we did what all civilized WASPs do about everything—we didn't discuss substantive matters and we acted like we had no issues between us.

But we both knew we did.

Dad as a new father was, well, something I'd never considered as a wild possibility. Yet, last night when Gil Kelley punched Dad on the arm and gave him the "sly dog" routine, Dad had grinned from ear to ear. His face lit up in a way I've seldom seen it. He'd looked positively radiant as he thanked Gil for his good wishes.

George was quick to jump in with his congratulations, too. I had spit coffee all over myself and left the table abruptly.

So far, I hadn't actually said anything to Dad or Suzanne about the baby. I truly didn't know what to say. I was tempted to just keep running, away from my home and my issues.

But now I was really cold. The wind continued to whip around the island and was even worse on the west side as I came close to the house again.

This time, although the dogs could have easily completed another lap, I stashed them in their outdoor run and trudged heavily up the back stairs. I wanted a hot shower and hotter coffee.

If the weather didn't warm up before the Distance Classic, I might have to rethink this plan. I was running for my favorite charity, Young Mothers' Second Chance, a home for single mothers, and they really needed the money. But still, there had to be an easier way to capture the public's compassion—and their cash, I thought, as I tried to catch my breath and prepare to face my demons.

CHAPTER SIX

Tampa, Florida
Sunday 9:30 a.m.
January 28, 2001

LATER, IN THE KITCHEN, I found George sitting alone with coffee and the Sunday papers.

"Morning, darling. I hope I didn't wake you," George said, without glancing up, as I made preparations to brew my *café con leche*. He looked relaxed and happy, unshaven, hair mussed, like a man at home on a Sunday.

Honestly, I thought, does nothing faze my husband? A man died downstairs last night and George seemed untroubled. I envied him his tranquility and I felt worse for Margaret.

I couldn't imagine my life without George. I was sure Margaret felt the same way about her husband. I wouldn't believe she murdered him, no matter what Ben Hathaway suspected. Ben has been wrong before. I willed him to be wrong this time.

"Actually, I've been out running. Are you the only one up?"

I waited for the coffee and heated the milk in the microwave.

"Your dad and Suzanne went downstairs with a few of the others for breakfast. I decided to stay here and read the papers. Great news about your new sibling, huh?" he asked me, as he folded the front section over and looked up briefly.

"Sure." I said, with all of the joy I usually display for trips to the gynecologist. "Wonderful."

"You don't like the idea of being a 'big sister' at the age of thirty-nine?" George turned his full attention to me now, in his concerned and compassionate way.

"Not really. Should I like it?" I snapped, a little more crossly than I had meant to.

"Sorry. No need to be so touchy." He sounded wounded. George and I rarely had personal disagreements, although we argue issues all the time. And it wasn't his fault.

I relented. "I'm sorry, too. I just haven't quite sorted out how I feel about this yet. Can we drop it for now?"

He studied me a few seconds, then changed the subject. "This is a great story in the paper here today about how Americans are constantly reinventing themselves." He pounded on the paper with his index finger. "Did you see it?"

I sat down at the table with him and looked at the story he'd pointed to in the front section of The Tampa Tribune. I read the headline aloud, "'Change Your Identity, Change Your Life.' Well, that would be one way to do it." I sipped the hot coffee like a heroin addict shooting up. "Seems a little farfetched, though. Who would want to do that?"

"You'd be surprised. Jim Harper is making himself over into a husband and father," he said. I had to concede, so I nodded. "Think of people who change their names for professional reasons, like actors and musicians. Or just because they don't like their names, they're too hard to spell or too hard to pronounce."

He seemed like he was really getting warmed up. "Or maybe, they've done something illegal and they want to cover it up." George sipped his coffee and grinned at me. "There must be hundreds, if not thousands, of reasons to change your life or your identity."

"Maybe," I responded, knowing there was more coming.

He waited a beat or two, like a stand-up comedian before delivering his punch line. "Like maybe your father has embarrassed you by marrying a woman half his age and getting her pregnant, and then showing up at your house when you have several hundred guests, to tell you the happy news?"

The absurdity of it all did make me laugh, a little. "I don't think that would be enough to make me change my name and leave town, but it might be a motive for murder," I teased.

George relented. "Read this article later. It's quite interesting."

To please him, I reviewed the Tribune article more carefully. A former member of the FBI wrote a book telling ordinary people how to hide their assets and disappear. He was traveling the country giving seminars on the subject and had been in Tampa yesterday.

Even with all the Gasparilla festivities, over 2,500 people had attended the guy's presentation. The book had already sold over a million copies. Clearly, reinventing oneself was a more popular topic than I'd realized.

When Margaret came into the room, I set the article aside to read later and turned my full attention to her

She appeared rested. Although, dressed in the clothes she'd

slept in and with yesterday's makeup smudged around her face, Margaret looked far from her best.

"I can't really believe he's gone," she said to George and me, after we'd gotten her settled and fortified. The dry bagel she chewed slowly and washed down with coffee seemed to strengthen her somewhat, but she still seemed an exhausted and bewildered shadow of dear, kind, petite Margaret Wheaton.

Some lawyers have office wives who partner with them at work as their spouses partner with them at home. I had Margaret, my office mother. She cared for me, watered my plants, dusted my desk, kept me from working too hard and prohibited others from over-scheduling my time.

Margaret even stood up to the CJ, my pseudo-boss. She chastised me for antagonizing him, but when she thought he was out of line, she stood right up to her full height and went toe-to-toe with the old despot.

From long experience, I knew Margaret had reserves of feistiness in her that would see her through her husband's death, even if they weren't apparent at the moment.

"We knew he was going to die, of course," Margaret said aloud. "We'd been preparing for it for months. He had a living will, made sure we transferred all the titles to my name. He gave me everything he had. So we were ready."

I didn't know how to respond to that, so I said nothing. Neither did George.

"We thought it would be the ALS. I'm glad he had a heart attack instead." She sounded anything but ready or glad.

George reached over and covered her small hand with his large one. She stared at the plain gold band he wore on his left hand for a while. Fresh, quiet tears, started down her cheeks again.

"What can we do, Margaret?" I felt as anguished as she was. I'm not good at death. I don't do funerals, wakes or memorial services, if I can avoid them. Death is a part of life's circle, I know. I even sort of believe in reincarnation of some kind. But the loss and sadness the survivors feel when a loved one dies is just too hard to observe and revives too many bad memories for me.

Watching Margaret's grief confirmed my belief that she had not killed her husband. Nothing would make me believe it. Not even a full confession. Hathaway was just wrong.

But Margaret had to know the theory the police were pursuing. So I took a deep breath and just said it. "Margaret, Ben Hathaway isn't convinced that Ron just passed away." She flashed me an alarmed glare that shook my resolve. "He's checking that," I assured her.

"But?" she asked, for she knew there was a condition.

I inhaled courage. "But he's checking other possibilities, too. He has to. It's his job."

The alarm on her face resembled a small child watching a car speed toward her beloved cat lying in the street. "Other possibilities? Like what?"

George listened intently to my answer.

"Well," I stalled. "Ben has ordered an autopsy to see what caused Ron's death."

"Why?"

"Because it's the law," I said, as gently as I could. "They have to rule out other causes of death."

"Like what?"

My discomfort grew as I tried to avoid explaining exactly what I knew Ben Hathaway believed and would try to discover. "Well, like maybe suicide or homicide."

Now, Margaret's expression was even more horrified. As if the car had hit her cat and splattered its body all over her face.

I would have said anything to wipe that look off her face. I backpedaled quickly. "I mean, not that that happened here. Just, that's the reason for the law requiring an autopsy."

Margaret shook her head, slowly, as if to say "No, no, no, no." "Who would want to hurt Ron? He was the kindest man in Tampa. He didn't have an enemy in the world. For all the years we were married, I don't think he ever raised his voice to me, even once." She kept shaking her head. "No. That's not possible. No one killed Ron. It's not possible."

Real tears and sobs began again, then, and I helped Margaret back to bed. She collapsed into sleep almost immediately. As if the world was too much to face.

Grief is like that, I remembered all too well. It comes in great, overwhelming waves. And although grief subsides, like the tide, it comes again and again. My mother had been dead for more than twenty years. Yet, when I saw Jim Harper with Suzanne or worse, when I heard her called "Mrs. Harper," fresh grief ambushed me again.

Margaret would be all right in a while, but she'd have bad times, too, for the next few months. Maybe for years. I hoped Hathaway would wrap this up soon so Margaret could deal with her grief and move on with her life.

Hathaway's suggestion was outrageous, I thought again. The woman just lost her husband. She wasn't a killer. I may not know everything, but I knew that much. Margaret didn't have anyone to help her except me, now that Ron had died.

It's not that I'm all that experienced with killing. But I knew Margaret didn't kill Ron and I wouldn't let Ben Hathaway try to prove she did.

Still, it nagged at me. Ben has been wrong before, but not that often. He's good at his job. Tampa's crime rate is declining and very few cases remain unsolved.

When I came back from Margaret's room, I heard the front door to our flat open and Dad and Suzanne walk in, laughing and chatting, right past the kitchen and on to their room down the hall.

George chuckled, "Afternoon delight, hmmm?"

I hit him in the arm and he yelled, "Owwwwwwww!" loud enough to wake the dead. We were both still laughing when a couple of our other house guests came in to join us.

We exchanged pleasantries for a while, spent the rest of the day being social, and tried, unsuccessfully, to forget Hathaway's suspicions.

CHAPTER SEVEN

Tampa, Florida
Monday 8:15 a.m.
January 29, 2001

MONDAY MORNING, AS I drove over the bridge off Plant Key away from Minaret and turned right onto Bayshore Boulevard heading toward downtown, my favorite view of Hillsborough Bay unfolded. Some days I see dolphins and manatees on my way to work.

My daily drive east on Bayshore, over the Platt Street bridge, toward the Convention Center, and on to the old federal courthouse to my office is one of many aspects of my life for which I am truly grateful.

I felt my mood lightening and I actually felt better, physically. Even though I was running late, something I detest in judges, especially myself, I tried to focus on the view as it sped past.

The old courthouse itself is circa 1920, about twenty years newer than our house. As the most junior judge on the bench,

I'm stuck in the least desirable office. It's the RHIP rule; I have no rank and no privilege. My courtroom and chambers are on the third floor in the back. Moving quickly from the parking garage helps me keep my schoolgirl figure.

Only slightly out of breath, I got to my chambers a little before nine and had to dig out my key to open the door when my repeated impatient buzzing failed to raise Margaret to release the lock.

Margaret wasn't at her desk, but her computer was on, her chair was away from her desk like she'd just gotten up for a moment, and a cup of hot tea was steaming near her phone.

Before she left our home on Sunday, I'd tried to convince her to take some time off, but she'd declined. She said she'd rather work. "I need to get on with my life, Willa. Let me do that, okay?"

I hurried into my office, dropped my minuscule purse into a drawer, and plucked my robe off the hook on the back of the door. I flipped through my pink telephone slips quickly and found one from the "CJ," that is, the Chief Judge of the United States District Court for the Middle District of Florida. He'd called at seven-thirty this morning, knowing I wouldn't be here. I never get here much before nine. I'm not a morning person. The message, written in Margaret's hand, said CJ wanted to talk with me before I took the bench.

I was tempted to ignore him. If I went out right now, I'd be seated on the bench at eight fifty-nine, keeping my self-imposed rule of timeliness. The CJ isn't really my boss, although he acts like he is. I'm appointed for life and there isn't a darn thing he can do about it, as much as he'd like to.

I inadvertently took his parking space my first day on the job and he's been on my case ever since, a reaction more than a little bit drastic for such a minor infraction. I got the worst case assignments, the smallest chambers, the most meager courtroom budget. At meetings he ignored my suggestions and generally made it known, without saying so, that I was far from his favorite jurist.

When his sister and brother-in-law both committed suicide a while ago, CJ acted like it was my fault. Then, when George was accused of murder, according to CJ, I should have resigned before the masses had a chance to impeach me. He's still pissed off that I didn't.

My thinking was, hell, if the Chief Justice Earl Warren could withstand an impeachment attempt, let 'em try and get me for nothing more than being married to a guy who was wrongfully accused.

The CJ has aspirations to higher office and I've been his biggest supporter. Moving him to Atlanta would be a very pleasant surprise.

So talking to the CJ was never high on my list of priorities, and especially not when I'm already late taking the bench. Regardless of whether he acknowledged our true relationship, this was a request and nothing more. I could honor it. Or not.

But it would be good for me to take the high road, I reasoned, if I was ever going to convince him to give me a chance to move my office to the new courthouse with the rest of my colleagues. No point in creating trouble if it's unnecessary.

So I picked up the phone, hoping he'd be busy. Unfortunately, CJ had left instructions to put my call through immediately.

I sat down wearily in my chair and looked around at my minuscule office, decorated in what I call ugly green and uglier brown but that a decorator probably once had called "avocado" and "copper." The beat-up client chairs and this stupid platform my desk sat on were put here by my predecessor, who was clearly a little Napoleon.

I wondered when I would ever get to move. I refused to redecorate, although CJ had several times offered me the money to do it. I didn't want to give the impression that I was planning on staying here long enough to make redecorating worthwhile.

Maybe if I could force myself to be a little more gracious to the CJ he'd find the money in this year's budget to let me relocate to the new courthouse with everyone else. Maybe that was why he'd called.

"Good morning, Willa," he boomed into my ear. Why is it that some people who are hard-of-hearing either shout at you or whisper? He continued right on through my greeting, "I understand you have Armstrong Otter in your courtroom this morning."

Really? I had no idea. I hadn't had time to prepare for my docket of conferences today and didn't know exactly what was scheduled. I'd been just a little preoccupied with the party preparations, Jim Harper's new wife, and now, a death in my home.

Besides, one case begins to look like another after a while. The CJ knew more about today's calendar than I did.

CJ continued to shout, "I have personally known Armstrong Otter for several years. I've bought a number of pieces of jewelry for my wife from him and I've always been completely satisfied."

Really? I thought again, and my mind began to wander. Nothing CJ said ever held my interest for very long

"Most everyone in South Tampa has been his customer, one time or another," CJ said. "There's not a damn thing to this case and you ought to dismiss it so you can get on to the real cases on your docket."

What? My eyes blinked and I shook my head, as if to clear it of the outrageous remark.

The CJ was so far out of line that if he hadn't been shouting I would have thought I'd misheard him. He wasn't really asking me to dismiss a case. He couldn't be.

CJ took my non-response for consent, and said, "Good. I'm glad we got that resolved. You have over eight hundred cases on your docket, Willa. Surely some of them deserve your attention." And he hung up!

I pulled the receiver away from my ear and stared at it, as if the receiver itself had uttered the offending remark. I returned the receiver to its cradle slowly, but I was still nonplussed as I walked out into the courtroom and took the bench to hear pre-trial motions on my first case, which I obviously knew very little about.

The courtroom deputy called *Fitzgerald House v. Armstrong Otter* and we were about to begin working when Margaret entered the courtroom from my chambers, walked toward the bench where I sat and handed me a ceramic mug filled with *café con leche*.

Seated at the defense table was a local lawyer, Armstrong Otter, and his insurance adjuster. As Margaret glanced over toward them, all color drained from her usually placid, small, olive face. She stared at the three men, her mouth open, speechless.

I reached to take the coffee cup from her, a split second after she dropped it. The cup shattered into a thousand pieces. Just before Margaret fell to the floor.

I stood up immediately and motioned to my court security

officer. He picked Margaret up, carried her into my chambers and placed her onto the ugly brown couch that did nothing to enhance the adjacent ugly green chairs. She looked too pale. I put a shaky hand on her clammy forehead. I felt a shallow pulse.

Margaret could have simply fainted. Heaven knows she probably hadn't gotten much sleep or taken care of herself since Ron died two days ago.

Yet, Margaret is a pretty tough little woman. She didn't faint when we found her husband dead and it was nothing short of amazing that she had now.

I instructed one of my clerks to call the court's medical team and, once they arrived, to call the housekeeping department to clean up the floor.

Then, I returned to the courtroom, stood in the position Margaret had occupied moments before, and turned to look out into the courtroom, just as she had done.

My gaze fell squarely on the three men seated at the defense table, but so what? Margaret had met the lawyer, the adjuster and Otter before. What had caused her so much distress that she'd fainted?

Today, Otter looked much as I had seen him Saturday. He wore a business suit, which made him appear somewhat more conventional. The suit's style was recent enough, but the suit and its inhabitant didn't seem to be comfortable companions or even well acquainted.

All in all, Armstrong Otter wouldn't even rate a second look on the street, I thought. Margaret's reaction told me to wonder whether he had a totally different impact on older women.

Still thinking, I looked back into my chambers where Margaret was sitting up now, sipping tea, and well cared for. Because I had a courtroom full of work to do, I returned to the bench, making my way around the broken pottery and coffee on the floor, vowing silently to ask Margaret about the entire matter later in the morning.

When the clerk called the Fitzgerald House case again, Otter, his lawyer and his insurance adjuster were still there looking pretty much the way they had a few minutes ago, except that Otter appeared even less comfortable.

Fitzgerald House was present in the form of the chair of its board of directors, a bent, grey-haired, elderly woman who looked like my elementary school librarian. Her lawyer was young and inexperienced, probably because no more experienced lawyer would have taken this case.

I glanced briefly at the case summary my clerks had provided to me. Privately, I had to agree with the CJ that this case didn't appear to deserve the court's time. Unfortunately, I don't get to make that decision *sua sponte*, or on my own.

This was a relatively small matter involving a business dispute between two parties. Ordinarily, my view is that such matters should be resolved without my time or energy. However, anyone with the filing fee and a typewriter can file suit. It's called open access to the courts for the redress of grievances. Our government is founded on it. True, many cases were frivolous and got dismissed, and this one might, too, at some point. But we weren't there yet.

After a brief recitation of the facts by the young lawyer on behalf of Fitzgerald House, I tried to settle the case. Not because the CJ had asked me to, but because I try to settle all my cases. I tell litigants, "All cases are settled. The question is whether you do it yourself or whether you let the jury do it for you." Sometimes litigants listen to me.

"No, Judge," the adjuster said in response to my suggestion

that the insurance company simply pay Fitzgerald House the appraised value of the property in dispute. An elderly widow had bequeathed certain jewelry to the charity in her will.

The adjuster took a deep breath and delivered his prepared speech, all in one take. "The widow knew full well the necklace and earrings were fakes when she bought them. They weren't even insured, which she surely would have done if she'd thought they were really worth a million dollars. No. This is just another frivolous lawsuit and we will win this case. And if we don't, it's because Mr. Otter misrepresented the jewelry, which is an intentional act, and not covered by the policy anyway. We will pay no money to settle this claim."

The adjuster was puffed up with righteous indignation, settling in for a long, cold trial.

I looked at Otter and his lawyer. "You know how it is, Judge," Otter apologized. "Insurance companies always want to collect your premiums, but you're never covered."

He stared bleakly at the adjuster, who glared back. The lawyer was sitting, literally and figuratively, in the middle.

I'd dealt with this adjuster before. He would never budge. So I appealed to the board chair. Fitzgerald House is a museum, allegedly a modest home that F. Scott Fitzgerald once owned and where it is claimed he wrote part of The Great Gatsby. I've always been skeptical of the claims. But it was true that Scott and Zelda Fitzgerald used to spend vacations at the Don CeSar hotel on St. Pete Beach, and I've always felt a small connection to him.

Maybe the Fitzgeralds did own the little house in Palm Springs once. Beyond that, the connection to Gatsby seemed tenuous to me, based on what I've read of Fitzgerald's life.

"Can you afford a scandal like this?" I asked the board chair as kindly as possible. "And what if you lose? It's going to cost you a lot to take this case to trial. You could have to pay Mr. Otter's costs, too. Does Fitzgerald House have that kind of money to risk?"

The board chair and her lawyer looked uncomfortable, but she answered me truthfully. "Judge, we believe we're right about this. I talked to the widow myself about the jewelry. Many times. She absolutely believed it was real. She thought she was giving Fitzgerald House a gift that would finally bring us financial prosperity."

The young lawyer inserted, with the righteous certainty only the young can muster, "We can't afford not to try this case in the face of absolutely no offers from the defendant."

I felt a deep sigh escape my lips. *You can lead a litigant to water but you can't make her think,* I reminded myself silently.

"Well, then we have no choice but to get started. I'll take the plaintiff's motions first," I said, and we worked straight through all the motions until lunch. I recessed the matter for the day and went to take care of the pile of work on my desk, already feeling exhausted.

CHAPTER EIGHT

Tampa, Florida
Monday 2:00 p.m.
January 29, 2001

MARGARET HAD GONE OUT for lunch, which was unusual but not unprecedented. I didn't see her before she left, so I couldn't ask about her fainting spell this morning, but I was worried. I picked up the phone and called Chief Hathaway's office. He wasn't there. I left a message. I drummed my fingers on the desk, thinking about who could give me some answers. I picked up the phone and dialed Marilee Aymes.

"Dr. Aymes' office," the receptionist said, with as much enthusiasm as I display for over-cooked spinach.

"This is Judge Carson. Is Dr. Aymes in?" I asked, brusquely, and she agreed to check. I've learned that if you don't act important with these receptionists, they actually think they don't have to let you talk to the doctor. It's easier to call the CEO of Microsoft than to get past a physician's receptionist.

"What's up?" Marilee's office persona is about the same as

her personal and private ones. For years, she was Tampa's only woman cardiologist and she was still the best. She's also brash, bossy, brusque and more than a little overbearing. I think she's a hoot, but George says I shouldn't be seen with someone so "unsuitable." I suspect he thinks she's unsuitable because she does whatever the hell she wants. To George, such conduct isn't becoming, honorable or appropriate. He can be awfully stuffy sometimes.

"Sounds like you're busy?" I asked tentatively. This wasn't a conversation I wanted to have without Marilee's full attention.

"Always. But it's Monday. Everybody saved their heart attacks from the weekend for today. The waiting room is jammed. I'll be lucky to get done here by seven o'clock."

"So I guess a drink around five-thirty is out of the question, then?" I looked at the gold and platinum Cartier watch George had given me for our last anniversary. It was about two o'clock now. I needed to get home to my guests, but I wasn't impatient to do so. It was clear that Dad and Suzanne knew how to amuse themselves and George would be working until much later.

"Lemme look. Hey, girls, what's the wait look like?" she shouted to someone in the other room. "Umm. Ok. I could make it by six-thirty. How's that? Wanna meet at your place?" She asked me.

"How about Bella's? That's between here and there." I suggested a local Italian bistro with a nice bar and some quiet booths on South Howard, or "SoHo" as the area was now being called. She agreed and hung up without signing off. I called George's office and left a message that I'd be later than usual, but home by seven-thirty at the latest.

I'd finished my tuna sandwich and now I wanted a cookie. I had just enough time to run down to the cafeteria to get one before my next conference. So, I picked up my purse and, preoccupied with my thoughts, made my way quickly past Margaret's empty desk and through the door to the hallway.

Without watching where I was going, I literally bumped into Otter, who had his hand on Margaret's elbow as they argued in hushed tones outside the door to my chambers. When I practically knocked them down, Otter stepped away from Margaret and looked up, but Margaret was so engrossed she didn't notice I was there.

"But we're not young enough to waste any more time. Ron is dead now. Nothing will bring him back," she pleaded.

"Hello, Judge," Otter said, loudly enough to interrupt Margaret and too loud for the quiet hallway of our surroundings.

"Hello, Mr. Otter. Margaret." I nodded at them both. "Something I can help you with?"

"No, Judge," Margaret had composed herself. "We were just talking."

"You two friends?" I asked the obvious question.

"We were. Once. A long time ago," Margaret said. "I need to get back to work. Excuse me."

She left us to return to the office. Otter watched her go and continued to look uncomfortable standing there alone in the hallway with me.

"What was that about?" I asked him, not really sure I wanted to know. Margaret was all alone in the world. I didn't want to think she had any relationship, ever, with Armstrong Otter.

Based on what I'd heard this morning he wasn't the kind of man I'd want anyone involved with. If he had taken advantage of the widow in the Fitzgerald House case he might take advantage of Margaret, too.

She had told George and me that Ron's life insurance and

other assets would leave her financially well off. And she was particularly vulnerable right now. Exactly the kind of situation I had imagined the Fitzgerald House widow was in when she'd had her unsavory encounter with Otter.

The morning's fainting spell had proved that Margaret was unhappy and upset and trying valiantly to stay composed. Nothing good could come of any association between Margaret and Armstrong Otter. I didn't have to know more about him to know that.

I was in a position to rescue Margaret from herself, right now. So I went into what George calls my Mighty Mouse routine. You know, from the old cartoon where the mouse dresses up like Superman and flies through the air singing, "Here I come to save the Daaaaaayyyyy." It's a bad habit that I've tried to break.

George tells me, "Willa, if someone wants your help, they'll ask for it. You don't have to be everyone's hero. Some people don't want to be rescued, you know. If they want your help, they'll ask for it."

I know that. But it's against my nature to turn my head when my friends are in trouble.

Maybe Margaret's wish right now was not to be rescued. But that could only be because she didn't realize what she was dealing with. If the fraud claims Fitzgerald House was making against Otter were true, I didn't want Margaret involved with this guy, whether she thought she wanted to be or not. Especially until Ron Wheaton's autopsy came back and Ben Hathaway was satisfied that he'd died of natural causes.

Nothing makes a cop more suspicious than a new widow with a man friend who has a questionable past.

"Margaret recognized me as an old friend, that's all. We

were just catching up," Otter said, like it was true. Maybe it was.

"Mr. Otter, you are a defendant in a case in my courtroom. Please don't contact Margaret again until this case is over. After that, what you do is your own business," I told him, not as harshly as I could have.

He shouldn't be having private conversations with Margaret about the case. Otherwise, litigants have social conversations with court personnel all the time. It's not a problem. But I was hoping he didn't know that, and that he wouldn't discuss it with CJ. If Otter did as I asked, it might give Margaret time to come to her senses and decide on her own not to become involved with him in any way.

Beyond that, my staff isn't supposed to be personally involved with litigants in cases in my courtroom. It appeared that Margaret and Otter had been arguing. That suggested more of a personal relationship than I could ethically allow.

If any member of my staff did know Otter personally, the knowledge would have to be disclosed to all parties and dealt with. I might even be required to recuse myself from the case, if the involvement had gone too far.

"Of course, Judge, I understand. I'm sorry," Otter said as he turned to leave the building.

I watched him until he reached the elevator lobby, pushed the button, got in and the doors closed behind him. My sweet tooth had evaporated, but I went quickly, bought my cookie and returned in less than fifteen minutes to finish my conferences.

After the last of the lawyers left, I should have spent the rest of my time on my work, but of course I spent the time dwelling on Margaret instead.

What was Margaret's connection to Armstrong Otter? Ordinarily, she wouldn't even know the man. Otter traveled in circles that were way beyond Margaret's usual social life.

He was a local celebrity, in a small town way. He'd been an award winning jeweler in Pass-a-Grille, the little beach community just south of St. Pete Beach in Pinellas County, across the bay from here, for at least as long as I'd been in Tampa.

Yet I'd never met him before Saturday. Who was this guy and why had he upset Margaret enough to cause her to faint? Because, although there were other people in the courtroom when she collapsed, somehow I felt that Margaret was involved with Armstrong Otter. I was concerned based on what I'd learned about Otter today in the Fitzgerald House case.

Fitzgerald House claimed that the deceased widow hadn't just spent a million dollars on jewelry that Otter sold her, she had spent every cent she owned. She believed, because he told her so, that the jewelry was "one of a kind," with a "special history."

He'd told the woman that the necklace and earrings she'd bought had been designed by the legendary Tiffany's designer, Paulding Farnham, and had belonged to Marilyn Monroe. He showed the widow pictures to prove it.

Otter sold the pieces to her as an investment that would increase in value more significantly than any other investment she could make. The widow died believing that she had left her favorite charity, operated by the little woman who was now the chair of the Fitzgerald House board and the widow's closest friend, a legacy.

When the widow died, Fitzgerald House had the necklace and earrings appraised to be sold. They had an actual value of about forty thousand dollars.

The pieces did look like the pictures of a set Marilyn Monroe had worn to the Academy Awards in 1953, and they might have been. But if she'd worn these particular gems, they were fakes then, too.

Otter's only defense so far was to admit that the stones were not real, but to claim the widow knew that when she paid him more than twenty times their value. He said that Marilyn Monroe had actually worn the jewelry, and it had been costume jewelry at the time.

As memorabilia, Otter claimed, the gems were actually worth a million dollars, and suggested that Fitzgerald House simply sell them. Otter had counter-sued for defamation and damage to his business reputation caused by the claim, too. That was a pure intimidation tactic, I thought.

Working at my desk, I got caught up in the Fitzgerald House file as the time passed me by. Margaret stopped to talk to me on her way out at five o'clock.

"What happened today, Margaret? What caused you to faint this morning? Are you all right?"

"Willa, I know you're trying to help," she stood in the doorway to my office with her purse in her hand and her coat on, tying a scarf around her head against the wind.

Margaret got her hair done once a week and didn't touch it between beauty appointments. It always looked exactly the same. Her style was short, teased and varnished, not merely sprayed—a product of a bygone age.

"I mean this as kindly as I can say it. Please don't interfere in my private life."

"Margaret, you're not yourself right now, and you know how much George and I care about you." I jumped in without really hearing her or letting her finish her sentence. "Ron's illness and his death have been so hard on you. The stress must be overwhelming. It's not a time for you to make any big decisions."

"I appreciate your concern. Truly. I do. But I've been on my own since I was a young girl, long before you were born. Let me handle myself."

She said this in the same tone everyone uses to tell me to mind my own business, as she buttoned her coat and turned to go.

"If you need anything, you'll let me know?" I asked her.

She smiled her indulgence. "Sure, Mighty Mouse. I'll yell for help before I need it. Goodnight." She turned around to leave, but changed her mind. "There is something you can do for me, though. Talk to your friend Dr. Aymes and tell her not to sue Otter, okay?"

"Why is Marilee Aymes going to sue Otter?"

"You'll have to ask her. All he told me was that it was a big misunderstanding." This time she did turn and leave quietly.

Margaret had no idea what kind of trouble she could be in. I had to help her, whether she wanted me to or not, I persuaded myself.

Margaret was all the way out of the building before what she'd said actually resonated with me. When would Otter have told Margaret anything about Dr. Marilee Aymes?

CHAPTER NINE

Tampa, Florida
Monday 5:30 p.m.
January 29, 2001

I HAD ABOUT AN hour before my date with Marilee and I spent my time wisely. I turned around to my computer and accessed the files that are available to me as a U.S. District Court Judge.

Computers made researching individuals fairly easy, although limited information was available without the consent of the particular individual in question. I could get access to certain FBI files if I needed to do so, but not without a good reason. Furthermore, I'm not allowed to investigate cases on my docket.

So, all I looked for was whether there were any more cases involving Armstrong Otter.

I punched in "Armstrong Eugene Otter," after looking up his full name in the Fitzgerald House file. While waiting for the data to process, or whatever it does, I continued looking at the

Fitzgerald House file. I'd have to know it fairly well for trial anyway.

A few seconds later, the computer came up with a list of cases involving Otter. According to the screen, there were several closed civil actions in various jurisdictions. Some reflected Otter as the plaintiff and some were claims against him.

From this search, I couldn't discern the disposition of the files. Had Otter ever been brought to trial? Or were all the cases settled? I'd have to look at the actual files to know and most of them were either in storage or over at the new courthouse.

I saw one pending criminal complaint, *U.S. v. Armstrong E. Otter*, and, according to the case number codes, it was also on my docket, although I hadn't had any involvement with the case yet.

I wrote a short note to one of my clerks to pull the file for me and have it on my desk in the morning. I didn't have time to look into it further if I was going to make my date with Marilee Aymes.

But I put it high on my priority list for Tuesday, along with a note to do a similar search on Ron Wheaton

I had about ten minutes to make it to Bella's. Fortunately, even with today's traffic, you can get just about anywhere in South Tampa in ten minutes. Ten years ago, you could do it in three. I picked up my purse, pulled my electronic key to my car out of the side pocket, skipped the ancient elevator ride and loped down the stairs and to the parking garage.

Minutes later I'd pulled onto Florida Avenue, a one-way street north, which took me past the new Sam M. Gibbons Federal Courthouse containing the courtrooms I lust after. I looked again at the killer palm trees out front, so called because one of them had rolled off a truck during construction, landed on a worker and killed him. Not funny.

I turned left onto Tyler and drove past the Tampa Bay Performing Arts Center where the marquee said Tony Bennett was performing. There was a crowd of twenty-somethings out front, lined up to get in. To see Tony Bennett. Go figure!

I pulled into Bella's parking lot at six o'clock on the nose. I love living in South Tampa. Everything is so close, so easy. Except finding a parking spot at Bella's on a Monday night in January. I finally found one at the far end of the lot, locked the car and rushed up to the front door.

They had plastic walls up outside against the cold winds still blowing in the winter chill and snow birds.

Bella's is cozy, with a large wood-burning oven in the back. As I walked in, I was thankful for the oven's warmth.

Like most nights, the bar was busy with the South Tampa crowd, while the tables were filling with diners of all ages. I looked quickly at the bar stools to see if Marilee Aymes was waiting there. She wasn't. Then I checked the booths along the bar side and saw her in the back. I waved the hostess away and maneuvered through the martini-drinking, upwardly-mobile young professionals.

I ordered Bombay Sapphire and tonic with lemon. Marilee had a fairly hefty glass of bourbon on the table. It's not nice to make your friends drink alone. Besides that, the Queen Mother drinks gin and she's over a hundred years old. What's the problem?

Marilee was ensconced in the booth, her short, hefty body taking the entire bench on her side. She wore no make-up, a no-nonsense haircut, and a belligerent stare, a combination that made her a target of gossip and rumor around town. Add to that her tell-it-like-it-is style and it was fairly easy to understand why she was a guilty pleasure for people who cared about the opinions of others.

That group had never included me. Being a federal judge, I'm appointed for life. I'll have my job unless and until I do something truly outrageous. That day may come, but drinking with Marilee Aymes didn't keep me from getting appointed and wouldn't put me over the line now.

After greetings, Marilee lit one of the new Gasparilla cigars. I declined her offer to join her in another of our shared vices. I came straight to the point, which is the best approach with Marilee.

"I'm here to ask you a favor from my secretary." It was a direct, but not elegant, start to the conversation.

"You're kidding, right?" Marilee interjected as she puffed.

"Let me finish. You know Margaret Wheaton, don't you? She's worked with me for years. She helped us with our pet project, Young Mothers' Second Chance, several times?" I explained Margaret's pedigree in terms Marilee would remember.

"That's right. A very nice woman. Doesn't her husband have some kind of terminal illness?" Everyone always remembers what's of interest to them. Sometimes, getting information from people is easy. I'd wanted to ask Marilee about Ron's death so I could head Chief Hathaway off at the pass if he kept going off in the wrong direction.

"Yes, that's right. ALS," I said. "Or, at least he did. He died on Saturday."

Marilee shook her head, finished her bourbon, and ordered another. "Nasty death, ALS," she said around her cigar. "The lungs lose the ability to breathe air. The victim suffocates, fully aware of what's happening. Makes you believe in voluntary euthanasia."

"Yes," I said again, startled that her thoughts were mirroring the police chief's suspicions without knowing the facts. "Chief Hathaway is suggesting Ron's death might have been a mercy killing. By Margaret."

"Couldn't blame her. If I had ALS, I'd kill myself. Wouldn't need anyone to help me," she said, as she knocked back another swig of bourbon.

"How would you do that?"

She eyed me speculatively through the purple haze of her cigar smoke between us. "Well, as a doctor, it would be easier for me to do than it would for someone who didn't have easy access to drugs. The nicest thing would be to inject myself with an overdose of morphine. I'd just go to sleep, rather peacefully, too."

We sat quietly, both thinking about Ron falling peacefully asleep; Marilee thinking how much better that would be than the alternative at the end of the course of his disease.

I don't know what I was thinking. I'm not sure how I feel about voluntary euthanasia. Being a lawyer, I can argue all sides of the issue. But if I'd been in Ron Wheaton's shoes, what would I have wanted to do? And when would I have wanted to do it? Would it have been better to wait my turn, living out my life until the last minute, experiencing all there was to this life before moving on to the next?

I knew Ron Wheaton was a religious person, like most Americans are. He and Margaret had attended Hyde Park Methodist Church on Swann Avenue every Sunday for all the years I'd known them. Ron was a member of the administrative board; Margaret played the piano for the choir. Would his religious beliefs have made Ron less likely to take his own life?

"How far along was he?" Marilee asked me.

"Medically, I don't know. I saw him the day he died. He

looked very thin, frail, like a strong wind could blow him down," I told her, taking a sip of gin.

"Was he ambulatory?" she puffed in my direction.

"He was walking, but he had a wheelchair nearby, which he used when he got tired. They found his body in it. On our veranda. After the parade on Saturday." The telling of it made me shudder. I recalled Ron's pale body in death.

"Then he probably had the dexterity to inject himself. Maybe he did. Make it easier on the wife," Marilee offered her brand of compassion.

"What else could he have been injected with?" I asked her.

"Almost anything in large enough doses will kill you. Cocaine, heroin, insulin, household bleach, even air, to name a few."

"Then again, he could have had a heart attack, couldn't he? He was the right age for it. He had a history of angina. Couldn't that explain it?" I asked her, hearing the hope in my own voice and thinking it odd to hope for such a thing as a heart attack. Everything's relative.

She nodded her head on her short, stout neck. "Yep. Saw three heart attack patients over the weekend myself and a couple more today. No reason he couldn't have been one of 'em. So, what's the favor?" she asked, reminding me of the second reason I'd asked her here.

"Margaret asked me to persuade you not to sue Armstrong Otter. So I said I would talk to you about it. What's going on?"

"What do I look like, the answer woman? How should I know what's going on with that bony little troll?" she snapped at me, pounding her glass on the table to remind the bartender that she'd ordered another drink and it wasn't there yet.

"Well, are you involved in any lawsuits?" I asked her,

feeling a little uncomfortable now. It was a pretty personal question, particularly for a doctor. Most doctors are fairly touchy about being sued.

I used to defend doctors when I was still in private practice. I'd never met one who thought he'd done anything wrong. When I was a young lawyer, I had the chief of medicine say to me, "Willa, doctors are never negligent."

If only that were true. More people die of medical errors in our country each year than heart attacks. Hospitals are places you go to die, it's been said. At least, you should keep your wits about you while you're there.

Marilee looked at me through narrowed eyes and a bigger cloud of blue smoke. I didn't mind the smoke. In fact, I was rather wishing I had broken my self-imposed rule about not smoking Partagas, my cigar of choice, in public.

I took a second-hand whiff of pleasure. Bad habit, I know, and I don't have the Queen Mum to justify this one.

Marilee's bourbon arrived just as she was about to resume the glass-pounding routine, for which I and the rest of the patrons were no doubt equally grateful.

She drank half of the bourbon down quickly. I had no idea how much Marilee drank on a regular basis or how well she held her liquor. And I didn't want to find out. I was still nursing my first gin, hoping the bourbon would make her more loquacious but not obnoxious.

"Several, actually, and perpetually," she said, jerking my thoughts back to our conversation.

"What?"

"Lawsuits. I'm involved in several lawsuits almost all the time. It's the bane of a cardiologist's existence. People with bad hearts and bad arteries just don't live without care and treatment.

88 | DIANE CAPRI

And sometimes, they die anyway. Or they have a stroke. Then, the family sues the doctor. Hazard of the profession." She dared me to contradict her.

In my experience, people sued other people because they were angry and felt cheated. I could believe Marilee's bedside manner left much to be desired and might easily get in the way of her medical skills. When a loved one died, she'd be the natural target of the family's anger.

"I don't mean to pry into your business. I had the impression that Margaret believes you're suing Otter, not the other way around. Is that possible?" I was a little sorry I'd started this and wondering why I wasn't home, relaxing, with my own cigar.

Then I remembered my child stepmother and that answered my own question. Maybe I was so interested in Margaret today because it gave me a legitimate excuse not to go home. That didn't bear thinking about.

"Anything's possible. But in answer to your question, maybe because I get sued all the time, I don't sue anyone myself. I usually try to resolve everything out of court," she said.

Then, she decided to give me a break. Maybe the bourbon was mellowing her some.

She lowered her voice and I bent closer to hear her over the dull roar of the bar crowd. "And I am trying to resolve a dispute right now with Otter. Confidentially."

"So what is it?" Marilee might be the only person I know that I would ask so bluntly.

In Tampa, no one asks anyone anything bluntly. Nor do we tell each other what we really think or how we're actually feeling. We tell everyone else what we think, but not the object of our affection, or rejection, or disdain. It's just not done. Bad form, you know. But it's okay to shoot them. Go figure.

Not Marilee, though. She was one tough cookie. Cool, strong-willed, and used to having her own way, all the time. Someone had once taken advantage of Marilee Aymes, but that was a long time ago, and she'd spent a lifetime making sure it never happened again.

"That asshole," she hissed, her nostrils flaring and her mouth set in a hard line across her ample face. "He sold me a multi-color sapphire-and-diamond pinky ring for a gift awhile back. Charged me over fifty thousand dollars."

"Wow. That's a lot of money for a gift."

Marilee ignored my comment. "I took it in to be appraised for my insurance and they said it was a fake. Can you believe that? I went right to Otter and told him he'd give me my money back or I'd sue his scrawny little ass and make sure it got on the six o'clock news every night for a year. Do you know what the toad had the nerve to say to me?" With each sentence, her voice increased in volume until she could be heard plainly over the din of the bar crowd.

I shook my head and kept quiet.

"He said the ring was real when he sold it to me and whoever I gave it to must have had the stones switched. He threatened to sue me for defamation if I went public with this. And then the pony-tailed twerp offered me ten thousand dollars to settle!"

With this last exclamation, she slammed her glass on the table so hard the ice cubes popped out onto the floor. The bartender, having learned his lesson the last round, rushed over with a fresh drink just in time.

CHAPTER TEN

Tampa, Florida
Monday 8:00 p.m.
January 29, 2001

"WHAT ARE YOU LOOKING at, Dad?" I asked as I
approached him in the Sunset Bar at George's a little while later.
I sat down across from him in the booth after I stopped at the bar
and ordered a Perrier, thinking I might be careful about the
drinking so I could avoid turning into Marilee Aymes in another
twenty years.

"What do you know about the old masters?" my father
responded.

"Not much. What I learned in the required art history classes
as an undergraduate. Why?"

"I was thinking about how the smallest things can trip you
up. If you want to embezzle from your bank, that is," he warmed
to his subject, leaned back and clasped his hands behind his
head. I saw he was drinking coffee. Which meant he was
working.

Dad's insurance agency issued errors and omissions insurance, bonds against employee theft in banks, brokerage houses, art galleries, jewelry stores and other places where theft can be a serious loss to a business.

As the selling agent, claims came to him from his customers for initial investigation before they were passed on to the carrier. He loved his work and always had interesting tales of larceny to report.

"Take the case of Miami's CenTrust Savings and Loan, for instance."

"Now there's an old case, Dad. You're too young to be wallowing in the glory days," I teased him.

"True. But seriously, when your Florida banking officials figured out that the bank's chairman had purchased a famous Rubens painting and two dozen other artworks for over $29 million, it didn't take long to discover where the money came from." Dad smiled a satisfied grin. "He's been sitting in prison for quite a while and is likely to be there a bit longer before he starts collecting art again."

Dad thinks of himself as an all-American hero, a real John Wayne, one of the good guys who makes sure thieves go to jail.

"And this is relevant to our lives today, why?" I said, smiling, too. I guess we all get to create our own illusions, especially of ourselves.

Jim Harper looked nothing like the Duke. More like Gig Young with salt-and-pepper hair, actually. He was taller than me by about two inches. He played squash and liked to ski, so he kept himself in shape. But Dad's crime-stopping role was strictly cerebral. He tried to out-smart those who stole from his clients.

Today, he had on a black cashmere turtleneck and a tan suede blazer. Gray slacks, socks and brown shoes completed the outfit. He reminded me of a black and tan Doberman; slim, sleek, and stealthy.

"I'm thinking about a new claim I got recently and how I'm going to prove that the bank's president has been embezzling for a long time. It'll be something small like that."

We'd always been able to talk about work. It was one topic where we were completely comfortable and compatible. It was about the only topic we ever discussed.

"If I recall correctly, that Rubens sold for over eight million dollars not long ago. I'd hardly call that a small thing," I reminded him.

"True. But it's not usually like that. Usually, it's something smaller and easier. Like the guy who cheated on his expense report by claiming he'd been having dinner with the auditor and then the auditor caught it. Or the time we were looking through a stack of paid bills and we saw that some were folded in half where others from the same vendor weren't—because the folded ones were phony and the clerk was paying himself. That's the usual way we catch these things."

He set aside his coffee cup and reached into the file sitting next to him on the bench, handing me an unsigned letter dated about six months earlier and postmarked in New York. "Maybe you'd like to help me with this one. Besides wanting to see you, it's one of the reasons I came here."

Dear Mr. Harper:

I am a bank stockholder. I have reason to believe that the president is taking bank funds for his personal uses. I've asked him about this and he denies it. But he has a lot of perks for a guy with his salary and our stock isn't worth nearly as much as we expected.

He has all the money in the world, but we never get any. And the bank is doing well. I'm elderly and don't have many assets. I need my money. Please look into this.

I handed the letter back to him. "Won't this be a problem for you? I mean, if the president has been embezzling funds, won't you have to pay the bank on the bond?"

"Yes. But that's what insurance is for, Willa. It's important that my insureds feel like they're getting what they paid for. And this is a complaint from a shareholder. If you're a bank, you can't have many of those before you have the Feds coming after you. My insureds expect me to take these things seriously and to investigate them right away. Whether or not there's anything to this complaint, the sooner we find out, the better."

"You must get hundreds of letters like this every month. Do you investigate them all?"

"To one degree or another, we do. The reason I'm getting personally involved in this one is that there's a lot of money at stake and the carrier is one of my biggest insurers." He put the letter back in the file. "And it gave me an excuse to spend a few days with you."

I couldn't help the warm glow in which his words bathed me, surprised at his expressed desire to visit. It wasn't something I'd heard him say often.

"So you read this letter and you looked into it?" I asked.

"Kind of. I gave it to one of the younger guys to look into. And he didn't find anything. But one night, I was just flipping through the stuff he had accumulated and I came upon this." He reached across the table and handed me a list of transactions.

I studied it for a while but couldn't make any sense out of it. "What is this?"

"It's a list of transfers, all the deals the bank has done in the last ten years. Notice anything?" From the look on his face, I knew there was something to notice. But for the life of me, I couldn't figure out what it was.

Accounting is not my strong suit. I like unraveling mysteries, but it's words that interest me, not numbers. I pay someone to do my taxes and I'd pay them to do all my bookkeeping if I didn't have George. He's the numbers man. He loves it. To me, numbers are Sanskrit, close to voodoo, cave drawings—well, you get the idea.

"I give up. What does it reveal, Oh Great One?" I asked with mock reverence.

"Let's take an example. Look here," he pointed to a transaction about halfway down the first page. "He moved one hundred thousand dollars from Company A to Company B, both of which he controls. Then here, the first company shows a receivable on its books for one hundred thousand from Company B, but the second company shows no payable back to Company A."

"So what?"

"Where did it go?" He said, both hands palm up toward the ceiling.

"I give up. Where did it go?"

"Check the next page. The only one hundred thousand dollar deposit recorded anywhere at the time was into the president's personal bank account. Voilà! Elementary, my dear Watson. He stole it. Plain and simple." Dad looked pleased with himself.

"Why didn't the big auditing firm catch that, if it's true?"

"Good question. Which is what I spent the day asking them. And you know what they told me?" He stopped again. His timing was almost as good as a stand-up comedian's.

"I'll bite. What?"

"They said they were never asked to compare all of the president's personal holdings to the bank records. They were only asked to audit the bank. Which they did. Quite competently."

"So how much are we talking about here? How much do you think the president has taken from the bank?" Which really meant how much had he taken from depositors and shareholders.

Dad answered me as he collected his documents back, put them in his folder and then inside his briefcase. "I'm thinking several million over the years," he said, almost nonchalantly, like several million dollars was gas money.

To signal he was done working for the day, he ordered a draft beer and I ordered Bombay Sapphire and tonic with lemon, not lime.

"Who has several million dollars?" Suzanne asked, as she approached our table.

Today, she was wearing another of her silk designer warm-up suits. This one was silver and the underlying silk tee-shirt was bright teal. She wore silver flats with the easily identifiable Prada look, meaning they cost more than a good dinner for four at George's restaurant.

I'd been wondering how she could hold up her left hand under the weight of the obscenely large diamond engagement and wedding bands she wore, but even the addition of the notoriously heavy diamond-beveled platinum Rolex didn't seem to keep her hand from fluttering to her perfectly styled hair.

"That's what I intend to find out, darling. That's what I intend to find out." Dad's determination made me shudder and think that I didn't want to be in that bank president's shoes right now.

He not only looked like a Doberman tonight, he fairly growled, reminding me that Dobermans can be effective attack dogs as well as good for personal protection and defense. Like a football team, offense or defense just depends on who has the ball.

Later Monday evening, George and I sat in the dining room of his restaurant with Suzanne and Dad, having put off the quiet family meal as long as we could. I was once again admiring the china, crystal and silver that George had inherited from his Aunt Minnie, along with her house. The pieces were worn and well-used, which made us believe Aunt Minnie had had a wonderful life here, a tradition George and I intended to continue.

The four of us had ordered dinner, but I had little appetite for the heavenly Salmon with White Wine Sauce and fresh snap peas that was usually one of my favorite dishes. George's chefs had won so many awards that he couldn't keep all of the plaques on the wall in his small office off the kitchen, so he stacked them on the floor.

George felt it was gauche to display one's achievements in the plain view of others, even if his competitors did so.

Salads, complete with the dried Traverse City cherries that George orders every year from American Spoon Foods, were before us on the table and the talk had turned to sports, as it always did on social occasions with Dad.

Suzanne and I were bored with the conversation, but our reactions to it were quite different. I was grateful that I didn't have to contribute, while Suzanne seemed annoyed that she was being excluded.

Get used to it, I thought. Dad had about as much desire to discuss social topics that would be of interest to Suzanne and me as he had to discuss his deceased first wife. Which is to say, no interest at all and no intention of doing so.

It's not that I don't love Jim Harper. Just the opposite, actually. I've loved him devotedly all my life. I've begged him to visit us, to stay awhile, to leave those cold New York winters and enjoy the sunshine.

Yet, I see Dad rarely. I wanted to get to know him better, to leave my adolescent feelings for him, both positive and negative, behind us. To forge a new, adult relationship.

Since Mom died, Dad has been rather scarce in my life. He'd loved mother deeply and just never seemed able to cope with her loss. Instead of the two of us helping one another through Grace Harper's death, his solution had been to run away and hide, leaving me to live with Kate and work things out on my own.

We'd been wary strangers since, although I suspected he wanted to change our relationship as much as I did. It had been more than a year since I'd seen him briefly in New York the last time, and then we'd just had lunch.

All of which explains why I never know how to act around Dad. He's a good man, but he can't deal with emotional issues, so he ignores them. He never wants to discuss Mom and he doesn't want to hear anything remotely unpleasant. He only talks about work and superficial things: sports, the weather, vacations. He's a good guest, though, and entertaining.

Despite my unease, so far, Dad had been an excellent Gasparilla guest, I persuaded myself with the help of the wine. He'd been pleasant, fun, entertaining and the other guests liked both him and his beautiful young wife. No one appeared surprised.

In Florida, the February/December marriage is almost as accepted as it is in Hollywood.

I was the only one who seemed to notice how much younger Suzanne was and to find the relationship embarrassing. But then,

I was the only one who saw in Suzanne what Jim Harper saw in her.

I concluded I could work out my relationship issues with him some other time, and raised my glass of Stag's Leap Cabernet in a silent toast to my father. The wine was much too good to sour with a bad mood.

Suzanne, less tuned in to the reactions of her new husband than I, waited for a lull in Dad's replay of last week's Super Bowl and jumped right in, with gusto. She started talking about the wedding, redecorating Dad's apartment, the honeymoon, and finally got around to the new baby.

Every comment she made, it seemed, was followed by, "Isn't that right, Jimmy?" leaving Dad no space to reply and forging into the next sentence without expecting one.

By the time Suzanne took a breath, we were through with our main courses and the waiter appeared to take dessert orders, which resulted in a few seconds of sound other than Suzanne's constant, high-pitched, meaningless prattle.

Since I'd been running eight to sixteen miles every day to train for the Gasparilla Distance Classic, I could eat with abandon. I ordered the Gasparilla Goldbrick, a sundae the chef created especially for the festival and makes only during Gasparilla month. It's golden vanilla ice cream, coated with butter toffee chocolate sauce that hardens into a sort of classy Eskimo Pie with crushed pecans on top.

On the side of the pirate ship-shaped dish it's served in is a chocolate coin wrapped in gold foil. The coin is embossed with the face of the legendary José Gaspar, for whom the month's festivities were named, on one side, and his pirate ship on the other.

Like most signature dishes, once created by George's chefs,

the Gasparilla Goldbrick is now copied all over town. But none of the copies are as good as the original. When the dessert arrived, I ate mine with gusto. Having a mouth full of sundae had the added benefit of preventing me from talking.

When Suzanne finally excused herself to go "to the little girls' room," with a kiss on Dad's cheek before she left the table, and George was called away to address a shortage of California wine he'd been experiencing since a fire burned all the stock in a Napa warehouse last year, I was face-to-face with Dad with nowhere to hide.

CHAPTER ELEVEN

Tampa, Florida
Monday 9:30 p.m.
January 29, 2001

WITHOUT THE CONVERSATIONAL COVER of work to engage us, he didn't seem any more comfortable about our forced unity than I did.

"I loved your mother desperately, you know," he finally said, playing with his wine glass and watching the light reflect off the crystal.

"I know, Dad."

"I waited over twenty years to remarry."

"I know."

"Suzanne makes me happy, Willa. She's bright and she's bubbly. She's as sweet as any girl I've ever known." He was almost begging me to like her, but he didn't look at me while he asked.

"Except one," I reminded him.

"Yes. Except for Grace," he sighed and looked up. "Grace

was so much more than that. She was loving, kind, gentle." He skipped a couple of beats.

"Quiet," he said, and we both laughed at his reference to Suzanne's unfortunate habit of prattling.

"It's just a coincidence that Suzanne looks so much like Mom, hmmm?"

He seemed uncomfortable again now, never one to honestly discuss things that were unpleasant to him. "No. Of course not. It's what drew me to Suzanne in the first place. I met her at a client's office in New York. She's an MBA, Willa. Did you know that? She's not an airhead."

I must have looked as doubtful as I felt. I'd seen no evidence to support that idea.

"She was working on a marketing campaign that her company wanted some extra insurance for. I was selling it to them. We just hit it off," he said. "It only took me about two minutes to realize she wasn't Grace, but, I don't know, something about her appealed to me. Is that so terrible?"

He wanted my approval, asked for it, pleaded, really. What could I do? My demons were not his demons, after all.

He'd known my mother as an adult, and he'd loved her desperately. How long did I expect him to mourn?

But that wasn't it, really. It wasn't that he'd married that bothered me, although I would have appreciated a little notice and an invitation to the wedding. It was the choice he'd made.

I couldn't look at Suzanne without thinking of my mother.

She looked nothing like Mom, in truth, when you studied Suzanne carefully. She had freckles and blue eyes like Mom, but where Grace Harper had been delicate and willowy, Suzanne was impish and childlike. There were other differences.

Suzanne was taller, broader, had more physical substance

than Mom had. And the personality difference was so striking that it jarred me every time Suzanne opened her mouth.

Mom was a nurse and Suzanne's expertise is sales. That said it all.

I knew Grace Harper wouldn't be one bit satisfied that her husband had stayed single and alone all these years. Grace expected Jim to remarry, told him so and told me so, too, before she died.

Nor would she be happy with me if I was less than kind to Suzanne or to Dad. Grace would want me to try at least, and a lot harder than I had been trying so far with Suzanne.

I reached over and took Dad's hand where he had laid it open on the table between us like he used to do when I was a child, like he was offering his heart to me, too, gently and without insistence, allowing me to make up my own mind but clearly communicating what he wanted.

"I feel blessed to have another chance at happiness at my age, Willa. I know I wasn't the best father to you. I'm hoping to do better this time, to learn from my mistakes. I'm older now. Wiser, I hope. Will you help me?"

"That's a little unfair, isn't it?" I wasn't really pouting. "I was five when you married Mom. I needed a father, too."

"Yes. And I wasn't good at that then. I was young. Just getting started in my career. And I made the biggest mistake a man can make. I thought I'd have more time. It never occurred to me that Grace and I wouldn't be together forever."

"Me, neither," I told him.

Before I could say or do anything else, George and Suzanne returned to the table. They both noticed our clasped hands and smiled hugely.

George clapped Jim on the back and Suzanne gave him

another kiss. Then she sat down quietly and allowed everyone to talk pleasantly for another hour.

She and George discussed the stock market's recent plunge. She told me how much she admired our federal judiciary, explaining intelligently why she felt so.

I recognized, with a guilty twinge, that Suzanne must have been nervous about meeting us, unsure of her reception. Empathy is a sign of maturity. Maybe I was developing some.

When Dad reached over, took her hand, and suggested they go upstairs to bed, Suzanne said, "Good night, Aunt Willa. I so hope our baby has that cute little gap between her two front teeth that you have. Good night, Uncle Georgie. See you in the morning."

Dad at least had the good grace to mouth the words "I'm sorry" as he herded her out the door, leaving "Uncle Georgie" and me at the table.

George had some things to do in the restaurant's kitchen and I didn't want to go upstairs, so I wandered into the Sunset Bar looking for some quiet time to think.

I picked up a Bailey's Irish Cream and a cup of coffee and took it over to my favorite booth, which was always reserved for me. One of the perks of being married to the proprietor.

Just as I started to contemplate the vagaries of the universe, Marilee Aymes sat down across from me with a drink and a cigar. Since I was an outcast from my own flat, I broke my self-imposed rule and joined her in a satisfying Partagas.

I looked at the cigar, smelled it, tasted it, and wondered not for the first time whether fifteen dollars was just too extravagant for something that would intentionally go up in smoke.

According to the propaganda, Partagas cigars come from the Dominican Republic and are made from tobacco originally from Cuba. Hand-rolled, of course, and aged until just the right flavor was to be experienced. It was the aging, along with the Cuban tobacco, that made the limited reserves special. I lit this one with a sigh of pleasure.

"Penny for your thoughts," Marilee said to me. Then, with a grin and the type of self-deprecating humor I liked her so much for, she said, "Since Otter got through with me, a penny's all I have. I was supposed to meet the little toad here, but he hasn't shown up. I'll sit with you while I wait for him."

I was searching for a safe topic of conversation. I really did not want to talk to Marilee about my father and Suzanne. But I wasn't going to tell her that, either. "I was thinking about Gil and Sandra Kelley," I said.

"Really? Whatever for?"

Because I'd seen them in the dining room at dinner, I thought. "Do you know them?"

"Sure. Knew Senior Kelley, too. He was a regular fixture around town. A philanthropist of the first order. And a really decent man. I liked him a great deal. His funeral was very, very well attended, so you know how folks felt about him."

I hadn't known Senior well. I think George did and had a lot of respect for him. Senior had dined here a few times, we attended the same parties, he belonged to the right clubs, gave to the right charities, had his picture made with the right people.

I'm told the bank prospered under his guidance. Since George's restaurant is a large depositor and we're the type of high-profile couple bankers like to get to know, Senior had made it his business to eat here, as does his son, who succeeded him as president when Senior died.

Then, being Marilee, she had to spice up the conversation. "Sandra's been telling people that Senior stole money from the bank."

"Why would she do that?"

"Who knows, where Sandra is concerned. That woman is as vindictive as a rattlesnake. Maybe Gil's been having an affair again. But I've heard her say it myself. And heard about it from several folks in the last two weeks."

"Do you believe it?"

"That Senior was a thief? Hell, no," Marilee said, re-lighting her cigar. "But he might have used the bank's money on the theory that it was his anyway. He owned the bank, you know. Or at least he did until it went public in the late 1970s."

Marilee and I pondered in silence awhile. Senior had been a wonderful, courtly Southern gentleman. I knew, but wasn't about to say, that Gil, a man of only modest success in town, must have been a great disappointment to his father.

Whereas Senior had been honest, hardworking and straightforward, Gil was a party boy, more interested in having a good time than living the staid banker's life. I'd heard that quite a few Old Tampa depositors had left the bank when Senior died.

George only continued to deposit there out of respect for Senior and concern for Sandra. The Kelleys had been posted at the club for failure to pay dues a few times. George was worried that they were having financial problems.

And he felt pretty secure in that Federal Deposit Insurance on his accounts.

"My favorite story about Senior's character was why he sent Gil away to Miami to learn the business back in the fifties." Marilee puffed her cigar and drank her bourbon straight while she told me. "Gil was a pretty wild kid around here in his high school days and his momma petted him like he was the future king of England. She had lost a couple of babies and Gil turned out to be an only child. She treated him like a miracle and Senior indulged them both."

She paused for a swig and a puff before she continued.

"Gil got into a bunch of minor scrapes that his daddy had to get him out of, but nothing that would have sent him to jail. Still, when he went off to Duke and then on to Florida for his MBA, the local mamas were pretty glad to have him away from their girls. Even then, he was a ladies' man, flirting with any female in a skirt old enough to drive and young enough to walk unassisted."

Marilee lifted her glass to the bartender and he brought her another bourbon. I could see she was just getting wound up, so I ordered another Bailey's Irish Cream on the rocks and more coffee, but I was sipping slowly and listening carefully.

"Anyway, when Gil came home from school, he started up with his old tricks."

"Like what, specifically?"

Marilee looked at me with one eye open, peering through the amber liquid in her glass. "Gil had a pretty rip-roaring summer that year. He dated several local girls, bedded a few, crashed a couple of cars, stayed out late, drank, gambled, and generally just sewed his wild oats, as Senior put it to the local cops more than once."

"Was he actually arrested?"

"I doubt it. In those days, Tampa cops didn't arrest a guy like Gil Kelley. But they picked him up and brought him home, and Senior felt obligated to smooth it over. Until Gil went too far."

"In what way?"

"Well, it turned out that one of the many local girls Gil had taken a shine to was the daughter of the McCarthy citrus empire. You've heard of those folks, haven't you?"

"Hasn't everyone?"

McCarthy had sold out to one of the big conglomerates right after we came to Tampa, for several billion dollars. They made everything from orange juice to sausage.

Every grocery store in America had examples of McCarthy labeled products in their produce, meat and dairy aisles. In Tampa, you could hardly buy anything else.

"Yes. Well, old man McCarthy was fit to be tied. Threatened to pull all his money out of the bank. He wasn't about to have his daughter messed up with the likes of Gil Kelley. No-siree-bob." Marilee slapped her glass down on the table and ordered another bourbon.

This had to be her standard practice for getting served, I guess. It worked. The bartender scurried over with another bourbon and I made a mental note to get someone to drive Marilee home later.

"So what happened?" I asked her, impatient for the punch line.

"Mariam McCarthy got pregnant, that's what happened. And Gil Kelley 'borrowed' some money from the bank to send her to Paris for an abortion. Or at least that's the story that made the rounds at the time. Senior found out about it and shipped Gil off to Miami for two years until Old Man McCarthy could get over it and find his daughter someone else to marry."

Marilee finished her story with the bulldog look I've seen on her face a thousand times. The one that said she was telling the truth and if you didn't believe it, well, then, that was just your problem.

But I believed her. And I felt sorry for Mariam McCarthy. "What happened to her?"

CHAPTER TWELVE

Tampa, Florida
Monday 11:00 p.m.
January 29, 2001

"SHE STAYED IN FRANCE for a while, but then she came back to live in Tampa and married Ozgood Richardson. Didn't you know?"

The CJ's wife? Had a torrid affair with Gil Kelley? Hard to believe, even if they were both young and foolish at the time.

Actually, it was hard to believe Mariam McCarthy Richardson had ever been young and foolish. All the times I've been around her, she's been about as interesting as paint dust.

I couldn't believe she had suffered a broken heart at Gil Kelley's hands, but I did believe that if she had, she'd be mortified to be living in the same town with him.

And I also understood why Kelley was a reluctant member of the Tampa social scene. He wasn't welcome at many clubs and parties. Old Tampa has a long memory and wouldn't have condoned such behavior, even in a young man. Especially if

Mariam Richardson was there to put the kibosh on it.

Marilee and I talked for another hour or so before I got one of the waiters to drive her home and gave him cab fare back. Then, I went in and talked to George for a while before going up to bed with a great deal on my mind and hoping that all of our house guests had already retired for the night.

Tuesday morning, the *U.S. v. Otter* file was on my desk, along with stacks of other files, mail, and stuff that had spontaneously generated in the night. I looked at the notes I'd left for myself on what I'd planned to do today.

A few years ago, I started making a list at the end of every day for tomorrow's work. It was the only way I could make any sense of my workload. Otherwise, I'd start the day with a plan and within minutes, be completely overtaken by the waves of work that flowed into my office as the tide overflows our beach.

While the tide ebbs and flows on a regular daily cycle, my work remains for years. Since I became a judge, I understand the story of Sisyphus on a personal level.

The Greek who was condemned to forever push the boulder up the hill was a perfect mascot for judicial work.

Today's project list said: "No. 1 – Check Ron Wheaton's history; No. 2 – Review *U.S. v. Otter* file."

While my ancient government-issue computer was booting up, to use my time wisely, I pulled the *U.S. v. Otter* file over toward me and took a look at it, once again lusting after the new courthouse where the judges had much newer, faster computers.

The second I started reading the *U.S. v. Otter* file, I forgot about my computer search altogether. Otter was being prosecuted for conspiracy to commit fraud, money laundering, witness tampering and fraud.

What was surprising was the number and caliber of people

who claimed to have been fleeced by this rather ordinary man. People who should have known better. Educated people, who were obviously wealthy to have paid Otter the millions they claimed, but must have had more dollars than sense.

The indictment charged that Otter had sold, cleaned, cut, appraised, and consigned diamonds and other jewelry to the listed twenty complainants, and countless unnamed others.

All along, the indictment said, Otter had given his customers cheap imitations. When sued by fleeced customers, Otter counter-sued for slander and reached confidential settlements for less than his customers' losses, so complaints about him never spread.

Like Fitzgerald House, several of the complainants were also involved in civil suits against Otter. Many of the complainants were names I recognized and a few were people I knew personally: celebrity golfers, performers, national and local businessmen.

The claims were eerily similar. In paragraph after paragraph, the indictment named individuals who had bought jewelry created by famous designers, now deceased.

The most frequently mentioned was the award-winning Paulding Farnham, one of the world's most talented and artistic designers of fine jewelry. At the Paris Exposition of 1889, Farnham had received the gold medal for his Tiffany & Co. jewelry designs.

Farnham's exquisite designs helped Tiffany's become the leader in the field of fine jewelry and silver.

In several paragraphs, Otter was alleged to have sold copies of Farnham's award-winning, twenty-four karat gold-and-enamel orchid brooches, and other pieces of Farnham's original work, to unsuspecting customers.

In some instances, the original designs were now featured in public collections at the Metropolitan Museum of Art, the High

Museum in Atlanta, and others, the indictment said.

But Otter told his customers that Farnham created designs for private customers, as well, selling his copies as Farnham's originals.

Because Farnham left Tiffany & Co. in 1908, when he was just forty-eight years old, the claim that he had continued to create one-of-a-kind jewelry for many years thereafter was certainly plausible.

People who should have known better believed it.

Otter had sold a pin consisting of a cluster of white tigers to a famous illusionist. It was made of diamonds in several colors. The diamonds were later determined to have been treated with radiation, and so were less valuable than the illusionist had believed.

On other pieces, Otter was alleged to have inflated the weight and value of the stones, charging his customers several times the market price for such jewelry.

A particularly unbelievable allegation concerned a 40-karat cubic zirconium that cost less than two hundred dollars. The stone was given a celebrity name and sold by Otter for over a million dollars.

As authentic looking as these manufactured stones have become, it was still hard to believe someone would part with a million dollars without a valid appraisal. Human folly among the wealthy was more rampant than I'd realized.

In all, the indictment claimed that Otter had fleeced customers for a total of more than $170 million. Punitive damages and recoverable attorney fees would also have been available in civil actions based on each individual fraud.

If convicted in the criminal case, Otter faced up to 165 years in prison, in addition to a potential order to make restitution.

No doubt about it, if Otter was convicted, his pampered

lifestyle would be over. Prison would not be kind to anyone used to the finer things, to put it mildly.

If Otter could make restitution, the criminal case might be pled down to lesser charges or dismissed altogether. The complainants might be persuaded to go away quietly if they got their money back.

The negative and outraged responses I'd gotten from Otter's insurance adjuster to my suggestion that the insurance company pay to settle the Fitzgerald House case, suggested that Otter would not have any better luck getting money for the claims in the criminal case.

Where would the money come from?

So Otter must be desperate to find enough money to settle these claims. Where would he get $170 million? Tampa isn't Palm Beach. That kind of money would be hard to come by here.

The assistant U.S. attorney assigned to the *U.S. v. Otter* criminal case was someone I'd known for years, and had always considered an astute lawyer. Briefly, I considered picking up the phone and dialing his office, but decided against it.

Judges are not supposed to seek or obtain information about cases on our dockets except through the litigation process. Because this was a criminal case and would be tried to a jury, I would have a little more leeway than if I was to sit in the trial as the finder of fact.

I considered how to discover what the federal "fraud squad" had learned about Armstrong Otter. The only way I would feel comfortable investigating now was if I transferred the case to another judge, or if both of the parties consented. That was about as likely as rain in the desert.

I could think of no appropriate way to learn more about Otter and I was out of time to think about it further. The *U.S. v. Otter* case was up for a pre-trial conference in two weeks and I'd learn more about it then.

But now, both my law clerks stood in my doorway with lists of questions, the computer flashed to tell me I had mail, all four buttons of my telephone were lit up with phone calls holding for my attention, and Margaret reminded me of my afternoon calendar. My "To do today, first thing" list was buried under a mountain of paper.

I didn't give Ron Wheaton's computer check another thought.

The rest of the week passed swiftly and uneventfully. Fitzgerald House requested a short adjournment of the trial, which I granted, giving them time to resolve the case. I'd been required to make some pretrial rulings that would give certain advantages to Fitzgerald House. Perhaps Otter and his insurance company would agree to settle the case.

I called Ben Hathaway several times, but he wasn't available to speak to me. Apparently, the Tampa police chief had a few things on his "To do" list, too. I hoped no news meant he didn't have the results of Ron Wheaton's autopsy. I allowed myself to be lulled into complacency on the investigation, thinking there was nothing to investigate.

I tried to talk to Margaret several times, but she remained uninterested in my help. She seemed to be dealing with Ron's death just fine, and I even heard her singing in the office several times.

Margaret looked better, younger and happier than I'd seen her in months. I knew she was a bereaved widow, but someone who didn't know her history would never have guessed that she'd just lost her husband.

She hadn't planned a memorial service. Margaret said she was the only family Ron had, and she didn't need a memorial to remember him. I feel the same way about funerals. The point of them is to provide closure for the living, I'm told. They do nothing for me but make me sad. I didn't find Margaret's decision bizarre.

Citing the need to resolve some problems with Ron's finances and life insurance, Margaret took a couple of days off at the end of the week. I didn't wholly believe her, but I felt she was giving me a clear message to stay out of her life, so I allowed myself to be deterred and occupied by a couple of applications for emergency temporary restraining orders and my other cases.

Dad's investigation was moving relentlessly forward. He'd left a note on the refrigerator door before I got up Wednesday morning saying he'd found a paper trail taking him to Miami to investigate the bank and would be out of town. Thankfully, he'd taken Suzanne with him.

He was due back Saturday and I looked forward to hearing about his progress. It gave us something to talk about besides the baby, Suzanne and my hurt feelings.

Dad and Suzanne offered to get a hotel room at the Marriott Waterside when they returned on Friday. Both George and I prevailed to keep them at Minaret, if for no other reason than to avoid the awkward explanations the move would require.

After being around her for several days, Suzanne continued to make me uncomfortable. Every time I saw her, Suzanne and Dad's adoration affected me like fingernails on a chalkboard. It was going to take me a while to get used to the idea of Dad having a wife and a baby. It would have been a little easier to deal with if Suzanne wasn't so good-natured, obviously in love with Dad, kind to everyone, and just generally so damn likeable.

My soul mother, Kate Austin, had gone on an extended vacation to Italy before Gasparilla started. She was the only person who could give me some objectivity on this thing with

Dad since she had been there since he and Mom married. Without Kate to discuss everything with, I was adrift in emotions that likely had no basis in reality. Dad had known Kate would be in Italy this month, which made me wonder whether he'd chosen to bring Suzanne to Tampa now so that he wouldn't have to deal with Kate and me at the same time.

I couldn't imagine that Kate, who had been my mother's best friend, would approve of Dad's marriage any more than I did. I tried to call Kate in Italy a couple of times, but she was always out of her room. I'd left messages, but she hadn't called back.

George was certainly no help. He kept telling me that Suzanne was Dad's choice and I would do well to accept her, unless I wanted to alienate Dad further.

Men can be so obtuse sometimes. Of course, I knew that.

But knowing and doing are two different things. I would come to terms with Suzanne in my own way, but the marriage was still too new, too much of a shock, to resolve itself so neatly in a few days after almost twenty-five years of the status quo.

George removed the restaurant's money from Gil Kelley's bank and re-deposited it elsewhere after hearing Marilee's story about Gil's youthful and distasteful indiscretions.

Sandra Kelley's allegations about Senior, which George had heard from a couple of other sources, caused further disquiet. George didn't believe Senior had embezzled from the bank, but he felt it was better to be safe than sorry. Besides that, if Marilee's stories were true, which George didn't wholly believe because they came from Marilee, he didn't want to be associated with Gil Kelley anyway.

Between my personal life and my work, I had little time for Margaret. And that was before the Friday, when, for the first time in my life, I got served with a subpoena.

CHAPTER THIRTEEN

Tampa, Florida
Friday 3:00 p.m.
February 16, 2001

THE SUBPOENA COMMANDED ME to testify before a panel appointed by the Judicial Counsel, who seemed to investigate judges at the drop of a gavel in Tampa these days.

We'd had several of our state court judges resign under pressure from The Florida Bar's Judicial Qualifications Commission. We all knew the JQC was investigating alleged improprieties by other judges. Ranging from allegations of gambling using county computers, to sexual misconduct with subordinates and case fixing, the investigations were alarming.

But the state JQC investigations hadn't reached the federal judiciary. Until now.

The process server came into my chambers respectfully enough. He asked me my name and handed me the folded subpoena in an envelope. As he left, I removed the subpoena and began to read it.

118 | DIANE CAPRI

I was being called to testify in the matter of a confidential investigation into allegations of misconduct by one of our federal judges. The judge remained unidentified, since the investigation was confidential until charges, if any, were filed.

But whoever had put the subpoena in the envelope had enclosed a copy of an article from the Tribune reporting the story of sexual harassment allegations by two female magistrate judges against "an unnamed federal judge."

Someone had penciled the letters "CJ" in the margin.

According to the newspaper account, the "unnamed judge" had made "unwanted passes" at the magistrate judges, left suggestive messages on their answering machines and asked them out on dates. In writing, yet.

All the women judges were being subpoenaed to testify. If more instances of harassment were found, the investigation would be spread to other women in the courthouse, including law clerks and support staff.

The old geezer! Who'd have thought he had it in him?

Truly, I didn't.

I wasn't fond of the CJ, and I was surely annoyed at his refusal to move me to the new courthouse, but I knew his wife. I didn't think he'd dare look for a date at work or anywhere else.

Men are often falsely accused of sexual harassment and it's a hard claim to defend. The CJ struck me as dumb enough to leave messages to women that could be traced, but smarter than to try to date women he worked with.

Besides, I knew both of these magistrate judges. While they were somewhat strident and opinionated, I didn't believe they would falsely accuse the CJ. Among other things, they did not have the luxury I had of a lifetime appointment. They liked their jobs. If, as the paper said, they were complaining, it was because they had something to complain about.

What was it with men and sex, anyway? Did the recent impeachment of a United States president teach them nothing?

I was figuratively shaking my head over this development while remaining sure that there was more to this story than met the eye. The CJ had a number of detractors and he was unpopular with the junior jurists. I figured there was a hidden motive in this story that I'd have to wait to learn.

Part of me just rebelled against everything. I felt both exhaustion and an overwhelming need for solitude. I was tired of the "George Knows Best" show, Dad's mid-life crisis, Suzanne's sweet disposition, constant smile, extended fashion show and incessant twittering, and, most of all, tired of worrying more about Margaret than she was worrying about herself.

I was even tired of Kate's absence. If I wasn't running ten miles a day, I would probably have strangled someone that week.

It was a good thing that Margaret didn't need my help and compassion, I thought on my drive home Friday night along the Bayshore toward Plant Key. Help and compassion were in short supply with me right now and they didn't seem to be on the immediate horizon, either.

Such was my mindset as I drove across the Plant Key Bridge in the dark at 6:30 Friday night, with a full briefcase, a head full of troubles, and a heavy spirit in need of care.

The tranquil vista of Hillsborough Bay was obscured by February's early nightfall, the avenue of palms was dark as pitch, and Minaret blocked the lighted downtown Tampa skyline from my view.

Our house, Minaret, is a grand old building. It was built in the 1890s when Tampa's richest citizen, Henry Plant, wanted a family home. Plant was constructing the Plant Hotel, now the University of Tampa, which he believed would be a Mecca for the rich and famous. When they came to the hotel, he wanted to show off a fabulous home, as well. He wasn't going to be outdone by his rival, Henry Flagler, who had created such a magnificent hotel in Palm Beach.

Before he could build his house, Plant had to build Plant Key itself. When the Port of Tampa channels were being dredged to allow passage of freighters, Plant persuaded the Army Corps of Engineers to build up enough land mass for Plant Key at the same time.

Plant made his island oval-shaped, with the narrow ends facing south toward Bayshore and out into the Gulf. It's about a mile wide by two miles long. Plant also built Plant Key Bridge, which connected Plant Key to Bayshore Boulevard, just east of Gandy. Marine life ecosystems weren't a priority then. If you had an island, you had to have a way to get there, didn't you?

I pulled under the portico and let the valet park Greta, my Mercedes CLK convertible, and grabbed my briefcase out of the trunk. I prepared to trudge up the front stairs to our flat with all the enthusiasm of Marie Antoinette on her way to the guillotine.

So lost was I in my own thoughts that I ran right into the broad back of Chief Ben Hathaway, standing in the doorway, waiting for a larger party in front of him to be seated.

Ben turned around, saying, "Hold on a minute, there, partner—Oh, Willa, it's you."

"Sorry, Ben. Didn't see your tail lights." I flashed him a weak grin. "What seems to be the hold up?"

"I don't know. Looks like round two of the drunken revelers you had here last Saturday to me," Ben replied.

I looked through into Aunt Minnie's tastefully decorated foyer.

When Aunt Minnie had lived here, the house was a private home and these were her secretaries, breakfronts and sideboards. Even the small butler's table, between the upholstered camelback sofas in the center, were Aunt Minnie's pieces, and they were filled to capacity with small children climbing over the arms and the graceful backs.

The soft blue *fleur-de-lis* wallpaper had been restored to match its former gilded excellence. Even using modern materials, the wallpaper wouldn't hold up long after we scrubbed off the sticky paw prints prevalent about three feet off the floor.

Would Aunt Minnie be pleased to have her beautiful things returned to usefulness, or horrified that strangers came into her home for lunch and dinner seven days a week? I felt sure she'd be horrified at the disrespect those unruly, excited children were showing for her furnishings tonight.

"Good grief!" I said, turning on my heel. I left Hathaway there waiting for a table, retraced my steps back down the stairs and around to the back entrance. I'd forgotten that Minaret Krewe would be here in force for the pre-event party to celebrate tomorrow's Knights of Sant' Yago Illuminated Night Parade in Ybor City. The grounds were quickly filling up with cars and guests.

I put my head down, watched my path, and carefully made my way around the house in the semi-darkness.

I heard them before I saw their shadows. Two men, close together, were speaking softly. I couldn't see them clearly. They were too engrossed in their conversation to notice my approach. I recognized the CJ's voice, raised in stage-whisper anger.

"Damn you, anyway. Why the hell did you have to come

here? And why now? I already told you I don't have any more money." CJ shoved the smaller man roughly.

He whispered something I couldn't hear before he pushed back.

Inadvertently eavesdropping, I couldn't hear the smaller man. Whatever he said angered CJ further, because CJ gave him a push hard enough to challenge his balance.

"Forget it!" CJ said. "Just forget it! It won't happen! Go crawl back into the hole you came from and leave me alone!"

The smaller man righted himself, said something further, walked around out of my sight and behind a parked van. I thought I saw a flash of white hair, but I couldn't be certain.

CJ stood there a little longer, raking his hand through his hair and muttering curses loud enough for me to hear. Then he turned and saw me standing, watching.

Not knowing what to do, I simply continued to walk toward the back of the house. As I passed CJ standing in the shadows, I said, "Good evening. Anything I can help you with?"

"No, thank you," he said.

I'm not sure whether he realized I recognized him or not. I kept my head down. CJ didn't stop as he walked past me, but he was close. I could feel his heavy breathing and the anger that blew off him like radiating heat from an out-of-control bonfire.

I let out the breath I hadn't known I'd been holding, marched directly up the back stairs and into the flat without another word. But I was trembling so hard it took me three tries to unlock the door.

Inside, our Labradors, Harry and Bess, were laying by the door, waiting for anyone who happened to come in so that they could immediately lick them to death.

Bess is black and Harry is yellow. Like their namesakes,

Harry and Bess Truman, they're fiercely independent dogs, thoroughly devoted to one another. We got them originally for protection and guard dogs because so many strangers come into what is, after all, our home. Of course, anyone who spends five seconds with Harry and Bess realizes what useless guard dogs they are. They do have big barks and that counts for something, at least to strangers. We still pay the alarm company every month, just in case.

Both Harry and Bess were wild to get out. I went over and opened the back door. If they found the CJ and scared him off the property, so much the better.

"What was that all about, I wonder?" I said to no one as I sat heavily onto the couch to gain a little self-control. I'd recognized Armstrong Otter as soon as I'd seen him standing there. It was the second time the CJ's connection to Otter had been thrown in my path.

I worried that their connection to each other somehow related to Margaret, and I didn't know what to do. I would have gone downstairs and found Chief Hathaway, but I didn't want to give him any more reason to upset Margaret. At least, that's what I think my motivation was.

George would be working until well into the night. I was beginning to feel like a prisoner in my own home and I couldn't wait for Gasparilla month to be over so that I could get some of my life back.

I decided to eat scrambled eggs in the kitchen rather than face the crowd downstairs again. George wouldn't even notice I was missing. Tomorrow night would be another long one as we kept the restaurant open until the wee hours of the morning for folks going to the Knight Parade. I felt entitled to a quiet dinner before the onslaught.

Dressed in yellow pull-on knit slacks and a matching sweatshirt with brightly colored fish on the front, I sat at the dining room table and ate my infamous "Eggs *a la* Willa." I'm not sure exactly what I put in the eggs. It's never the same thing, but just whatever we happen to have that isn't growing mold.

This time, the final result was heavenly, and I don't even like eggs. Pumpernickel toast and hot tea completed the meal, which was fine enough to support a great French chardonnay. Not that it matters what I eat with a great French chardonnay.

I intended to think about Margaret, Otter, the CJ and Ron Wheaton. I meant to figure out what the connection was between them and why I felt so uneasy about it all. But by the time I had finished my eggs and wine, I could hardly keep my eyes open and called it a night.

I slept fitfully, and my dreams that night were vivid snapshots of one disjointed scene after another. Ron Wheaton was walking around Minaret, kicking up his heels every now and then, square dancing at the Minaret Krewe Gasparilla Ball with Sandra Kelley as the Queen, wearing a sparkling tiara, diamonds dripping around her neck.

Gil Kelley with his King's crown, leering after my stepmother, who sported the swollen belly of her near-term pregnancy, giving her lanky frame the look of a pencil carrying a basketball.

Dr. Marilee Aymes in my courtroom arguing that Sandra Kelley should be executed for embezzling from her husband's bank.

And, just to be sure I recognized these as nightmares, the CJ in a cartoon version of prison garb, peering at me from behind the bars of our holding cell in the old federal courthouse.

When I sat bolt upright in bed, my heart pounding wildly, I

was grateful for whatever had awakened me, although it took me a few seconds to figure out what it was.

I thought I heard the cannons on the José Gasparilla firing off just as they had on the day of the Pirate Parade, when Ron Wheaton had died and Chief Hathaway suggested that Margaret could have been a mercy killer.

Once I came fully awake, I realized it was still dark out and the cannons wouldn't sound again until next year's parade.

So what woke me up? George was snoring gently in the bed beside me, exhausted from the party tonight, for which I had never made it downstairs. Both dogs were sleeping peacefully, too. Why did I wake up?

And then I remembered the final snapshot in my dream. Margaret Wheaton gleefully injecting her wheelchair-bound husband with a lethal dose of morphine.

CHAPTER FOURTEEN

Tampa, Florida
Saturday 4:00 a.m.
February 17, 2001

SATURDAY BEGAN EARLY. I couldn't get back to sleep after that last nightmare. If a real noise had awakened me, I never learned what it was. Otherwise, it must have been an over-active imagination, or messages from my subconscious. Or something.

In any event, when I woke up at four o'clock, it was pitch black out and colder than a frozen daiquiri in our flat.

I wrapped myself in the warm terrycloth bathrobe that George had bought me for Christmas from the Don CeSar hotel. The robe was pink, like everything else associated with the hotel, and had an emerald green crest on the pocket. I snuggled my feet into the matching lamb's-wool lined slippers and headed to the kitchen.

Temperatures were well below normal for February. Our nineteenth-century home was long on charm, but drafty and short on heat. When we renovated the house, we did the best we could with insulation. But the old clapboard siding had cracks in some places that gave Old Man Winter free passage.

Both dogs and George were sleeping soundly and the rest of the flat was quiet. I went into the kitchen and started my tea ritual, the one I use when I want to calm my nerves. I'd picked up my journal on the way through the den, too.

I'd started journaling recently at Kate's suggestion. She had given me a black spiral-bound journal with Andy Melon's words on the front, "When your heart speaks, take good notes."

I was resistant to it at first, but now I found writing in the journal to be a comfort. Kate, who is more than a little metaphysical, feels strongly that keeping a journal is a way to reach your inner guidance, whatever that is. I just feel it helps me to organize my chaotic thoughts.

I still didn't believe Ron Wheaton had been murdered, Chief Hathaway's suspicions, Dr. Aymes' suggestions, and my over-active dreams notwithstanding. But I'd found during a spot of trouble George had been in recently that it helped me to figure things out if I wrote them down.

After the kettle heated, I poured the hot water over chamomile tea in my mother's Royal Albert teapot and covered it with the rose tea cozy she'd loved. This ritual with Mom's tea things comforts me somehow.

While waiting for the tea to steep, I carried everything in on a tray to my favorite chair and ottoman in the den, where I lit a small fire in the fireplace. The last piece of the ritual is to select one of the animals from my Herend zoo to share my contemplation.

I studied the animals inside the curio on the wall in the living room. The zoo had been Aunt Minnie's. I think she had a Hungarian admirer at one time. He gave her a beautiful set of Queen Victoria china and the whimsical porcelain figurines painted in the technically difficult fishnet pattern.

Judging from the many animals in her zoo, the relationship must have lasted for a while. Aunt Minnie had given all the animals Hungarian names that she left in the inventory we received when George inherited the house.

To the extent Aunt Minnie's ghost or spirit still lives with us, she must be pleased that I admire her zoo and George is adding to her collection. Whenever a particularly special opportunity arises, George orders an unusual piece from Hungary to give me.

The animals are now available here in the States, but all of Aunt Minnie's pieces, and mine, were specially made for us.

Tonight, I chose Szabo, Aunt Minnie's blue cat, stretched out and lying down, looking as if she was as content with life as a cat could possibly be. Seeking some tranquility myself, I settled in with her, picked up my journal and began to write down everything I knew about Ron and Margaret Wheaton.

I found I needed to shorten my musings because in the past ten years, I'd learned a lot about Margaret.

For instance, I knew she was an only child, like me. That made us feel closer to one another.

I'm technically an orphan, I guess, since both my natural parents are dead. But I don't feel like an orphan. James Harper adopted me when he married my mother. I was five years old and he is the only father I've ever known.

Kate Austin was my mother's best friend and has been my soul mother since I was sixteen, the year Mom was diagnosed with the breast cancer that eventually killed her.

But Margaret felt like the orphan she was.

Both of her parents had died when she was young. She didn't marry Ron Wheaton until she was twenty-five. Ron had adored Margaret. That much was obvious to anyone who ever saw them together.

Although she was grateful for Ron and felt affection for him, when she married, Margaret's heart had belonged to another. She'd never told me much about him but, once, when another friend had been having marital problems, Margaret said, "Not everyone has the storybook marriage you have, Willa. Some of us can't have our one true love. We've had to make the best of what we've been offered."

It's one of life's ironies that everyone always assumes my life is so perfect. People feel free to accuse me of being beautiful, rich and, most dismissively, lucky, as if such luck was a personal affront to the speaker.

Margaret had done so that day, telling me that my life was blessed in a way few lives are, that I should be grateful. What she didn't say, but I heard, was "more humble."

The truth is that I feel attractive enough, most days, although I'm far from beautiful. We live comfortably, but George and I both have full-time jobs, and not just because we want to contribute to the world, except in the sense that we have to pay cash for groceries, like everyone else.

I am lucky, though not in the way people accuse me of.

The most significant thing that's ever happened to me was that my mother died of cancer. While she was ill, we spent as much time together as we could: I wanted to savor every moment of the life she had left. Mom wanted me to go to school and the truant officers insisted that I go at least half a day. But the last few months of her life, they let me stay home.

That was such a glorious time. She taught me how to make bread, arrange flowers, put on a dinner party. She told me all of the secrets a mother imparts to a daughter about dating and dealing with men.

Mom and I had our own little world then. Dad was traveling, as he always had, even at what was clearly the end of his wife's life. On some level, I never forgave him for that.

But on another level I was glad for the time it gave my mother and me to be together. Maybe that was his present to both of us.

It was while Mom was sick that she told me she'd wanted to be a lawyer instead of a nurse. And I promised her that I would do what she had not done.

Eventually, Mom died and her husband never came home. I was sent to live with Kate, graduated from high school, and then went directly to the University of Michigan.

What doesn't kill you makes you stronger. I know now that I was lucky to have loved my mother for sixteen years, and to have had her unconditional love while she lived.

She sent me into the world with that—the love, desire and support necessary to make something of my life. Every time I think of her, I think, "I could be better," not just as a lawyer, or a woman, but as a person.

She believed that what's important is how you live your life, how you treat others. She taught me always to do my best and to help those who need it. It was a hard lesson to learn at sixteen, but I learned it, and it sustains me. It also gets me into trouble. Mighty Mouse does save the day, but it's not easy.

Of course, I am grateful for my life. But anyone who really knows me understands that things are not always what they seem.

And that was the remark I'd snapped at Margaret at the time, causing her to stop talking.

I cursed my impatience now, because I missed the opportunity to learn more about Margaret Wheaton's relationship with her husband, why she married him and what had happened to the love of Margaret's life.

Ron Wheaton was a janitor and later, maintenance supervisor, for Hillsborough County Schools. He was a big man, capable and well-liked, from all accounts.

He and Margaret didn't travel in our social circles for the most part, but when we did see them at events or around town, Ron was always pleasant to me.

We invited Ron and Margaret to Minaret on the day of the Parade of Pirates, just as we had invited almost everyone we knew. Before Ron was diagnosed with ALS, both were active members of Minaret Krewe. They would come to the parties every year and celebrate until the wee hours. Ron was a party person, even then, and so was Margaret.

After his diagnosis, Ron deteriorated fairly slowly for an ALS patient, but it was just too much of a struggle for them to socialize as they once had done. Indeed, I was surprised when they showed up for the Minaret Krewe party last week.

Ron's condition had gotten much worse than Margaret had led me to believe. He was mostly confined to his motorized wheelchair, which he could still maneuver himself but couldn't get out of without help. They had twenty-four hour care at home, where Ron slept in the guest room in a hospital bed most days.

I'd been pleased they had come because Ron wouldn't allow visitors to the house. He hated people to see him so debilitated, unable to care for himself and dependent on Margaret.

I refilled my teacup, poked the fire and gazed at Szabo's peaceful countenance, imagining I could hear the ceramic cat purr.

Returning to my journal, I recorded all the curious behavior I'd witnessed this week, from Margaret, the CJ, Gil and Sandra Kelley, Marilee Aymes, and Armstrong Otter.

Was there a connection between them all? And, if so, what was it? Did it have anything to do with Ron Wheaton's death? Or to Otter's legal problems? As I wrote these questions down in my journal, I felt better.

Asking better questions is the first step to solving problems of all kinds. I knew the answers would be revealed to me in due time. Thinking about everyone else left me free to ignore the issues I was facing with Dad and Suzanne, too, although I knew I'd have to do something about that soon.

The chamomile tea wasn't making me sleepy, and I'd written about all I knew of Ron and Margaret Wheaton. The sky was slowly beginning to lighten in the east. I made a list of all I had to do today. Yet another celebration this evening was scheduled here before and after the Knights of Sant' Yago Illuminated Knight Parade in Ybor City.

Whatever it was that caused George to think having a Krewe named after Minaret and sponsoring them every year would be a good idea, I can't imagine.

Yes, the Krewe did a lot of good works for the community and George was always wanting to "give something back," but really—we just could have written a check or something.

Which made me smile. After all, I was the one training for the 15K Gasparilla Distance Classic next weekend just to raise money for Young Mothers' Second Chance.

A small light dawned in my head—that was another thing I knew about Margaret Wheaton. She sits on the board at Young Mothers' Second Chance. She told me once that these women and their babies were her own children and grandchildren, since she and Ron had never been blessed with a child themselves.

I reopened my journal and wrote that down, too, where I'd previously written in "Children—none."

I closed my journal, and as I set it aside it fell to the floor. When I bent down to pick it up, I found the article from the Tribune George had brought to my attention last Saturday. I picked it up and returned it to my journal, promising myself I'd read it after my run. I replaced Szabo the cat, the tea things and my journal to the kitchen table, and began the day.

Dressed in a long-sleeved tee-shirt and long cotton pants, I pulled out my light-weight gloves and a headband to cover my ears, and left George snoring while the dogs and I crept down the back stairs.

It was too cold to throw sticks into the water for them today, so we started to run. Within seconds they were so far ahead of me that I could barely see them in the gloaming. They wouldn't leave the island, though, so I wasn't worried. It was peaceful to run in the pre-dawn without the dogs trying to lope around me every step of the way.

After two laps around Plant Key, all three of us returned upstairs. I headed directly for the shower while Harry and Bess had their breakfast. I could hear voices in the kitchen and noticed that George was out of bed as I walked through the bedroom and our dressing room to the shower.

I missed my weekly golf game during Gasparilla month. Usually, I spend every Saturday morning at Great Oaks Country Club, playing golf with my former law partner and whomever else we could get to make up a foursome.

With every Saturday taken by one festivity or another, golf was impossible. Yet another reason to look forward to March, I thought, smelling the ginseng shower gel that promised to deliver energy today.

When I toweled off and dressed in black jeans, Topsiders, lime green socks and a matching lime green sweatshirt, I spent about two minutes with the blow dryer, which is all it takes to dry my short auburn hair. I applied light makeup and quite a bit of concealer over the dark circles under my eyes.

Thinking I was prepared, I shrugged and faced the day.

CHAPTER FIFTEEN

Tampa, Florida
Saturday 8:30 a.m.
February 17, 2001

BY THE TIME I made it to the kitchen, George was alone, reading the paper and drinking coffee in his white pajamas and the royal blue silk robe he favors. I smiled as I noticed the blue silk scuffs on his feet, too. How many men dress like that these days? Damn few, I figured, given the casual look that has become so popular with the Generation Xers.

I'm an old-fashioned girl. Give me Cary Grant in his silks anytime over those rugged Xers with their hip-hugging pants, tight shirts and scratchy, unshaven faces.

"Morning, darling," he said, eyeing my journal on the corner of the kitchen table and the leftover tea things. "Manage to run your cares away?" George knows me too well.

"Not all of them," I told him as I made my *café con leche* and Cuban toast. Usually I don't eat breakfast, but I'd been up so long this was practically lunchtime. "Where is everyone?"

"We should talk about Jim and Suzanne, you know. It's not the kind of thing that's going to go away by itself. In fact, I'd say we're soon going to have even more to think about," George told me gently.

"Like what?" I was still fooling around with the toast. It takes longer to toast half a loaf of Cuban bread than you might think, even if you don't put the cheese on it, which is the way I eat it.

"Jim told me they want to have several children. This isn't going to be the only one. You'll have a much bigger family than you expected. It's something you're going to have to deal with."

This wasn't altogether surprising, really. Suzanne is young and she told me she loves children. I expected her to want more of them, at least in the abstract. These things have a way of working themselves out once the reality of 3:00 a.m. feedings sinks in.

"I know," I told him.

"Then why are you so resistant to the whole thing? I'd think Jim's happiness would be important to you. Isn't it time for you to show him what you're made of?"

"Funny. I thought I was." I took the toast from the oven and added the cheese, returning it to the broiler.

"Meaning what, exactly?"

"Jim Harper wasn't much of a father to me. He thought of me as 'in the way' when Mom was alive and he wanted her all to himself. And he just left me alone for years after Mom died. If it hadn't been for Kate and her family, I'd have had nothing resembling a normal life." I put the cheese toast on the plate and sat across from George at the table.

"All of that was years ago, Willa. People often attempt to repeat their lives and improve on the job they did the first time around. You have the ability to be a hero, here. To show Jim, Suzanne and everyone else that you're a bigger person than most. To live up to everyone's expectations of you. Including your own." George was attempting his personal brand of gentle persuasion. What he meant was I had a chance to live up to his standards.

To George, it was always of utmost importance to do the right thing, the honorable thing; to go one's own way; "to thine own self be true" and all that.

George thinks the only one we have to please is ourselves, and that we should have exacting standards for our own behavior. This, of course, leads to constant disappointment when others don't behave as well.

Such as one's wife when her father marries a woman half his age and begins to act like the father he never was.

I said nothing as I ate my toast and reached for the front page of the Tribune. After a few moments of silence, George got up, put his dishes in the sink, and kissed my head as he walked by to get dressed for the very long day we had ahead of us.

A short while later, the telephone rang twice and I got up to answer it. "Is that son-of-a-bitch, Jim Harper, there?"

A woman's voice. One I recognized.

"Hello? Sandra? It's Willa Carson. Dad's not here right now. Can I help you?" I thought I heard growling from Sandra Kelley in response.

"Yes, you can help me. Did you know your father was in Miami snooping around Gil's bank this week?"

"Not really, I…"

"You can tell him that we don't appreciate him suggesting that Senior was a thief. Gil is damned upset about it, and so am I. You can tell him that for me." She was breathing heavily as she spoke to me in loud, angry tones.

"I'm sorry. I don't know anything about this, Sandra, but I'm sure you both are upset. I'd heard that you were suggesting Senior had embezzled money from his bank, though. Didn't you expect people to take you seriously about it?"

"You just tell Jim Harper to keep his nose out of our business or he'll have someone else to answer to!" she actually shouted at me—just before she slammed down the phone.

I looked at the receiver and then replaced it as George came back.

"She hung up on me," I said.

"I figured that. If I was an eavesdropper, I could have heard the entire conversation from the other room," he said. "Actually, I did hear every word she said. No surprise. Surely you didn't think she'd take it well—Jim going into her husband's bank and asking questions about thefts by Senior Kelley."

I frowned at him. It was okay for me to be upset with Jim, but I didn't like Sandra Kelley's tone. I'd always thought she was more than a little unstable.

"Do you have any idea what your Dad's been doing in Miami?" George asked.

"He didn't really tell me. He mentioned last week that he was doing a bank investigation. I didn't realize he meant Tampa Bay Bank."

The hordes would descend on George's restaurant later today. Using my downtime wisely, I headed over to Pass-a-Grille to see The Armstrong Otter Studio for myself. Driving over the bridge from Plant Key to Bayshore Boulevard, I turned left and then right onto Gandy, heading due west. As I drove, I assured myself the visit was not unethical.

Otter had invited me to come over. I didn't intend to speak to him. And I wasn't sitting in a bench trial, I rationalized.

Nor did I intend to rely on what I learned to make a decision in any case. Besides that, based on what I'd read in the *U.S. v. Otter* file, I was the only person in Tampa who had never seen the studio.

Some people, like the CJ, would say my visit had the appearance of impropriety. But so did smoking in my office, which I sometimes did, too. Nothing I said in my imaginary argument convinced me to turn the car around.

Gandy Boulevard begins at the Bayshore, runs for about five miles as a busy commercial highway, and then becomes a bridge connecting Hillsborough and Pinellas counties.

Gandy Bridge is the third and southernmost bridge connecting the two counties and helping to form the Tampa Bay Metropolitan Area, as the Chamber of Commerce likes to call it.

Until the advent of crass commercialism joined the counties in their search for tourist dollars, sports franchises, and business development, the two counties couldn't have been more separatist. Today, we're just one big happy family. Or so the Business Journal would have us believe.

In any event, I passed the beach areas where the thong-bikini clad hot dog vendors used to stop traffic—literally—until they were banned as "unhealthy." Those women had looked mighty healthy to me, but I easily believed they were a traffic hazard.

The fifty million tourists who visit us every year stop on the entrance ramps before merging on the freeway, turn right from the left-hand lane, and drive the wrong way on Tampa's many one-way streets to make driving a death-defying experience. We don't need one more traffic problem.

My opinion had absolutely nothing to do with my own personal appearance should I ever have considered wearing a thong-bikini. Really.

Once I reached I-275, I could put the pedal to Greta's metal and speed down to exit 4, the Pinellas Bayway. For a mere fifty-cent toll each way, this little stretch of highway connects St. Petersburg with St. Pete Beach, just north of my eventual destination.

Between here and there is Eckerd College, the road to Fort DeSoto Park, and quite a few golf courses next to high-rise condominiums. All of that passes before the Intra-Coastal Waterway that separates the mainland from the barrier islands, including St. Pete Beach and Pass-a-Grille, further south.

The Bayway ends right at the doorstep to my favorite famous old hotel, the Don CeSar. The Don was built in the 1920s and, as I said, was a vacation spot favored by Scott and Zelda Fitzgerald, among other flapper era swells. During World War II, the Don served as a hospital for recuperating RAF pilots. A recent multi-million dollar renovation brightened up its pink and white, birthday cake exterior.

The Don's current owner was an insurance conglomerate. They'd created a spa and resort that welcomed guests who would visit for a few hours instead of a few weeks. A sign in the lobby said, "You don't have to stay here to play here."

That philosophy had done much to return the Don's financial situation to the pink, too. We'd been invited to several weddings and parties here the last few years, and they were always beautifully done.

I turned left at the Don and drove under the second-floor entryway, traveling at the staid twenty-five miles an hour required on Pass-a-Grille Way, down to Eighth Avenue and the business district.

Being a Saturday in the middle of the high season, there was no hope of finding a good parking spot. I cruised up and down the short one-block street a couple of times before resigning myself to the ravenously hungry parking meters at the beach side on Gulf Way.

Overstaying the meter here can cost thirty dollars or more. The local paper boasted the amount of increased revenue the town collected from over-parked tourists each year.

I walked back to Eighth Avenue from the Gulf side and realized that I might never have really looked at these little shops before. There weren't many of them, but the shops they had were quite nice.

A hair salon with a small lending library; an upscale sportswear store, two gift shops that didn't have a single pink flamingo in the window but displayed pottery, oil and watercolor works by local artists.

On the south side of the street was the famous jeweler, Evander Preston's place. The beautifully painted Chinese red doors had a doorbell on the left doorjamb and a sign beneath it listing Preston's "hours of availability."

On the north side of the street was Armstrong Otter's gallery. It wasn't as impressive as Preston's, but it had the same look about it.

Otter's door was painted a bright green and his doorbell had a sign listing his hours. He was open "by appointment" on Saturday from ten until two o'clock. It was eleven-thirty.

I pushed the lighted nose of a Newfoundland, hearing the discreet chime of the bell inside.

A woman opened the door. "Welcome," she said, "have you been to Armstrong's before?" When I told her I hadn't, she said, "Only the jewelry is for sale. Everything else is for your viewing pleasure. Please look around and let us know if we can help you."

As I said, I'd been to Preston's shop before, so I expected Armstrong Otter's copy to be similar. Otter displayed an eclectic collection of autographed and personalized lithographs, hand-thrown pottery, brass sculptures and, on the walls, a few photographs of himself with celebrities.

There were pictures of Otter with Donald Trump, Ted Kennedy, Jimmy Buffett and other celebrities with ties to Florida.

The jewelry itself was avant-garde in most respects. Stashed behind glass, on the walls, and in jewelry cases near the discreet cash register, several different artists were credited with design.

The most interesting display was one entire wall of jewelry devoted to designers Otter employed who had, at various times, won the Gasparilla Festival of the Arts' Emerging Artist Award.

After I'd been looking for about twenty minutes, the rail-thin hostess who'd greeted me returned. "Is there anything I can help you with?"

"I'm unfamiliar with Mr. Otter's work. Can you tell me a little about it?"

She handed me a small brochure with "Armstrong Otter" inscribed in gold calligraphy on a bright green cover embossed with the head of a Newfoundland, a large, black dog that closely resembles a St. Bernard.

Reciting what sounded like rehearsed lines, she began, "This tells Armstrong's story and gives you some examples of his work. He's probably most well known for nurturing new talent and allowing promising young designers to create new pieces under his tutelage. Armstrong and his protégés have won many national art prizes. The piece he plans to submit to the Gasparilla Festival of the Arts is in this display."

She directed me to a glass case in the middle of the room. In a voice that she might have used to introduce the Hope diamond, she whispered, "This is Gasparilla Gold. Isn't it fabulous?"

The piece was even more spectacular than it had looked in the photograph Otter showed us. The gold and jewels sparkled in the center of a white background. It was smaller, though, than it had looked in the photo.

"Do you think this piece will win first prize?" I asked her, feigning an equal level of reverence.

"Oh, we hope so," she gushed. She clasped her hands together as if in prayer.

I glanced briefly at the brochure she'd given me. "I see Mr. Otter is also well known for collecting and reselling 'Jewels of the World.' What are they, exactly?" I hoped my voice contained just the right mix of interest and curiosity.

"Let me show you," she said, as she led me to another cabinet on the opposite wall. "Here are several examples of what you're talking about."

She'd pointed to a photograph. "As you can see, this is a picture of Princess Grace of Monaco, wearing a sapphire necklace. And here, below the picture, is the necklace. Here's another one: a picture of Princess Diana with a pearl ring on her pinky. The ring is right here," she pointed to the ring as if I needed guidance to see the obvious.

Burying my annoyance at her patronizing attitude, I said, "This is amazing. How did Mr. Otter acquire such wonderful pieces? Aren't they dreadfully expensive?"

And, I was thinking, aren't they assets that could be attached to satisfy some of those claimants in the criminal case pending against Otter?

CHAPTER SIXTEEN

Tampa, Florida
Saturday 11:45 a.m.
February 17, 2001

THE STICK-SKINNY SALESLADY SMILED her own Grace
Kelly smile, a slight bending of the lips with evident amusement.
"Oh, Armstrong knows absolutely everyone."

I studied the pieces more carefully now and asked, "Does
Mr. Otter have any jewelry worn by Marilyn Monroe?"

"I'm sure he must have. He knew Joe DiMaggio quite well. I
would be surprised if Joe hadn't sold Armstrong some of her
pieces. I could ask him for you, if you'd like to leave your card."

"Hmm," I said. "How much would something like this
Princess Diana ring cost?" The question was indelicate, but this
was a store, after all, where things were for sale.

She gave me the look that said, "If you have to ask, you
can't afford it," and coughed a little behind her hand.
"Armstrong makes all sales of his 'Jewels of the World' himself.
You'd have to discuss that with him." Apparently, she'd decided

I was a deadbeat looker, not apt to haul out my credit card. When the bell sounded again, she said, "Would you excuse me for a moment, please?" and left me for a more promising customer

I wandered around a while longer. There really was something to see in every nook and cranny. I started to wonder how I'd been in Tampa all this time and never known this place was here. Or that its occupant was so famous.

I don't usually think of myself as isolated, but maybe I was. Partly, it was that I don't wear jewelry that much, myself. What I do wear regularly are a few good pieces that were given to me, mostly by George.

Although I find gems interesting and beautiful, my usual lifestyle doesn't allow elaborate jewelry. I look at the constant streams of catalogues that make it to my mailbox at the office but, otherwise, I'm woefully ignorant on the subject.

When the sales lady, or whatever her title was—curator?—didn't come back after a while, I took my brochure and left. I couldn't stay gone from home forever. Even with a few hundred people around, George would surely notice.

But the trip over here had been a nice break for me. I took advantage of it just a short while longer.

I zipped my jacket, turned up the collar, and stuffed my hands into my pockets. I walked on the beach from Eighth Avenue up to about Seventeenth and back. Then, I returned to the Hurricane restaurant and went inside.

The waitress seated me inside, on the second-floor balcony overlooking the Gulf of Mexico. She took my order for a grilled grouper sandwich with lettuce and tomato, claimed to be the best in the bay.

I reached into my pocket and pulled out the bright green Armstrong Otter Studio brochure while I awaited my lunch.

The brochure was sealed with a gold crest sticker in the shape of Newfoundland, and I recalled that I'd noticed the same crest on the door of Otter's studio. Pulling the sticker open, I then had a sort of envelope that had five flaps and a few four-by-six cards inside.

On each of the cards was an example of jewelry creations by several of Otter's protégés, with both the designer and the pieces described on the back.

The flaps of the envelope contained short comments about Otter, himself. Mostly promotion pieces about his training, awards and commitment to creative jewelry design.

The "Jewels of the World" were mentioned only in a short paragraph that said: "Armstrong is pleased to be able to offer select customers a limited number of truly special Jewels of the World owned by the most gracious women of our time. By appointment."

Nowhere on the promotional material was a disclosure that the jewels might be faux.

What I did see were several pieces of jewelry I recognized as belonging to a number of Tampa socialites.

For instance, the diamond and black pearl drop earrings set in platinum were worn by the Queen of Ye Mystic Krewe last week during the Parade of Pirates. And the last time the CJ and his wife had been at the cancer foundation fundraiser she'd worn the large Atocha coin set in diamonds and sapphires on a platinum chain around her neck.

The prices for these pieces weren't listed, but I'd bet my greatly devalued stock portfolio that they weren't cheap.

When my sandwich arrived, I put the brochure aside and spent a fairly leisurely forty-five minutes enjoying the Gulf, the sand and the sunshine. I left reluctantly, walked down the beach and back to where I'd parked Greta—only to find a neon green envelope holding a parking ticket on the windshield.

When I returned to Minaret, the members, friends and family of Minaret Krewe had already begun to fill George's again for makeup and pre-festivities revelry. I pulled her over to the side and surreptitiously slipped the electronic key to the valet on my way through the front door. The valet would park Greta later, after he took care of the paying guests.

The makeup artists were again set up around the lobby and the perimeter of the dining rooms. Pirates and wenches in various stages of preparation wandered around, carrying drinks and unlit cigars. Some had heavy, gold-tone coins in small bags hanging from their waists, and most had the brightly colored beads they would throw to the crowds later draped around their necks like Floridian stoles.

I noticed Gil Kelley and his wife Sandra making the rounds, gleefully preparing the men and women who were brave enough to participate in what the weatherman was calling one of the coldest nights of the year.

By the time the parade was in full swing, the temperatures would be down into the high thirties. These costumes were clearly meant for warmer weather and I saw some of the women, in particular, attempting to find a suitable wrap for their bare shoulders and legs.

When George and I had agreed to be in the parade tonight, I'd had no idea it would be so cold. But we couldn't demur now, so I trudged upstairs to find my costume and to discover whether I'd saved some long underwear from my prior life in Detroit.

When we lived in Detroit, we'd have considered forty degrees in February a heat wave. I smiled to myself as I thought of the whining I was doing over a little cold snap and picked up the pace up the stairs.

A short while later, I'd donned my wig of long, red ringlets covered by a bright blue bandana, which was bound to keep me warm. "Half your body heat escapes through your head," Mom used to say as we bundled up for sledding or ice skating. I was counting on that bit of folk wisdom tonight.

I'd found some pink silk, long underwear in the back of the dresser, and they didn't show under the flounce skirts and petticoats of my wench's costume. Short black boots completed the outfit, which I normally wear with sandals or no shoes at all. Not tonight.

The pre-parade preparations were in full swing when I returned to the party downstairs. I'd done my own makeup, accentuating my lips with deep red lipstick and my eyes with dark brown liner and blue shadow. I felt I looked as good as Margaret Wheaton, who'd had hers done by the professionals.

Of course, I was over twenty years younger than Margaret, but she looked young enough tonight. As she stood talking with Sandra Kelley, I thought they must have been made up by the same artist. They looked enough alike to have been sisters.

Armstrong Otter joined them and they had an animated conversation that might have been a quarrel, or could have been just the fun and spirit of the evening. Otter was dressed in a pirate's costume tonight. He had his ponytail tied low on the base of his skull with a bright yellow ribbon to match his blouse.

George came up behind me and put his arms around my waist while nuzzling his chin into my neck and pinching the big hoop earrings I had on against us both. "Ahoy, wench!" he sneered in his best pirate accent, which still sounded a lot like a mid-western banker. "What're you doin' later this evenin'?"

"I'm open to suggestions," I told him, laughing, as Dad joined us, a glass of something dark and foamy in his hand.

"Are you two a threat to my health and safety this evening?" he asked, getting into the spirit of things.

"Perhaps, sir. Perhaps we are." George told him. "You might want to return to the safety of your home."

"Exactly my plan, dread pirate. I have a big thick file to work through and I've just come in from outside. I think a good seat in front of the television is the best place for this boy tonight." Dad raised his glass and turned toward the Sunset Bar.

"Landlubber!" George shouted after his retreating back.

Shortly afterward, the costumed ones were loaded onto busses to drive down to Channelside, where we'd get on the float and prepare to join the parade.

George and I stayed around to be sure his staff had everything on hand for the next phase of the celebrating while we were gone. The parade would wind through historic Ybor City. Afterwards, the buses would return us to George's for late night snacks and coffee. Our float was about number ninety-one in the procession, so we could avoid the cold a while longer.

Dad wasn't the only one staying in tonight. About thirty would-be revelers had settled into the Sunset Bar with the television on to watch the parade in the comfort of seats, food, drink and most of all, warmth. Suzanne sat close to Dad, all cozy in a booth. I bid them goodbye and boarded the last bus.

Channelside was a fine example of Tampa development. When we moved here, the land around the cruise ship dock was nothing short of an eyesore. Filled with abandoned warehouses and flat lots holding old beer cans and trash, it wasn't a credit to the chamber of commerce.

Today, the area houses The Florida Aquarium, Garrison

Seaport, Channelside Shops, a movie theater, and is just a short walk from Tampa's fabulous hockey arena. The only thing Tampans could find to complain about the area now is the increased traffic. On the evening of the Knight Parade, that complaint was more than justified.

When we arrived at our float, we found it already fully loaded with members of Minaret Krewe dressed in costume and weighted down with beads, coins and candy to throw to the crowds. The body heat generated by those milling around on the float made the cold more bearable. I was getting a little warm, myself, but not enough to make me want to take off my long underwear.

As I made my way to my assigned station, I noticed Margaret Wheaton and Armstrong Otter standing on the back of the float. I waved to Margaret, but she didn't see me. She was too involved in her conversation with Armstrong, as he held her arm and no doubt regaled her with tales of his celebrity customers.

I felt an almost involuntary scowl crease my features. Neither Margaret nor Armstrong were Krewe members. Why were they here? And together? There was no one for me to ask.

The float, a replica of Minaret, the Krewe's namesake, had been funded and built years before, when we first established the Krewe. The float required some sprucing up every year, but was mostly unchanged.

It was a flat barge with a Minaret in the middle, a banner with the Krewe's name on the front, and the shape of a pirate ship made it fit into the overall theme of the parade.

George and I took our places at the front of the float next to Gil and Sandra Kelley, this year's King and Queen.

"We seem to have some non-members on the float tonight,"

I leaned over and said to Sandra Kelley, who was standing on George's right.

"We probably had some people cancel out because of the cold and got some volunteers. The more the merrier, right?" And, to be sure I got her point, she rebuked me. "You don't own the Krewe, Willa. George just sponsors it."

Her tone raised my anger and I tamped it down for the moment.

The loud music someone had added to the float last year emanated from the miniature Minaret. The small tractor that would pull all of us along started up. I couldn't talk to Sandra over the noise, keep my balance, and prepare to throw away the beads and candy given to me all at the same time.

The conversation would have to wait, but I definitely intended to have it. I didn't like Sandra Kelley's short temper and angry threats against Dad.

Unstable or not, I didn't think she was dangerous. She just needed to understand that her behavior wouldn't be tolerated. Not by me, on my own behalf or for Dad.

The illuminated Sant' Yago Knight Parade has been following the Parade of Pirates for more than forty years. The group that sponsors it, the Knights of Sant' Yago, has about 275 members and claims to have roots in the ninth-century Spanish Brotherhood of the Royal Order of St. James.

Like most of the clubs, or krewes that participate in the various Gasparilla events, the Knights use the revenue from the parade for good works. In this case, to fund renovation of historic club buildings in Ybor City, community projects and scholarships. Mostly, their aim is to promote the Latin heritage in Tampa.

The parade route has been changed several times, but this year it wound down Channelside Drive, over to Ybor City, down Seventh Avenue, and terminated on the east end of town at 22nd Street.

Wall-to-wall people lined the sides of the narrow streets from curb to storefronts. Most of them raised their arms and their voices as every float went by, seeking to catch whatever booty was thrown out to the spectators.

The bars were open, selling beer and soft drinks out of barrels, both inside and out on the sidewalks. Beer, wine, soft drinks, hard liquor, and who knows what else flowed literally and figuratively all along the parade route. Already, the streets were a goocy mess.

By the time we reached the end of the parade route, I was hoarse from yelling to George and the others over the noise of the music and the crowd. My arms were tired from throwing beads and coins to the spectators. The long underwear I'd so happily put on at the beginning of the night had turned into a cocoon of hot silk that had me sweating like I'd just completed a marathon at the head of the pack.

George had to return to the restaurant so we were one of the first ones off the float, onto the bus, and back at home.

As quickly as possible, I excused myself and headed upstairs. I peeled the wench's garb off, followed by the now soaking wet silk underwear. I threw the clammy duds into a heap on the bathroom floor, hoping never to see them again.

Beneath the steaming shower I began to feel a little revitalized. Once out, I managed my quick change: hair (three minutes), makeup (two minutes), clothes (three minutes). Usually I can do the clothes faster, but it took me a while to decide on the medium-weight, long-sleeved pink cotton dress and jacket from Fresh Produce. I had been very warm in my costume, but it was still only about forty degrees outside.

When I had dawdled as long as possible, I returned to the restaurant. Most of the revelers had returned as well and were making their way through the buffet line. Everyone looked a bit worse for wear.

I approached George and suggested he go upstairs and change, offering to play hostess while he was gone. Making my way around the tables of seated pirates and wenches, I deliberately took my time, and avoided the tables where the CJ and his wife sat, as well as where Sandra and Gil Kelley held court. George could deal with them when he returned.

Dad and Suzanne were seated in the small blue room that was originally a parlor, and where dining was more intimate. They saw me and waved me over to join them, which I found myself curiously happy to do. Maybe that was because they had a free chair.

Dad smiled while Suzanne squeezed my hand when I sat down. They shared the details of their television viewing experience with me, telling me all about the Knight Parade as if I hadn't been one of the participants. It was actually fun to hear Suzanne's take on the whole event, so childlike was she in her enthusiasm.

When Dad excused himself to wash the barbecue sauce off his fingers, Suzanne took the opportunity to bend my ear about her latest shopping experience for "Elmo," the name she and Dad had humorously given to my soon-to-be sibling until its sex was determined.

She described the layette, toys, wallpaper, paint and accessories until my eyes glazed over. Being Suzanne, she never noticed how little I contributed to the conversation.

I almost missed it when she uttered a startled, "Oh!" and allowed a momentary lull into her stream of chatter.

CHAPTER SEVENTEEN

Tampa, Florida
Saturday 10:15 p.m.
February 17, 2001

"THERE'S THAT POLICE CHIEF, Willa. I don't want to talk
to him again. Sit up straight so he won't see me," she said, as she
crouched down across the table from me.

"Why don't you want to see Ben Hathaway?"

"I just don't want to tell him the same story over and over
again, that's all. He keeps asking me if I saw anybody with Ron
Wheaton out on the veranda, and I didn't. I wish I had. But I
didn't even know Ron was there. Until I found him alone and not
breathing." She shuddered again, remembering the experience
that had upset her so much last Saturday.

Hoping to avoid further waterworks—I'd had plenty of
that—I said, "I've been thinking about the same thing, Suzanne.
I tried to remember seeing Ron with anyone else during the
party, but there were so many people here, I just don't recall."

Of course, the entire discussion made her nervous and

Suzanne started her incessant chattering again. "Well, I didn't know him at all, so I wouldn't have thought anything about it, except that he was in that wheelchair and I felt bad for him. I had talked to him a little bit. He was with that nice Armstrong Otter. And since I didn't know very many people here, I went over and talked to both of them for a while. They were discussing Mr. Wheaton's wife, and I don't know her, either. Both of them were talking about how nice she was, how kind and loving. I remember because I thought that it would be wonderful if Jimmy felt that way about me after thirty years. But that was the only time I saw Mr. Wheaton before he died."

How could she go that long without breathing?

I tuned her out. I'd seen Ron and Margaret talking with Armstrong Otter last Saturday, too. But that was earlier in the day. Surely, Hathaway had been able to determine whom Ron was with just before he died. I determined to find Hathaway and ask him.

When Dad returned, I left them to continue visiting with our other guests.

By the time I'd circled through the crowds, all the way around the dining room, the restaurant had started to thin out. Buses were again available for those not ready, willing or able to drive home.

When I looked at my watch, it was after midnight. Feeling I'd done more than my duty today and that it had been a very long time since I'd awakened at four o'clock this morning, I waved goodbye to George, went upstairs and fell into oblivion.

WHEN I FINALLY RETURNED to the land of the living, it was late Sunday morning and the flat was empty. George was gone to parts unknown, leaving me with two sleepy dogs, an empty coffee pot and papers strewn all over the kitchen table.

Cherishing the unexpected gift of peace and quiet, I made my *café con leche* and settled in the den with it and the four papers we get every Sunday morning. They were a jumbled mess, so I tried to sort them out before I started reading them, not wanting to get my current events from four cities mixed up.

Then, I started with the *Tribune*, although I expected all the coverage to be about the Knight Parade yesterday and the festivities before and after.

I spent the rest of the morning this way and then decided I needed some exercise, so I'd go to hit a bucket of golf balls. I'd been off the course for two weeks now and I was getting restless.

When I'd dressed in light-weight slacks and a sweater, I snuck down the back stairs, leaving a note for George on the kitchen table, the place we'd decided all notes would be left after a fiasco a few weeks ago when he'd left me a note I hadn't seen.

The short drive to Great Oaks, the country club where I play golf, invigorated me as it always does. As I approached the large, plantation style clubhouse, I realized anew how amazing it is that such a beautiful 36-hole golf course is nestled right in the center of South Tampa.

Actually, Great Oaks was the only place to play golf that didn't require a twenty-minute drive, so most golfers in South Tampa were members here.

Fortunately for me, Great Oaks has a very liberal admissions policy: anyone who applies gets in. As a federal judge, I can't belong to any discriminatory societies, and I wouldn't want to, anyway.

It was about two o'clock in the afternoon by this time and all the serious golfers would be off the course and back home. I went into the pro shop for a bucket of balls and asked to have my clubs brought around. In no time, I was out on the driving range, the bright Florida sunshine warming the still cool temperatures, and not a soul around.

This was my idea of heaven on earth.

After a few stretches to warm up, I began hitting the balls, five strokes with each club, rotating through all the clubs in my bag. Soon, the repetition of the swing allowed me to trance into a deep meditative state that gave me a chance to examine my issues.

Avoiding the obviously more important issue of Ron Wheaton's death in my home, I focused on attempting to come to terms with the new family I would soon be getting.

George was right that I had nothing to say about all of this and I could either choose to be closer to my new family or more estranged from it. Living half the country away didn't seem to be as much estranged from my Dad as I would be if I didn't accept Suzanne.

I believed in my heart that Suzanne wouldn't stay with Dad long. She'd get bored with his empty conversation, tired of his low-key life style, angry with his failure to emotionally connect, and leave him heartbroken one of these days.

Until that happened, if I wanted to have any kind of relationship with my father, I had to accept Suzanne. Of course, after she left, there would be the problem of half-siblings to cope with, too.

Unlike some adult children in my situation, I wasn't worried about my inheritance because I never expected to get one. I'd long ago told Dad I wanted him to spend all his money, prepay the funeral and put the last five dollars toward the party he'd be at when he died a happy old man at the age of 102.

I was only kidding about the "prepay the funeral" part.

George and I had done fairly well in the stock market, riding the long-term bull for the past ten years. George's restaurant was profitable and I had a very decent salary from my job as a U.S. District Court judge for the rest of my lifetime, or as long as I wanted it.

I knew Dad had made a provision for me in his will and that Suzanne could get him to change it, but that was a long way down the road and I truly didn't care.

Everything about the situation would have been easier if I hadn't realized that Suzanne was such a nice kid. While her nervousness had made her early conversations and behavior seem vacuous and tedious, once she began to feel more comfortable around us, I noticed the character Dad loved.

Suzanne was truly likeable and everything about her now made me want to take care of her. I'd enjoyed talking with her this past week about a variety of subjects—where I could get a word in.

In some ways, living in New York City had made her sophisticated beyond her years. She looked smart, well educated and savvy because she was. I couldn't honestly say Suzanne would be bad for Jim Harper. Indeed, he was lucky to have attracted her.

What I was worried about, truly, was me. That I'd refused to face this until now was typical of my Pollyanna attitude toward most of life.

But now, the truth stared me full in the face. I was worried about being displaced in Dad's affections by Suzanne and, worse, by his new children. His own natural children. Which I wasn't.

This wasn't particularly noble, or even novel. It certainly

wasn't a mature attitude. Maybe deep emotions never are.

People call me strong and intrepid. I think they mean it as a compliment. And most of the time, I am.

But the Achilles' heel I have is a deep, abiding fear of abandonment. It's not rational. I've considered going into analysis about it, although I never have. Usually, it doesn't affect my daily life, so I can ignore it. But when it rears up and slaps me, I'm forced to pay attention.

This was one of those times. I rarely talked to Dad, saw him more rarely, and thought of him almost never.

Yet, he is my dad, with the emphasis being on the word "my." Now, he'd be her husband and their dad, too, for I had no doubt there would be at least one more after this child. That thought caused me to hit the last ball over one-hundred yards— with a pitching wedge.

It took two buckets of balls to get through all the clubs in my bag and the stuff in my psyche but, afterward, I felt stretched, limber and relaxed for the first time since Dad had shown up with Suzanne.

And I'd come to terms with my fears so that I could face my emotions and stare them down.

At least, I could do that at the driving range where my resolve wasn't being tested. That challenge was waiting for me back at Minaret when I returned to get dressed for an evening at the performing arts center to see a revival of Oklahoma with George, Dad and Suzanne.

"Sandra Kelley called the house looking for you," I told Dad, as we shared a glass of cheap—but not inexpensive—white wine at intermission.

"I know. She told me when she bitched me out at the Knight Parade. She said she was pretty rude to you."

"You could say that," I told him, wryly. "But, if she was rude to me, she was positively offensive about you. What's going on?"

Instead of answering my question, he asked his own. "Why don't you tell me the local view of Gil Kelley?"

"You already know that Gil inherited Tampa Bay Bank from his father, who acquired it by marriage to Gil's mother. The bank was owned by the family until about 1990, when they sold off some shares." The bells chimed to signal intermission was ending. I sipped more quickly. "George would know more about that than I do. Gil tried to sell some of the shares to George at the time, but George didn't think it was a sound investment. I don't know who bought into it."

"I do. And I want to ask you about those other shareholders. But for now, I just want to hear about Gil Kelley."

I sipped my wine, thinking about what to tell. Most of what I knew about Gil and Sandra Kelley was secondhand information. Things I heard at George's parties, fundraisers, and on the golf course.

The only firsthand knowledge I had about Gil came from one Saturday afternoon a few years ago when he was at Minaret waiting for George. I later learned he wanted George to buy shares in his bank but, at the time, I didn't know anything about Gil except that he was a local banker.

George had been a banker in Detroit before we moved here, so I thought Gil Kelley was making a social call. Comrades in arms and all that.

Anyway, I had gone downstairs to greet him and he not only hugged and kissed me, he tried to stick his tongue down my throat. I pulled away from him and would have slapped him silly, except that George came in right at that moment and I didn't want to make an already bad situation worse.

I found out later that Gil Kelley had done something like that with every woman I knew. And I stayed clear of him ever after. I'd never told George why I didn't want to be alone with Gil Kelley, but George has a built-in radar for quality people. He never liked Gil and we didn't discuss it.

Gil and Sandra Kelley had joined Minaret Krewe, but they just never made it to our list of friends. Since I hadn't told George about my Gil Kelley encounter, I wasn't going to tell Dad about it now. So I repeated the gossip I'd heard from Marilee Aymes instead.

After I finished, I asked him, "Why are you so interested in Gil Kelley, Dad? It's not that he's been flirting with Suzanne so shamefully, is it?"

"Maybe," he grinned. "But that's not all. I believe Kelley has either personally embezzled several million dollars from the bank and its depositors, or he's covering up for someone else who's done it. I think it's been going on for years, and I plan to prove it."

"What evidence do you have so far?" I asked, just as the lights flickered and the chimes sounded again signaling that Oklahoma's second act was about to begin.

"I'll tell you about it later. At this point, I've reached a few dead ends. I'd like your thoughts," he said.

As we were returning to the play, Larry Davis, a lawyer with one of Tampa's better law firms, approached me.

"Willa, I'll need about an hour of your time tomorrow, if you can manage it. I can come over to your office," he said, over the constant chimes calling us back to our seats.

"I've always got time for my friends, Larry, but my calendar is very full. What's up?"

"I'd rather not discuss the whole thing here, but I was Ron Wheaton's lawyer and my firm did his estate plan. He came to see me about a month ago and changed his will."

"Yes?"

"The new will names you as his executor."

I couldn't have been more surprised if he'd told me Ron had left me all his money. I knew Ron, but we weren't confidantes. Ron hadn't called or said anything to me about being the executor of his estate.

"Does Margaret know?"

"I haven't told her, and I don't believe Ron did, either."

"Maybe I'd better come to see you, then. I don't want to upset Margaret until we have this figured out."

CHAPTER EIGHTEEN

Tampa, Florida
Monday 9:00 a.m.
February 19, 2001

MONDAY MORNING CAME WITH the precision of a universe still on its axis, time moving inexorably forward, as it normally does.

I have always been fascinated by the concept of time travel. Many times I've wanted to go back and change mistakes made during my course in Life 101. It would be fun to travel to other times and other cultures. I could see Mom again, know my grandparents, be present when great world events occurred.

I like the theory that everything in the universe now exists in the same time zone and that's why *déjà vu* happens—that you get a glimpse of other things going on in the space-time continuum simultaneously with your life.

For me, though, time marches forward, seconds at a time, to be sure, but steadily forward, leaving me no choice but to continue along with it.

Although her husband had been dead only two weeks, Margaret had arrived at the office before me and there was a waiting room full of fashionably monochromatic gray-suited, gray-tied, lawyers there as well. I nodded to them all, acknowledged them with the traditional, "Counsel," and strode forward into my chambers to prepare for the long queue of pre-trial conferences scheduled today.

My law clerks and the court reporter came in right behind me and we started to work. Four hours later, the last of the day's matters was being discussed between the assistant U.S. Attorney and defense counsel.

The case had been transferred to my courtroom from Miami by a judge who'd said the defendant couldn't get a fair trial there. This is often a euphemism for "I've got too many cases on my docket and now I have a legitimate chance to get rid of one, so I'm going to do it." Use this ploy too many times and other judges were likely to start returning the favor.

I was zoning out when the case started, so I missed the initial statements by counsel and was more than a little shocked when I heard the assistant U.S. Attorney say a word I hadn't heard in my courtroom before today.

I held up my hand in the traditional "stop" position, palm out, and said, "Whoa, there. Come again?"

He glanced at me as if I were a few bricks short of a load before he repeated it. "I said, the defendant, Mr. Aielo, was a member of a Philadelphia Mafia crime family in the 1980s, your honor. He's being charged with Federal murder and robbery there in the death of a housewife."

"Mafia?" I repeated the foreign word again. "You're kidding, right?"

"No. I'm serious as a heart attack, Judge." He appeared as seriously pained.

"This is outrageous, Judge," the defense attorney broke in. "Mr. Aielo is a legitimate businessman. He owns six popular nightclubs in Miami. Before the case was transferred here, several of his customers put up their personal property to secure a fifteen million dollar bail bond. What kind of criminal has those kinds of friends? The way our society works is that when someone comes from a rough neighborhood and turns his life around, becomes successful, they become a target. This is a vendetta by the U.S. Attorney, nothing more."

I was still shaking my head, as if my ears were stopped up. "Is this some kind of career case or something?" I asked the people's lawyer. "Because I'll tell you—Tampa is not Miami. We don't have a Mafia mindset here. Do you think you can make a Tampa jury understand what you're talking about?"

"We haven't had Mafia running things here in more than twenty years, Judge, that's true. But there was a time when the mob flourished here. There was a lot of illegal gambling, money laundering, loan-sharking. Mob guys were gunned down in the streets in the 1970s. Several high-profile cases were tried and mobsters sent to prison. There was even a Tampa mobster who was involved in the cases that resulted in the movie, Goodfellas."

He was attempting to impress me with a side to Tampa history I hadn't known. It didn't work.

"Well, all of that was before my time. I doubt our jurors will have such long memories. Even so, why would I want to keep a case like this? Shouldn't Mr. Aielo be tried in the state where his crime was allegedly committed?" I asked him pointedly.

Now, I had the chance to transfer the case to another court, and I was sorely tempted to do it. Here on the bench in the

Middle District of Florida, justice is too often delayed and denied in our courtrooms by the sheer volume of the work.

The CJ, who has the moral responsibility to resolve this problem, to his credit, had been working to get us more judges. But so far, we were just slogging along as best we could.

One case less would be a welcome gift, but would not lower the level of the water enough to cause me to transfer the case without good reason.

"Judge, Mr. Aielo is a Floridian now. It would be a real hardship on him and his businesses to send him up to Philadelphia. And these are Federal charges. Surely the court can apply the law as well here as they can up North," the assistant U.S. Attorney argued, in a blatant appeal to my vanity. I imagined myself as a strong legal scholar and he obviously knew that.

"Why shouldn't I grant the State of Pennsylvania's request for a transfer, then, Counsel? Surely, you have enough work to do down in Miami without this file? And," I said, turning to the well-known celebrity defense counsel, "surely you would be defending Mr. Aielo in Philadelphia, as well? Mr. Aielo fled Philadelphia in what, it says here, 1986? Haven't the people there waited long enough for justice?"

Both of them started to sputter at once, confirming my hunch that both the cases in Miami and Philadelphia had strong possibilities of success.

They argued a while longer over the various interests of the people of Miami versus the people of Philadelphia, while I snuck a surreptitious glance at my watch. It was one o'clock already. How time flies when you're having fun, I thought, sourly, as I took the matter under advisement, told them I'd review their briefs and issue an order shortly. Then, I shooed everyone out of my chambers and sat down behind my desk for the first time that day.

Margaret had brought me my usual working lunch of tuna salad on white with chips and a Diet Dr. Pepper. It sat invitingly on the right of my desk and today's newspapers were folded neatly on the left. Pink slips were piled in the middle, the voice-mail light flashed on my phone, the message that I had e-mail waiting was in the middle of my computer screen, and the mail was piled a foot high above the in-box. In other words, it was a typical Monday.

As I ate the sandwich, I flipped through the pink slips first. Three from the CJ. I threw those in the trash can with a small, rebellious smile.

Messages from several of my colleagues on the bench about committee meetings and such. I scribbled answers to their questions on the slips and put them in a pile for Margaret to return their calls.

We rarely talked to each other, my colleagues and I. Instead, our staffs called back and forth, relaying our questions and answers. We called it successful delegation. It was better than voice mail or e-mail because we didn't have to actually do it ourselves. And it was less formal than the letters between justices that were the norm on the U.S. Supreme Court.

After that exercise, I had three pink message slips left. One from Police Chief Ben Hathaway, with a note to "please call back," and no clue as to why. One from Dad containing the same notation. And one from George that said, "Check the Tribune. Metro. Page three." Curious.

I took another bite of my sandwich, pulled the newspaper over toward me, started flipping through it, looking for the Metro section, as I cradled the receiver to my ear with my shoulder and waited for Dad to answer the phone. This is what they call "multi-tasking"—doing three or more things at once—and I'm a master at it. What woman isn't?

Just as I swallowed, Dad answered the phone and a small item in the Metro section, on page three, caught my eye.

LOCAL MAN FOUND DEAD AFTER PARADE

Sanitation workers cleaning up after the Knights of Sant' Yago Illuminated Knight Parade found the body of Pass-a-Grille artist Armstrong Otter on Sixteenth Street in Ybor City early Sunday morning. Few details were available at press time, but it appears Otter may have fallen and hit his head on a sharp piece of broken concrete. Otter was taken to Tampa General Hospital where he was pronounced dead.

"Hello? Hello? Anyone there?" Dad was saying. I was so dumbfounded by the *Tribune* article that I couldn't answer. He must have heard something, though, because he said, "Willa? Is that you? Are you all right?"

I got it together enough to answer him in a few seconds. "Uh," I said. Not brilliant, but enough to keep Dad on the line.

"Is something wrong? Willa? If you don't answer me, I'm coming right over there. I see on the caller ID where you are." He was starting to sound stern now, although it only could have been a few seconds since he picked up the phone.

"Yes, Dad. I'm here. Just a second." I took a swallow of my Diet Dr. Pepper to wet a throat suddenly too parched for speech, took a slow calming breath or two, and put the receiver back to my ear. "Okay. Sorry. I was just eating my lunch when you picked up the phone. Something must have gone down the wrong way."

Not an entirely truthful explanation, but not really a lie, either. I try to make it a point never to lie, even white lies that are meant to save others' feelings. George believes lies diminish both the people who offer them and the people who accept them. It's one of the things we agree on.

It's harder to tell the truth and still be tactful. Sometimes I fail the second half of the equation. But I still try not to lie, even if it gets me into trouble, which the truth often does.

"What's up?" I asked him. "You called me."

"I did?" he sounded genuinely perplexed.

"According to this pink slip here on my desk, you called at three-forty-five this afternoon," I told him, still distracted.

"Willa, it's only two-fifteen," he said, gently.

"Yes."

"How could I have called you over an hour from now?"

I was not really listening. Or looking at the pink slip, either, apparently, which clearly said this message had come in last Friday.

"Willa? Are you sure you're okay?"

"Yes. I was just reading the paper. It says that Armstrong Otter died over the weekend. I guess I'm a little preoccupied."

I was thinking about Margaret and how she would react to this news; about the Fitzgerald House case, and what would happen to it; and most of all, about the man, Armstrong Otter, who was becoming such an interesting phenomenon to me and whose studio I had visited for the first time just two days ago.

"Really? I wonder where Gil Kelley was at the time of the murder?" Dad sounded sarcastic. He was single-minded in his pursuit of Gil Kelley. To him, if it related to Kelley, it was a worthwhile conversation. Otherwise, not.

I told him I needed to make some more calls and would see him at home tonight.

Then I looked at the message slip saying Ben Hathaway had returned my call, made sure he had called today, and punched his private number. He picked up on the third ring, sounding harried and rushed, "Hathaway here."

"Willa Carson, Ben. What's up?" I asked for the second time in the last ten minutes.

"Just a second, Judge," he said, covering the receiver with his hand and talking to someone else in muffled tones. I gathered up the rest of my sandwich and tossed it in the trash, collected my thoughts and waited. I heard what sounded like a door closing and Ben Hathaway was back on the phone.

"Sorry, Judge. I'm in the middle of two homicide investigations here. I'd like to come by and ask Margaret Wheaton a few questions about the death of Armstrong Otter and her husband."

"When?" I squeaked.

"Now," he said. "I'd like to hang up, get in my car, and be there in ten minutes. Is she there?"

I actually hadn't seen Margaret since I walked in this morning.

"I don't really know."

"Well, do you think you can check?" he asked me, with barely suppressed impatience.

I buzzed her and she answered.

"Yes, she's here." I warned him, "And so am I."

I didn't have much time to talk to Margaret before Hathaway arrived. She came in the room and I took a critical look at her for the first time since I'd seen her on the Minaret Krewe float Saturday night with Armstrong Otter. The night Otter died.

To hear Hathaway tell it, Margaret was some sort of Dr. Jack Kevorkian, the physician convicted of helping terminal patients commit suicide. Or maybe he thought she was another Lizzie Borden, killing men for her own personal reasons.

No one could have looked the part less.

Sitting in one of the ugly green client chairs in front of my desk, Margaret appeared tranquil and relaxed, the same Margaret she always was.

She'd been somewhat happier the last week or so, her face a little softer, fewer lines around her eyes. I imagined her improved mood was because she didn't have the burden of dealing with her husband's illness every day.

"Ben Hathaway is coming over to talk to you," I told her. I didn't say why, and she didn't ask. We discussed business until we heard the buzzer at the door, impatiently seeking entrance into my chambers. I got up and let him in.

Hathaway is a big man, but he moves quickly. He blew into my reception area like a windstorm and walked right past me into my chambers before I had a chance to stick my tongue in my cheek, point and say, "She went that-a-way, Chief."

Perhaps he was worried that I'd sent Margaret off somewhere to avoid him. And I might have, except that I wanted to hear what she had to say as much as he did.

"Mrs. Wheaton," he nodded to her, as he sat in the other ugly green client chair across from my desk, pulled out his old-fashioned notebook, the small one with the spiral on the top, and rested it on his wide thigh.

I closed the door to my chambers and sat behind my desk, my hands folded in my lap, watching them both closely.

"Where were you on Saturday night between the hours of

midnight and 3:00 a.m.?" was his first question, after the
preliminaries.

So that's when Otter died, I thought, and made a mental note
to recall where George and I had been, too.

"I was in Ybor City, on the Minaret Krewe parade float.
Why?" Margaret looked a little bewildered at this question.

"The parade ended around eleven. I'm talking about after
that."

"Oh. Well, I had coffee with Armstrong Otter at Joffrey's
down on Seventh Avenue, afterward. Why?"

Again, he ignored her question and asked his own. "How
long were you there with Mr. Otter?"

"I don't know. A half-hour or so, I guess. Why?" Margaret
was embarrassed to admit she was with Otter in front of me. I'd
specifically asked them both not to speak to each other, which
they'd ignored and flaunted their disregard on the float Saturday
night. I'd seen them together myself and done nothing. Now, I
was sorry I hadn't attempted to enforce my own advice.

CHAPTER NINETEEN

Tampa, Florida
Monday 2:45 p.m.
February 19, 2001

AS BEFORE, HATHAWAY IGNORED her question and asked his own. "When was the last time you saw Mr. Otter?"

"About eleven-thirty, I guess. Some friends came along and invited him to go to a party. I got on the last bus back to Minaret because I was tired and wanted to go home. Why?"

This was the fourth time she'd asked this same question and this time, Hathaway answered it. "Armstrong Otter was found dead on Eighteenth Street, near the corner of Seventh Avenue, early Sunday morning," he told her, bluntly and without much finesse, I thought.

A couple of beats passed as I watched the emotions her face revealed: first shock, then disbelief, then, grief. Margaret broke down completely then, sobbing and wailing. She crumpled onto the floor. Everyone in the office could hear her, which would embarrass her beyond redemption, I knew, once she regained her composure.

I stood quickly and moved around my desk, reaching Margaret on the floor just a couple of seconds after Ben. We both tried to calm her, to raise her up off the floor, but she wouldn't stand. Finally, Ben picked her up and put her on the couch in my office, while she continued to cry like I have never observed a person cry before in my life.

Too shaken to do much besides cover her with the afghan Margaret had knitted for me long before, I locked the door connecting my chambers to the courtroom. Ben and I left Margaret, crying more softly now, and went out into my reception area to be alone.

"I guess that answers that question," I told him, bitterly. He had the grace to look sheepish. "I'm shocked at you, Ben Hathaway. I never would have thought you capable of taking advantage of a woman that way."

"You knew he was dead, too, Willa," he accused softly.

He was right, of course. I could have told her about Otter before Ben arrived and Margaret would have at least been somewhat prepared. I didn't tell her because I wanted to see her reaction when Ben revealed the news as much as he did.

Now that I'd seen her reaction, I said a quick thank you because I wasn't there alone when she learned Otter had died. A river of shame washed over me. How could I have thought for one second that Margaret would hurt anyone? Based on what? Nightmares and an overwrought psyche? Unbelievable.

"Now what?" I asked him. "Surely, you don't think she killed Otter, after that reaction? She couldn't have known."

"You don't think that was the reaction of a guilty person

being found out?" he asked me, as if he believed that, which I knew he didn't.

I ignored the question, which wasn't worthy of a response. "Like I said, now what?"

"Now, I find out who did kill Armstrong Otter. And why. And hope that his death isn't tied to Ron Wheaton's somehow."

"That's the second time you've suggested that connection. Do you know more about Ron's death? Was it murder?" I wasn't going to let him sneak out without at least telling me what was going in.

"We're not releasing that information, Willa. Let's just say the autopsy's back and we have good reason to suspect Ron's death wasn't by natural causes."

"What reason?"

He studied me for a minute before making his decision. "Will you keep it to yourself?"

I nodded.

He said, "Ron Wheaton had three times the amount of insulin in his body than it takes to kill a man in his condition. That much insulin didn't get there by itself."

"I thought you couldn't detect insulin on autopsy. I had a case in my courtroom about that several years ago."

Hathaway shook his head. "That was true, once, because we believed that insulin dissipated quickly from the body. But now we know that the acidic conditions in the body at death preserve the insulin and the formation of lactic acid in the muscles after death prevents insulin breakdown. There's no question that Ron Wheaton died of insulin overdose."

"How long does it take an overdose of insulin to kill someone?" I asked him, making my mental pictures of the night

Suzanne found Ron Wheaton dead on our veranda repeat themselves.

"The reaction time is from five to sixty minutes," he replied, letting me reach my own conclusions.

"Meaning someone killed him while he was a guest at George's that Saturday night?"

"Exactly," he said.

I considered who was with Ron Wheaton when he died, and my mind didn't want to go there. "Where was he injected?"

"I'm not releasing all of the details at this point. Let's just say it was in a location where someone else could have done it." He picked up his hat and told me, "We'll need a list of everyone who was at Minaret for the party. We've already started to repeat the interviews we did that night." We walked toward the door. "I'm going to want to talk to Suzanne Harper again. I'll interview you and Margaret myself, when she pulls herself together."

We'd reached the entrance now. "And Willa," he said, one hand on the door knob as I pressed the release to allow him to open the door, "keep Margaret here for a while. We have a search warrant for her home that I'm about to execute. No point in upsetting her further."

I strode around Margaret's desk where I'd been standing to push the door release, grabbed his arm and said, "Not without me present, you won't."

"Oh, really? And just why would I allow you to be there?" He shook off my arm and headed through the door as I turned back to my office to get my purse and car key.

I stopped to tell my clerks to look after Margaret, cancel the remaining afternoon pre-trial conferences, and to lock up at the end of the day. Hathaway had about a fifteen-minute head start on me when I hurried out the door and hopped down the stairs, two at a time.

When I arrived at Margaret's home on Coachman Street, just off the Bayshore past Bay-to-Bay, there were two police cars on the street out front and the front door was closed.

I parked in the driveway, went around back and tried the back door. It wasn't locked. How convenient, I rationalized. I was meant to be here. Besides, Margaret or her lawyer could be present as the police executed their warrant and, since they weren't, someone had to protect her interests.

I heard Ben Hathaway directing officers to search here and there in Margaret's modest house. It didn't take me long to find him. "What have you found so far?" I asked him.

He gave me a sour look. "Why are you here?"

"Owner's representative," I said. "May I see your warrant?"

He grunted in a way that meant, "Yeah. Sure." But he handed me the warrant and didn't ask me to leave. Maybe he wanted someone to report back to Margaret. Or maybe he'd just given up trying to make me do things he knows I'm not going to do. In any event, he turned back to the officers conducting the search.

I glanced quickly at the warrant and saw that they had the right to search the entire house, looking for insulin, syringes "and any other evidence" that Margaret Wheaton did or had reason to administer a lethal dose of insulin or any other drug to Ronald Wheaton last Saturday.

They had started in the obvious places: the bathroom medicine cabinet, the bedroom that was still furnished as Ron's sick room, the kitchen where I had seen other medications on the counter when I came through the back door.

A photographer made still pictures of the house and another

was taking video of the search. I was torn between running back out to Greta for the small disposable camera I kept in the glove compartment to take my own photographs, and staying to watch the search. I figured I could get copies of the police photos later and make my own pictures after they left, so I stayed to watch.

The officers found and bagged several syringes, but they all appeared new to me, not used. Then they found a plastic container near the sick bed labeled "sharps," which they bagged unopened.

Margaret had not dismantled the last remnants of Ron's illness. The room was tidy and clean, but still full of the accouterments of a long-term sick room.

Hathaway and I watched as the officers took all of the prescription medication with Ron's name on the label and a few bottles that looked like over-the-counter medication.

Margaret's medicine was left intact and there seemed to be quite a bit of it. I didn't know she took so many drugs on a regular basis. I made a mental note to ask her about it. I also noticed an officer dusting for fingerprints in all of the rooms. Randomly, as if Hathaway didn't have anything in particular he was looking for but thought he might get lucky.

Finally, after the officers had done all they could, they picked up their things and left.

I stopped Hathaway as he was about to walk out the front door. "What did you find?"

"Nothing much. No 'smoking gun' at any rate. I'll have to wait until everything is analyzed to be sure."

"Let me rephrase," I said, lawyer-like. "What were you expecting to find?"

Hathaway appraised me and made up his mind, again for reasons he didn't deign to share, to answer my question. He raked a weary hand through what was left of his hair, chewed more furiously on the toothpick he'd been holding between his teeth in a death grip similar to the one he unleashed on unsuspecting T-bone steaks.

He said, "I thought we'd find the insulin and a set of syringes to inject it with. I thought we might find some financial evidence of a motive for killing him. A journal. A letter to someone. Something like that."

"But you didn't find those things."

He almost growled out his answer. "No."

"So, what do you think? About Margaret, I mean? Do you really suspect that she killed her husband?"

I didn't mention my nightmare the other night. There was no reason for me to ask him his opinions if I was going to credit my subconscious.

"Yes, that's really what I think. But I'll grant you I'd have a hard time prosecuting her for it. He was going to die anyway. A long, terrible death. I've checked up on it. That ALS he had is a terrible thing. For all I know, he asked her to do it. Or maybe he did it himself. I understand he still could operate his hands somewhat before he died?" I nodded yes and he went on, "So I figured they were either in it together; he did it himself to spare her, or she did it to spare him. I'll admit to you, though, that this Armstrong Otter thing has thrown me a curve."

"You think the two deaths are related?"

He looked at me like I was one brick short of a load. "Of course, they're related. I don't believe in coincidence. Especially when I'm investigating homicide."

"I'm sorry, Ben. But I honestly don't have any idea what you're talking about. Give me a hint."

He tilted his head to one side as if to say, "Okay, I'll humor you this time," and then told me, "Margaret Wheaton's husband and her lover are both dead within two weeks. Do you mean to tell me you don't think the two deaths are related?"

For the second time today, I was stunned to speechlessness. I tried to ask Ben another question, but no sound came out of my mouth. I choked on my own saliva and then coughed myself into the kitchen for a glass of water.

Ben, who is an uneasy friend of mine, followed me into the kitchen to help me along. When I'd finally gotten a hold of myself again, I managed to ask him, "You think Margaret and Armstrong Otter were lovers?"

"Willa, really. What planet do you live on? I've gotta go. Give me a call if you want to share information sometime. I figure Margaret will talk to you. Eventually. And that may be the only way we ever solve this thing."

Hathaway turned around and walked out of Margaret's house.

I stayed around for a little while, convincing myself that Margaret would want my help, now that Otter was dead and Hathaway had targeted her as his number one suspect. I'd need to get her a lawyer, soon, and I was preoccupied with thoughts about that as I walked back out to Greta for my camera.

When I returned, I took pictures of every room in Margaret's house, the medicine cabinet, all angles of the sick room, the bottles of medication on the counter, even the dishes in the kitchen sink.

I didn't know what these pictures might do for me, but I'd been helped by this procedure before, so I tried it again. Sometimes, things are hiding in plain sight, but I just can't see them because I don't know what I'm looking for. I hoped that would be the case with Margaret's house because the more I tried to resolve the conflicting sides of Margaret Wheaton, the less sense all of this made to me.

From my car, I called Dr. Marilee Aymes. Once again, the receptionist threatened not to let me talk to the doctor, but I insisted. She put me on hold for several minutes, which I used for thinking.

I knew Margaret was diabetic, of course. We'd talked about it many times. Whenever someone brought in a great dessert for a party; when people sent me Godiva chocolates, some of my favorite things; when she was invited out for drinks with colleagues.

Margaret was a type one, insulin-dependent diabetic. Her mother had the disease, too. Margaret was very careful of her diet. Although I'd never seen her do it, I knew she injected herself three times a day, and had done so for years. She kept her daily insulin supplies in her purse.

But shouldn't she have had more at home? Why weren't they there? Was it because someone had used them to kill Ron?

So Ron might have had access to the syringes and to the insulin. But could he have injected himself? And if he did, why would he kill himself at Minaret on Gasparilla?

The insight, which seemed like such a lightning bolt when it had hit me while I was standing in Margaret's house, now presented as many questions as it answered.

What did Ron Wheaton and Armstrong Otter have in common? Margaret.

CHAPTER TWENTY

Tampa, Florida
Monday 4:30 p.m.
February 19, 2001

"YES, WILLA? WHAT DO you want? I've got an office full of patients here." Marilee finally came to the phone, bringing her usual gruff manner with her. I asked Marilee Aymes the question and she thought about it before she responded to me.

"Sure, he could have done it. His ALS wasn't that far gone."

"What would have happened to him, if he'd injected himself?"

"Depends on how much pure insulin he injected. Too much, and within minutes he would have been in a hypoglycemic coma. Not long after that, he'd have been dead. Probably about thirty minutes. Less if he hadn't eaten in a day or so. Anything else?"

"Just one more thing. Where on the body would you have to inject enough insulin to kill a man?"

"Insulin has to be injected under the skin, or it can be given in an IV. Enough to kill would leave a pretty big lump under the skin, so somewhere on the body that has the ability to take a big lump." She was impatient to hang up, and I was glad to let her.

I was speeding now, needing to get there before Hathaway figured it out, too. I parked the car, jumped out, and ran. It didn't take me long to find it. In the azalea bushes about ten feet from where Suzanne found his body.

The killer must have thrown the syringe there after he injected Ron with pure insulin.

I picked it up carefully with a plastic bag I'd grabbed out of Margaret's kitchen and brought with me for that purpose. Then, I zipped the syringe up inside the bag and looked at it.

Now what? If I didn't give this syringe to Ben Hathaway right now, I would be obstructing justice instead of just the bit of tampering I'd already done. I ignored the CJ's voice I could hear in my head, warning me that I was putting my career on the line again. Obstruction of justice is definitely an impeachable offense.

The syringe might have the killer's fingerprints on it. Or it might not.

I looked around in the bushes for a pair of surgical gloves, but found none. If the killer had worn gloves, he took them with him when he left.

But if Ron Wheaton had injected himself, his prints would be on the barrel of the syringe. I put the syringe in my pocket and went back out to my car, where I stored it in Greta's glove box.

It took me ten minutes to drive back to the old federal courthouse. I parked Greta in my customary spot, across two spaces, and walked pensively through the courthouse to the ancient elevator.

I could have taken the stairs, but my spirit was dragging, so I just waited. The elevator took longer to arrive than my drive in from home. Another interminably slow ride up to the third floor reminded me why I never used this elevator. I've seen entire pregnancies come to full term in less time.

I pushed the buzzer seeking entrance to my chambers rather than dig out my keys. No one answered the door. When I looked at my watch, it was only four-thirty, so I kept buzzing.

Eventually, all the way back in the library, one of my clerks heard me and came to let me in. I thanked him and made my way into my office, expecting to see Margaret in exhausted sleep on my couch. Which is just where she was.

Before waking her, I made us a pot of hot tea, rattling the cups to create some noise at the same time so that she might wake up by herself and not be startled. When I brought the tea back to the couch, she was sitting upright, a sleepy face still, and seeming quite bewildered.

I handed her the tea, liberally laced with lemon and a dollop of whiskey, for fortification. She was able to hold the cup in both hands. We sipped in silence until I thought she was gaining composure.

"Margaret, Ben Hathaway wants to arrest you for murder. He's been searching your house. It's time to let me help you. Will you do that?" I spoke gently to her because she looked so small and fragile and just plain old, sitting there with the afghan she'd made me wrapped around her small shoulders.

Without her glasses on, her eyes seemed smaller than usual. She blinked at me as if she didn't quite understand what I was saying.

"Margaret." I touched her on the arm this time and said, still gently but more insistent, "Do you understand what I'm saying? You need a lawyer."

Ignoring the warning bells going off in the self-preservation section of my own mind, I told her, "You need to let me help you. If you don't, you're going to be in jail soon. Ben Hathaway thinks you killed Ron. And Armstrong Otter, too."

She continued to stare at me with eyes that widened to the size of saucers, completely bewildered. Then, she began to cry again, but more controlled tears this time. I put my arm around her and we sat there for quite a while until the tears finally stopped.

"Let me take you home with me for tonight. I'll call a lawyer to come over and talk with you in the morning." She didn't resist.

When I got her home, I gave her a sleeping pill and put her to bed in the same guest room she'd occupied before. For the second time in as many weeks, and the only times in all the years I've known her, Margaret Wheaton spent the night at Minaret.

Once I got her settled, George and I moved into the den with our drinks and my first Partagas of the day. It took about an hour to explain everything but, afterward, George furrowed his brows and suggested I call Olivia Holmes, the lawyer who had successfully defended him on a murder charge.

I had mixed feelings about hiring Olivia for Margaret's case. For one thing, I doubted Margaret could afford to pay Olivia's fees and I didn't think it was appropriate for George and me to pay them.

Besides that, Olivia was a little too flamboyant and self-assured to deal with Margaret, who had been quite intimidated by Olivia when she was representing George.

We considered a few other possible choices and decided to

discuss it with Larry Davis, especially since I'd completely forgotten about my appointment with him today. Besides, Larry had a temperament closer to Margaret's, as well as a large firm that could afford to wait for Margaret to pay her legal bills.

And Larry was unusual in that he specialized in both probate and criminal law. Margaret would need a lawyer with both of these specialties. Larry might decline to represent Margaret because he had represented Ron, and Margaret was a suspect in Ron's death. But since I didn't believe Margaret had killed Ron, I was hoping Larry would agree to do the work.

I placed the call to Larry Davis myself. After I'd outlined the situation briefly, he agreed to stop by Minaret on his way home. Dad came into the den with Suzanne and his evening beer and joined us.

Suzanne looked at our somber faces. "Somebody die in here, or what?" she asked.

Larry Davis has rapidly disappearing brown hair and a portly build. He wears thick glasses that conceal his hazel eyes. A piece of tape wrapped several times around the bridge of his glasses kept the two halves together. One of his five kids must have broken this pair, too.

He's got bad feet, so he wears Rockport shoes that get replaced every ten years, whether they need to be or not. They rarely, if ever, get polished. His suits are always old and brown or green. He told me once that brown and green suits don't sell as well as other colors so he can buy them marked down at the end of the season.

Tonight, Larry held his jacket by one finger over his shoulder and too-short shirttails had crept out of his trousers in the back. His tie acted as a bib and revealed the contents of several meals by the spots all over it, which we could see even in the dim light of the early evening.

In short, Larry looked the same as always: dumpy, happily married, happily poor, and a loveable father of five.

We told Larry the limited information about the deaths of Ron Wheaton and Armstrong Otter, Chief Hathaway's comments about Margaret as his most likely suspect, and the results of the search of her house today.

Larry had a few questions of his own, which forced me to tell him what I'd told George earlier: exactly how Margaret had behaved after she learned that her husband of thirty years had died as opposed to how she'd taken the news of Armstrong Otter's death.

The contrast was obvious and supported Hathaway's assumptions. We all saw that. But I refused to believe Margaret was a killer.

"Things are not always what they seem," I said, to the room at large.

"But sometimes they are," Larry replied, quietly. "It's not smart to overlook the obvious, especially if you're a police officer. Most criminals are just not that smart."

"You're telling me," Dad chimed in. "Did you hear the one about the bank robber who passed his hold-up note to the teller written on one of his own bank deposit slips, including his name and address? Or the guy who called in to report the theft of his heroin stash? I could keep going, but the tales of dumb crooks are legendary. They could make a good stand-up comic routine."

"But we're not dealing with a criminal. We're talking about Margaret," I said. Only George seemed to understand me, but he and I were the only ones who knew Margaret well.

I could see from Dad and Larry's responses that someone

who didn't know Margaret at all might believe she had killed two men in the past two weeks. That was a bad sign. It meant Hathaway could probably arrest her and the State Attorney could easily get a grand jury to indict.

I had been right to insist that Margaret needed a lawyer. I just wasn't sure how much Larry was going to be able to help her under the circumstances.

"Let's not panic yet." Larry was talking to all of us. "All they have right now is opportunity. They're having a big problem with means for both deaths and motive on Otter. Even the motive Hathaway hypothesized for Margaret killing Ron is weak."

"I thought you said it was believable," I scolded him.

"It's believable," he replied. "But it's not likely. I've defended mercy killers before. Usually, the killer is the husband."

"See?" George said, giving me a poke in the side.

I ignored his attempt to cheer me up and Larry continued. "Most wives don't feel as desperate when faced with the care-giving responsibilities. They're still a ways from arresting Margaret. But we do need to get some facts from her and get ahead of the police. Do you think we can wake her up and talk to her now?"

"I don't think that's a good idea. As much as another twelve hours will put you behind, Larry, I think you'd better wait until in the morning. Why don't you come over here early, say around seven-thirty? We can talk to Margaret then," I suggested.

"All right. In the meantime, I'll call Hathaway and see if I can get him to tell me anything else." Are there any witnesses I can interview?"

Larry didn't sound pleased at the forced delay in his

investigation, but Margaret hadn't even agreed to let him represent her yet, and I wasn't completely sure that she would do so gracefully. Particularly if she couldn't pay his bill.

We talked about everyone who participated on the Minaret Krewe float during the Knight Parade. We told Larry that neither George nor I had spoken with Armstrong Otter that night because we were stationed on the front of the float and Otter was on the back.

"I talked to him," Dad offered, surprising us all.

"When was that?" Larry was taking notes.

"Probably about midnight, I guess. He was with a group of people over on Seventh Avenue. The group included the Kelleys."

"Was Margaret with them?"

"I don't know. I've never met Margaret, have I? If I saw her, I might remember. There were probably six or eight folks. Men and women."

"What did you talk about?" Larry asked.

Here, Dad looked down at the floor and I saw the color rise in his cheeks. He turned to Suzanne, who was being blissfully quiet for a change, and asked her if she'd mind making coffee. When she'd left the room, he turned back to Larry and answered the question.

"I wanted to return some jewelry he'd sold me last week," Dad said. He went on to explain that he'd bought Suzanne a gift from Otter's studio after George introduced them. It was a diamond and emerald slide for her Omega necklace. Then, when they were in Miami this week, Dad saw the same slide in the window of a costume jewelry store.

"So I had the slide appraised and the appraiser told me the stones weren't real," he finished. Dad was embarrassed. The fraud buster should've known better. He would consider it a personal failure that he'd been duped.

"What did Otter say about it?" Larry asked him.

Dad cleared his throat. His complexion assumed a darker hue and he cast his eyes down. When he answered, his voice was steel.

"He said no. We got into a shoving match. I pushed him down and would have continued the fight, but his friends broke us up and I walked away while the jerk was still lying there."

I felt as if I'd just landed in a strange movie. I'd never seen Jim Harper even raise his voice. How could he have gotten into a fight? With Armstrong Otter?

"Did you say anything else to him?" Larry insisted.

More embarrassed now, Dad said, "I shouted that I'd sue him."

"Did he respond to you?"

Dad cast his eyes down and looked chagrined.

"He said, 'Take a number.'"

CHAPTER TWENTY-ONE

Tampa, Florida
Monday 7:00 p.m.
February 19, 2001

ARMED WITH HIS LIST of potential witnesses to contact this evening, Larry prepared to leave, promising to return early tomorrow to interview Margaret. He asked to see me for a minute, privately. We moved into the den, alone, and closed the door, leaving the others having cocktails without us.

Larry got right to the point. "I need to discuss Ron's will with you, Willa. I've got to tell Margaret about it in the morning and you need to hear it first."

"I know. I'm sorry I didn't get to your office today, but I had just a little bit of distraction," I said wryly. "Let's do it now."

"I was hoping you'd suggest that, so I brought things with me." Larry pulled out a thin file and began to tell me about its contents. "I've known Ron and Margaret Wheaton for a long time."

Larry explained that he had prepared wills for the Wheatons

when he first started his practice. Then, about a year ago, when Ron was diagnosed with ALS and they knew he would die before Margaret, the Wheatons came to see him for financial planning advice.

"We drafted Ron a new will and helped them arrange their financial matters so that Margaret would inherit everything they had as simply and reasonably free of taxes as we could make it," he said.

"I'm confused. I thought you said Ron had named me as his executor?"

Larry nodded. "About two months ago, Ron came back to see me. Alone. He said he was worried about Margaret. He was afraid that, after he died, someone would try to take advantage of her. Take her money. He wanted to restructure his estate so that Margaret would have someone else looking after her best interests." He looked at me directly now. "Ron specifically wanted you."

"But why? Margaret has a good head on her shoulders. She's been handling everything very well, I think. Why would he do that?"

"That's all he told me." Larry had tried to talk to him further about it, especially since he knew Ron was depressed. "Ron never suggested that he might commit suicide, Willa. He wouldn't say anything more except that he knew you would take care of Margaret."

Larry reached into his pocket and pulled out his hand, which he held out to me, palm up. "And he left this safety deposit box key for you. He said to give it to you after he died." Larry handed me the small envelope containing the key. "The downtown branch of AmSouth Bank. I've arranged it so that you can go over there and open it whenever you're ready."

I took the envelope from him, opened it and shook the small key out into my hand. "Okay, Larry. I'll check it out."

"Do it soon. Margaret probably has a few thousand dollars in her checking account and not much else. She'll need money. And she needs to have this all resolved."

Larry left me, bewildered, holding the key and its little cardboard envelope.

Had Ron Wheaton been worried about something in particular, or was he just being overly protective of Margaret when he changed his will? I had known that Margaret was somehow involved with Armstrong Otter before Ron died, and I didn't like it, then or now.

Maybe Ron had known, too. If Otter had been Ron's concern, it was not something we had to worry about any longer, now that Otter was dead.

I would go to the bank as soon as I could get there and hope that Ron had left me some explanation for his actions in that safety deposit box.

After Larry left, George and I discussed the facts as we knew them for a while longer before my growling stomach led me to suggest that we go downstairs for dinner. Dad and Suzanne joined us.

"Just what do we know about this Otter character, anyway?" Dad asked, when Suzanne left to powder her nose. After George had given him the thumbnail sketch of Otter's credentials, I told them both about my visit to his gallery in Pass-a-Grille on Saturday.

"According to the CJ, almost everyone in South Tampa except us had dealt with Otter at one time or another," I said.

"But I dealt with him, too, Willa," George responded. "He was recommended to me by several of our friends. I took some of Aunt Minnie's estate jewelry over to him for cleaning and restoration once. I thought he did a good job. That's when I saw his studio and first became familiar with his work. Then, I bought your anniversary gift from Otter two years ago. The platinum Minaret pendant with the tourmaline and diamonds in it."

"Really? I had no idea. Was he reasonable to deal with?"

"Well, the cost of the restoration work was not out of line, based on what I'd had done before. I can't say the pendant was cheap, but I thought it was reasonable at the time," George said. "Our insurance agent didn't demur when I told him to add the pendant to our homeowner's policy at the price I paid for it. But I've never had it appraised."

"Based on my experience, maybe you should," Dad told him. "Maybe you should have all of the jewelry Otter touched appraised."

George's beloved face took on an alarmed appearance. "Why would I do that? Otter had a sterling reputation. Everyone we know has bought from him at one time or another. I feel terrible about what happened to you, Jim. I even recommended him to you. I had no idea."

I told them about the Fitzgerald House case, how Otter had sold fakes to the widow and passed them off as "Jewels of the World," and collected a million dollars from her. I also told them about the allegations in the criminal case. I thought the civil cases might proceed against Otter's estate, but the criminal case would now be dismissed.

After hearing about the claims against Otter, George was champing at the bit to go to his own safety deposit box and get Aunt Minnie's old jewelry out for appraisal. Of course, the bank was closed.

George left to call another jeweler to schedule an appraisal appointment while Dad and I finished our coffee.

"I thought this was such a sleepy little town. In all the years I've worked in New York, there's never been a murder in a place I was sleeping. What kind of a city have you moved to here, Willa?" Dad teased me, but weakly.

In truth, I was more than a little shocked myself. We have relatively little crime here in South Tampa. The police blotter is printed in the *South Tampa News* every week and it's usually a few petty burglaries, one or two "throwing deadly missiles" and three or less "criminal mischiefs."

Deaths happen all the time around here. Indeed, the second highest volume of export from the Tampa International Airport is dead bodies, after tropical fish. All those retirees who come here to live their last days in the sun return to their northern homes to be buried in the cold when they can no longer feel it. I guess the theory is that if the departed are close by, the loved ones will take better care of the graves and remember them longer.

Ron Wheaton's death in George's restaurant had upset me more than it seemed to upset Margaret at the time. I had to acknowledge that. She'd returned to work two days later and seemed to be almost lighthearted. I'd thought she was just putting on a brave face, but maybe she was happy that Ron had passed out of the way.

I went to a memorial service for a minister's wife where a Dixieland Jazz Band played "When the Saints Go Marching In," because both she and her husband felt that the best of life comes after death. I had put Margaret's behavior down to similar feelings, particularly in light of Ron's terminal illness.

But, what if Margaret's actions were attributable to

something else? Could Margaret have killed her husband? Or at least, could she have known Ron was planning to kill himself? I had to at least acknowledge the possibility.

Armstrong Otter's death, from what I'd heard about it so far, could easily have been an accident. A fall, hitting his head, probably resulted in a subdural hematoma, which was eventually fatal. In the Ybor City crowd Saturday night, it would have been easy for him to have been jostled to the ground, with no one ill-intentioned.

Lying undiscovered on a side street north of all the main action for several hours wasn't outside the realm of likelihood, either. Not on such a cold and busy night. By the wee hours, most people would have tired of the struggle to stay warm and gone home.

So far as I knew now, Otter was a casualty of a few too many drinks and a few too many people on a busy and cold night.

Although Dad admitted to pushing Otter down, I wasn't about to disclose that to Hathaway as an alternative theory of death. When Dad left Otter, he was on Seventh Avenue, not Eighteenth Street. Otter yelled back at Dad from the ground. And Otter had friends with him who would have taken care of him then. No, Dad wasn't responsible. I wouldn't even consider that.

If Hathaway's investigation pointed in Dad's direction, I'd deal with that problem when it arose. For now, I wouldn't believe Margaret had pushed Otter to his death, either. She wasn't physically strong enough to kill him, even if she'd wanted to.

And I was certain Margaret had been genuinely surprised and devastated by the news that Otter was dead when Hathaway told us so today.

Margaret didn't kill Ron or Otter. No doubt about it in my mind.

Well, almost no doubt.

I HAD FOUR DAYS left to train for the Gasparilla Distance Classic. The race is one of the biggest running events in Florida, often voted the best race and among the top ten races in the United States. The Gasparilla Distance Classic Association has donated more than $2 million to local charities and sponsors other running events.

If I finished the race, Young Mothers' Second Chance would collect $10,000 from the corporate sponsors I'd lined up. If I won, which was highly unlikely, Young Mothers' would get $20,000. But I could place in the first five finishers and, if I did, the moms would get a five-figure check.

It was a powerful motivator to haul my butt out of a nice warm bed the next morning before daylight and pull on my running clothes. When the dogs and I got outside, I was tempted to go back upstairs for my polar fleece, but I resisted and started my run at a slow, loping pace to warm up. By the time I got to the north end of the island, I was freezing, so I stepped up the pace. One lap, I told myself, just one. I could do one lap. I'd have to do more in the classic, but I hoped it would be warmer.

I struggled through the entire run and finally made it back to the house. Harry and Bess beat me back and had plunged headlong into Hillsborough Bay. They were frolicking around in the water as if it didn't contain ice cubes. Figuratively, of course. I had to stand around, stomping my feet and watching my breath come out in huge white puffs while they worked off their excess energy.

Margaret was up and about when I returned to the kitchen after a long, hot shower. She and George were having coffee and toast in the kitchen. It was about seven o'clock and Larry Davis would be here in a half hour. I wanted a turn at asking Margaret my own questions first.

Looking her in the eye, I told her I'd asked Larry Davis to take on her case.

"Thank you, Willa," she said, surprising me by accepting my decision. "I've known Larry for years, of course. His parents were always kind to my mother. If I have to have a lawyer, I have a lot of confidence in him."

Her comment startled me. Larry hadn't said he didn't know Margaret well. But I'd assumed he didn't know her because he'd acted like he believed she was capable of murder. Which I thought preposterous. I'd assumed our difference of opinion was based on his lack of knowledge.

"I'm sure he'll be able to make payment arrangements with you if you need them," George told her.

Margaret's response was another surprise. "That shouldn't be necessary. I'll collect Ron's life insurance soon and then I'll be a rich woman." Then she said with some quiet irony, "That is, if they'll pay it to a woman suspected of killing him."

Which, I knew, the company would never do. Like many states, Florida law prohibits killers from profiting from their own actions. The insurance company would stop payment faster than a stockbroker can say "profits."

"Since you didn't kill him, it shouldn't be a problem," I said, "You didn't kill him, did you?"

She said, "I didn't kill him. I wasn't sorry that he died, though I do miss the man I spent half my life with. He'd been wasting away every day. He was weaker, he could barely walk. For Ron, it was a slow and certain, painful death."

She stared at her coffee and tears welled. "It was so hard for him. We talked about it every day. He was still mentally sharp as ever. He remembered things better than I did. That made it worse. I think it would've been better if he hadn't known how he would eventually die. Older people aren't afraid of death usually. We just want to die in a reasonable way. There is nothing about ALS that's reasonable. Nothing!"

She slammed the cup down on the table. Coffee splashed. She ruefully wiped the spill off the table with her napkin.

"Do you know what killed Ron?" George asked her.

"No. I guess I thought it was a heart attack. Most ALS patients die from respiratory failure, was what the doctors told us. But Ron was a long way from that. I just figured his bad heart got him. He should have had bypass surgery a couple of years ago. He was on nitroglycerine several times a day. He wasn't a good surgical candidate. And he wanted to die of a heart attack. He always said it would be better to die quickly." Her chin quivered at this, fresh tears glassing her eyes.

Larry Davis came in just at the tail end of her answer. He bent down to give Margaret a kiss on the cheek. "Good morning, everyone. Willa, George. Is there somewhere I can talk privately with my client?"

"Sure, Larry, but I'd like to talk to you when you're finished. Would you stop by my office? And Margaret, you're welcome to stay here as long as you like. Don't feel you have to go home or come into work today," I told her.

Margaret looked grateful and nodded without response. Larry promised to call me after his client conference. He looked at me over Margaret's head in a way that I interpreted as meaning he had information to share. I showed them into the den, closed the door, and prepared to leave for my office, feeling even better with the choice of lawyer I'd made.

If anyone could defend Margaret with the kind of quiet competence and dignity she deserved, it was Larry. We have quite a few flamboyant criminal defense lawyers here in town who would have taken the case. Particularly if they knew Margaret had plenty of money to pay them with. But the best ones weren't so well-known or expensive. Although a criminal defense lawyer isn't something you want to buy from a discount chain. One always needs the best money can buy. Criminal justice in this country is definitely more available to the rich than the poor. It's not a fact we're proud of, but there it is.

CHAPTER TWENTY-TWO

Tampa, Florida
Tuesday 8:30 a.m.
February 20, 2001

TUESDAYS ARE USUALLY A little slow in my courtroom, but Ron Wheaton's bank wouldn't open until ten o'clock and Larry would be tied up with Margaret for a while, so I went into the office to get some things done. I don't have any regularly scheduled hearings or conferences. When there is no trial going, Tuesday is a day of catching up. Reviewing orders drafted by my clerks, planning and scheduling, meeting with my colleagues, and so on. I was in no great hurry to get started, but I knew the various and sundry small tasks would grow into giant problems if left unattended.

Waiting for Larry, I started on my work. I didn't stop until one of my law clerks, who was sitting in for Margaret, buzzed me to say that Larry had arrived and had asked to see me.

Larry and I settled around my conference table so we could have a conversation between colleagues—I wanted Larry to treat

206 | DIANE CAPRI

me as a surrogate client in Margaret's case. Margaret had no one else to look out for her. She had no children, her husband had just died, and George and I were the only close friends who would support her. Such was my conceit at the time, anyway. Larry, who knew Margaret better than I did, soon disabused me of that notion, among others.

"So, how does it look?" I asked him.

"Not good. I'm talking to you because Margaret gave me permission to discuss her case. I need you to treat ours as privileged communications, though. You are a lawyer, after all. If you can't do that, then I'll have to censor what I tell you."

"I think that's doable. Unless you tell me something I'll be obligated to disclose. Since I'm convinced Margaret neither committed nor concealed a crime, I'm sure that won't happen. So, let's talk." I folded my hands together on the conference table.

Larry lounged back in his chair and looked at me appraisingly before he responded. "Willa, I've known you a long time, but I've known Margaret even longer. She's lived her whole life in Tampa and she's traveled very little since her marriage to Ron. She's not a worldly person."

"I know. That's why I'm so worried about her," I said.

"But, she's not naive, either," he warned me. "She's been in and around Tampa all her life. Margaret knows the score on a lot of things. She doesn't travel in the same circles you do, but she's taken care of herself for a long time."

I eyed him speculatively. "It sounds like you're warning me about something, but what?"

"Just that you, of all people, should know that things are not always what we perceive them to be. Margaret isn't the helpless little old lady you've turned her into in your mind. For one thing, she's not that old. For another, she's more feisty than you think. Don't be deceived by your own assumptions. That's all," he said.

I thought about Larry's words briefly, but didn't have the luxury of considering them fully right then. I had my own agenda. "Okay. I'll keep that in mind. Tell me what you've learned about Ron Wheaton's and Armstrong Otter's deaths since yesterday."

He pulled out a yellow legal pad in the fourteen-inch size— the ones I had banished from my office—and flipped through pages of notes. Most lawyers don't use the archaic long-sized pads any more since most courts will no longer accept fourteen-inch paper. Knowing Larry, he'd probably gotten the last batch in Tampa at a bargain-basement price, and would be the only lawyer in town using them into the next decade.

"I talked with Chief Hathaway last night after I left you. I told him I was representing Margaret and asked him what he had so far."

"What did he say?"

"He told me the toxicology screen on Ron Wheaton and the autopsy had revealed that Ron didn't die of natural causes."

"Yes, he told me that, too. Although Ron's symptoms would mimic a heart attack and he had prior heart problems. So, if it looks like a duck and quacks like a duck…" I allowed my voice to trail off on the thought that Chief Hathaway and the medical examiner could be wrong.

Larry was shaking his head. "Apparently not. They're treating the death as a homicide. Although they recognize it could have been suicide, as well. They aren't sure it killed him, or who administered it, but they feel certain he was poisoned with insulin."

"Is it possible he killed himself?"

"Yes, it is. He could have injected himself. He was depressed, and males account for more than seventy-five percent of all suicides. Suicide is also on the rise among the elderly. They're alone, with failing health and terrified of what lies ahead. Hathaway is treating suicide as an active possibility."

"Where'd Ron get the insulin?"

"That's what they were looking for when they searched Margaret's house."

"And they didn't find it," I told him. "I was there and I saw what they did. There's a video tape, by the way, and you should get it." He looked at me as if to say I shouldn't tell him how to do his job.

"I did ask for the video tape. Hathaway told me I'd have to get it from the State Attorney when charges were brought against Margaret and time came for him to turn over his file. That's one of the reasons I'm talking to you, Willa. I hope you can get Hathaway to give us his file now so we can head this thing off at the pass. If that's possible." Larry didn't sound hopeful.

I wondered whether Larry knew Hathaway had done this for me before. The Florida Supreme Court had more than once held that law enforcement was not required to turn over an active investigation file before charges were formally made against a defendant. I had prevailed upon my relationship with Ben Hathaway to convince him to do me that favor once. I didn't think he'd do it again. Nor did I plan to ask him.

"Extremely unlikely, Larry, and you know it. If he wouldn't give the file to you, why would he give it to me? We'll just have to rely on my memory." I could see how disappointed he was, so I added "And the still pictures I took of Margaret's house afterward."

He was somewhat appeased. Instead of arguing with me over

my decision about Hathaway's file, he asked me for the pictures, which I'd picked up at the one-hour processing place yesterday. I handed him the second set of prints. I'd already looked at them and found nothing interesting. Maybe that was because I didn't know what to look for. Or, maybe there was nothing to find.

"What else have you got?" I asked him.

"I asked a friend in the U.S. Marshal's office to search the U.S. Government files for Ron Wheaton and Armstrong Otter," he said, looking down at his notes.

"Good. I intended to do that today, too. What did you find?"

"Even less than I feared. Ronald John Wheaton was born in Tampa in 1933, three years earlier than Margaret. He'd served in Korea, receiving an honorable discharge. His social security file showed he'd worked for Tampa schools over thirty years and retired young. There was no record that he'd ever been sued or charged with a crime. In short, there wasn't anything to help me in Ron Wheaton's official background." His voice carried the disappointment we both felt.

"What about Otter?" I tried to keep my tone neutral.

"The same non-stuff. Armstrong Eugene Otter. Applied for a passport in nineteen fifty-eight. Fingerprints on file. No convictions, although there's an arrest and a criminal case pending on your docket," he read from his notes.

"I know. There's a list of cheated customers that's longer than your arm in the indictment," I told him. "Of course, the case will be dismissed now that Otter is dead."

"Sounds like a lot of folks with a motive for murder," Larry said. "Let me take the list and I'll start running them down."

"All right, but I'll take the ones I know personally," I said, as I handed him the copy of the indictment I'd had ready for his review. When he was about to object, I told him, "You'll need help, Larry."

He nodded. Larry flipped through more of his notes, obviously picking and choosing what he would share, unsure of the protection Margaret would have from me if I felt she was breaking the law in a way that I'd have to report. "Hathaway also said Margaret and Otter were lovers. He said he had witnesses who had seen them together at the Knight Parade on the Minaret Krewe float and afterward," Larry said.

"Doing what? Having sex or something? It was a little too cold for that, I can assure you." I spoke more crossly than I had intended, but it was just this kind of idle gossip that could get Margaret in real trouble. I remembered all too well how cold it was on Saturday night, my long underwear, the freezing wind. I doubted any legitimate person saw anything resembling incriminating behavior by Margaret Wheaton. Besides that, Margaret was from the old school. If she was going to show some man her affections, she would do it in private.

"Of course not," Larry said, wounded, too. "But sitting a little too close together, holding hands, talking with their heads bowed toward each other, laughing between themselves over things others couldn't hear. The typical behavior that movies tell us is reflective of those in love while they play romantic music and cover the dialogue."

"Not good," I said, in a serious bit of understatement Larry didn't bother to acknowledge. "What does Margaret say about it?"

"I'd rather not tell you that just now. But let's just leave it that she's not too happy with the facts Hathaway has uncovered so far. And it looks like Ron may have had a good reason to be concerned about someone trying to take advantage of Margaret.

Have you been to Ron's bank to see what he left for you yet?"

I shook my head, "I've been waiting for you. Why does Hathaway think Otter was murdered instead of just falling down in a drunken stupor and hitting his head? Isn't that just as likely, given the circumstances?"

Larry considered his notes again, making decisions about what to share and what not to share, shaking his head in the negative. "The autopsy isn't final yet. It's a busy time in the medical examiner's office, apparently. The cold has caused a few elderly people to die and each one has to be autopsied, I guess. But Hathaway seems to think that the wound to Otter's skull suggests he was pushed rather hard onto that piece of concrete, harder than if he had just fallen."

"Well, there were lots of people on the streets that night. Anyone could have pushed him, intentionally or by accident," I protested.

"That's true enough. Although not as many people had a motive and the opportunity to kill Otter, according to Hathaway," Larry said.

"But that makes no sense at all. If Margaret and Otter were lovers, why would she kill him?"

Larry looked at me appraisingly again, as if to say, "No kidding."

What he said instead was, "Hathaway won't tell me and Margaret claims she has no idea. I think she was truly devastated and surprised by the news that Otter had died. I was hoping you could help me out there, too."

I was already shaking my head before he finished the sentence.

"Sorry, Larry, I'd like to help. I really would. But we'll just have to find some other way for me to do it. I won't ask Ben Hathaway to break the law."

"He wouldn't be breaking the law if he voluntarily gave you the file, Willa. He can do whatever he wants to do with it. We just can't make him hand it over," Larry cajoled.

"Besides," I ignored his plea, "my real guess is that Hathaway doesn't know what motive Margaret could possibly have for killing Otter. Usually, whatever he knows, he's more than willing to share if it will help him arrest the right suspect and avoid public humiliation. We'll have to find another way. I'll think about it."

"Never mind. You're absolutely right. I'll just wait for the trial. It'll all come out then, anyway."

The relief in his tone was obvious, even to me.

After Larry left, I dialed directory assistance for Grosse Pointe, Michigan. One of the complainants listed in the *U.S. v. Otter* indictment was the owner of a restaurant George and I had frequented when we lived in Detroit. I had the telephone number for Jake Miller's Chop House restaurant in less than five minutes.

Twenty seconds later, I was talking to Jake, himself.

CHAPTER TWENTY-THREE

Tampa, Florida
Tuesday 12:00 p.m.
February 20, 2001

"IT'S UNNECESSARY FOR YOU to tell me who you are, Willa. I always remember my favorite customers, even when they go into competition with me," he schmoozed, since I hadn't seen Jake in over ten years and had never known him well.

I laughed. "George isn't competition for you, Jake. He has no intention of opening a franchise in the frozen tundra."

After we chatted about the state of the restaurant business, the economy, how cold it was in Detroit and how warm here in Tampa, I could finally get to the point. "Jake, I was hoping you could tell me something about Armstrong Otter," I started.

"Willa, I hope you're not involved with that man in any way. He's a liar and a thief. He stole over $90 million from me." Jake was truly alarmed.

"That's what I wanted to talk to you about. How did that happen?"

"Pride. And stupidity. I thought I was making a good investment. I thought I'd be able to resell the merchandise for much more than I paid for it," he said. "When I started to try to resell it all, these Paulding Farnham creations he'd sold me were trash—nothing at all. People laughed at me. I paid ninety million for a few hundred thousand dollars worth of nothing." He almost spat.

"But how did that happen? Why did you believe what he told you about these jewels?"

"A man hears what he wants to hear, Willa, and disregards the rest. Sometimes to his great loss and embarrassment. Otter was introduced to me by a man whose name you would recognize. He was duped, too, but neither one of us knew that. We thought we could trust Otter. So we didn't do what, as good businessmen, we should have done—gotten the jewelry appraised before we bought it." The chagrin in his voice traveled easily over thirteen hundred miles of telephone wire.

"Did you ask Otter for your money back?"

He snorted. "Of course, we did. The man has nothing. He owns nothing. The police say he covered up with money laundering, but who knows where it really went? If I could kill him myself, I would. It's too bad you don't use your 'Old Sparky' anymore," he said, referring to the State of Florida's infamous electric chair, or what the criminal defense attorneys snidely referred to as "our favorite barbecue grill," which had been retired. Now, Florida executes criminals by lethal injection. "I hope they send him straight to hell."

Miller was so bitter, so vindictive, because he truly had lost much more than money. A man has nothing but his good name. The Japanese call it "saving face." It's the same here. Either he didn't know Otter was already dead, or he'd been putting on a hell of an act. Jake Miller didn't kill Armstrong Otter. But someone else on the long list of people Otter had cheated did kill him. Who?

As I hung up the phone, my law clerk came in to remind me that I had been subpoenaed to testify in the CJ's ethics complaint matter in an hour. With everything else going on, I'd forgotten about it. I pulled out the subpoena and realized the hearing would be in the office of the lawyer for the Judicial Counsel, downtown in the new Sam M. Gibbons Federal Court House. I could easily walk, but I didn't have much time for lunch.

As I pulled on my jacket, I regretted my choice of attire today. When I'd dressed this morning, I had forgotten about the subpoena or that I'd be going over to the other courthouse, where there are many more people and more of my colleagues. I usually dress casually in my courtroom. Under my robe, no one can tell what I'm wearing. I think most judges do this. I've seen my colleagues in jeans and no socks many times. Of course, I don't for a second believe the rumor that one of my brethren on the bench goes nude under his robe so that he can masturbate at the bench during particularly boring testimony. Having heard a lot of boring testimony over the years, I can see how he'd be tempted, though.

I thought about going home to change, but then decided to hell with it. I looked okay. I had on olive Dockers, a long-sleeved pink shirt that had been pressed, and a pair of Topsiders. I did have on socks and I wore a tan suede blazer. I was sure the CJ wouldn't approve of my attire, but he was the one being investigated, not me. With any luck, maybe he wouldn't even be there. I'm a dreamer, so sue me.

Precisely at one-thirty, after a quick sandwich on the run, I knocked on the door at the small hearing room on the eleventh floor of the Sam M. Gibbons Federal Courthouse. I avoided going into the courtrooms of my colleagues, which I lusted after in my heart as many a middle-aged man has lusted after Playboy Playmates.

Even the magistrate judges here had better courtrooms than mine. I thought it was particularly unfair that the CJ could keep me over in the dungeon, as I had taken to calling it, long after everyone else had moved. It was a tactical mistake for him to let me be subpoenaed to testify in his case, in this building, rubbing my nose in what he wouldn't let me have. Oh, he claimed it wasn't his fault. Congress wouldn't approve his budget; he didn't have the money to relocate me; as soon as he got the money, he'd be sure I got moved. Right. And the check's in the mail.

These were the excuses he offered whenever the subject came up. Yeah, sure, I thought sourly. And in that mood, I went into the room to see a three-member panel, a court reporter, two counsel tables, and the CJ sitting there next to one of the most obnoxious criminal defense lawyers in Tampa. This just kept getting better and better.

They were respectful to me, anyway, I'll give them that. They didn't ask me any unnecessary questions or keep me on the stand too long. They didn't ask me about my alleged sexual harassment, so the newspaper article that came with my subpoena was wrong, just as I had suspected. The panel didn't go into my personal and well-known mini-feud with the CJ, both sides apparently understanding it would help neither to do so. Nevertheless, what the panel did ask me after the preliminaries was shocking.

"Judge Carson," the lawyer for the Judicial Counsel asked, "have you heard that Chief Judge Richardson has attempted to influence the clerk's office to tamper with the random assignment of judges?"

"No," I answered, truthfully. The second question followed quickly and was more outrageous than the first.

"Have you heard that Chief Richardson has improperly handled the court's funds, misplacing funds allocated for the court's business or funds paid into the court by litigants?"

"No," I said, a little more forcefully than I'd intended. What an outrageous suggestion! I thought, just before the zinger—the third question.

"Have you heard that Judge Richardson has improperly tried to influence other judges by contacting them about the handling of their cases?"

They asked me these questions in rapid succession, trying to get me to answer without thinking. Okay. I was under oath here. I had to tell the truth. But the question was whether I'd heard about CJ's efforts to influence judges, not whether he'd actually done it. To me. In the *Fitzgerald House v. Armstrong Otter* case. Just last week. But did I have any obligation to help the CJ by ducking this question? Lord knows, CJ had gone out of his way to be as unhelpful to me as he could possibly be without attracting overt criticism from all corners. He hadn't actually ordered me to dismiss the Fitzgerald House case against Otter, but he'd strongly suggested it. Was that improper influence? Or just a reminder of my heavy workload and an effort to make the courthouse run more smoothly? My reaction at the time was that CJ's conduct was absolutely improper. Was I right?

Had I heard about CJ making similar calls to other judges? Yes. I'd heard about it. According to my colleagues, it was not unusual for the CJ to offer his unsolicited opinion on a variety of issues. But that's how we all took it; as a statement of his opinion. Was he trying to influence us? Probably. In the way that anyone is trying to influence someone else when they offer an opinion. CJ's "suggestions" never influenced any of us to do anything one way or the other. I really believed that. At least, he never influenced me. I usually went out of my way to do the opposite of whatever it was that CJ wanted. Childish, I know. But true.

So what was this investigation about? And why was I here? Were all the judges being asked to testify? If they were, everyone already knew about the CJ's opinions and how and when he expressed them. Or—and this may have been just the tiniest bit paranoid, I'll admit—were they really investigating me? The CJ had been out to get me for years. Maybe this question was an effort to catch me lying under oath. Maybe they wanted to try to impeach me. Maybe... Oh, what the hell.

I did the lawyerly thing and answered the specific question they asked me. I told the examiner that I had heard of instances where the CJ had tried to influence judges.

Which had the result of keeping me on the stand for the next four hours explaining every incidence when I had heard that the CJ had called one of my colleagues to give them unsolicited advice on what to do with their cases. And a promise that I'd be called back sometime before this was all over.

They never asked me about the CJ trying to get me to dismiss the Otter case.

But they would next time.

I left the hearing as bewildered as before I arrived, unclear as to what this investigation was about. It was the first time I'd ever been deposed, and it wasn't a pleasant experience. I vowed to have a lot more compassion for witnesses from now on, as I walked back to my car in the early twilight cold. The hour was

SECRET JUSTICE | 219

long after the bank had closed so I couldn't go to open Ron
Wheaton's safe deposit box. With more unanswered questions
and a heavy heart, I bundled up and headed home.

George and I had been in the Sunset Bar sharing today's
experiences for about twenty minutes when the CJ walked
through the door and came over to our table. He looked as wrung
out as I felt. Naturally, George asked him to sit down.
Sometimes, being married to a socially correct gentleman isn't
all it's cracked up to be.

CJ ordered a scotch and water, pulling off his tie with a hard
yank. He tossed his suit coat onto the bench beside himself,
without regard for the wrinkles. He made small talk until his
drink was served. I hadn't had time to tell George that I'd been
subpoenaed to testify in the CJ's hearing, so George was in the
dark as to the reason for CJ's presence. I wasn't so blissfully
ignorant.

"What can we do for you, Ozgood?" I asked CJ, wanting
him to get it over with and leave. I spend as little time with CJ as
possible at work; I certainly wasn't interested in sharing my free
time with him.

"I came to talk to you about Armstrong Otter," he surprised
me by saying. CJ is, like me, a fan of the direct approach. Still, I
expected him to dissemble awhile before he tried to influence me
again.

George looked even more puzzled than I felt. "Whatever
for?"

CJ looked at him. "Willa knows." Turning to me, he said, "I
wanted to explain why I called you last week about the Otter
case. Otter asked me to do it. He's been a friend for years. I
bought several anniversary gifts for my wife from him. He's well
known around town. And he knew the case would damage his

reputation. So he asked me to call you and see if you could get the case settled."

George was annoyed now. "You mean, you tried to influence how Willa handled the case?"

"No, George. Not really. I just wanted to share with her that this was a case that would be better settled. As all our cases are." CJ took a big gulp of his scotch as he tried to make us swallow this revised version of his conversation with me. Talking to me while I was still under oath, about the subject of my testimony, might be construed as witness tampering. I said nothing. I was technically not through testifying. He was taking a big chance coming here, trying to explain himself, knowing I would eventually be asked, under oath, about this conversation, too. He was pleading with me, though, to hear him out. It didn't take a clairvoyant to see that.

"The Fitzgerald House case isn't something that should even be in federal court, we all know that. It's a minor dispute. There's insurance. The whole thing should never have gotten to this point." He looked at me then, directly. "And it's not like you don't have enough work to do. All judges try to settle cases, anyway. I wasn't suggesting how you should settle it."

But he had. He'd specifically said to dismiss the case. That isn't the same thing as settling it. Not the same thing at all.

"What did Otter have on you to make you suggest that I should dismiss Fitzgerald House's claim?" I asked CJ, all too directly.

CHAPTER TWENTY-FOUR

Tampa, Florida
Tuesday 5:25 p.m.
February 20, 2001

CJ'S FACE SUFFUSED RED with embarrassment and anger. But he knew he had to tell me before the entire situation got completely out of hand and he found himself on the front page of the paper. Not to mention out of a job and maybe in jail.

Perhaps my nightmare last week was a premonition. CJ really could end up behind bars in orange prison garb.

"I did buy quite a few pieces of jewelry from Armstrong Otter over the years, just like I told you. One year, I bought my wife a necklace that he said had belonged to Carole Lombard. He said it had been designed by Paulding Farnham. He showed me a book about Farnham and his creations, including a picture of Carole Lombard wearing the necklace at the Academy Awards. It was a beautiful thing. A large sapphire center surrounded by diamond baguettes. Mariam loved it. Just loved it. She wore it everywhere for a couple of years and told

222 | DIANE CAPRI

everyone she knew that I'd bought it and what its history was."

The pride in his tone was unmistakable. It must be hard to be married to an heiress of Mariam McCarthy Richardson's stature. Her family fortune was immense, her local celebrity unrivaled.

How did a husband impress such a woman on a civil servant's salary?

I imagined CJ had been a "good catch" when Mariam McCarthy married him. Although his pedigree was good, it was nowhere near as good as hers.

But, if the stories of Mariam's youthful indiscretions with Gil Kelley were true, when she married CJ, Mariam was already a woman with a past. If Mariam McCarthy Richardson "married down," I doubted she ever let CJ forget it.

What it must have meant to him to have given her such a special gift as a piece of Paulding Farnham jewelry.

And what a colossal slap in the face it was when the gift was exposed as a fraud. People had killed for less.

"So what happened to enlighten you about the jewelry's pedigree?" George asked him.

"We took the necklace with us to New York one year. Mariam wanted to take it in to Tiffany's, to show it to them because it was a Paulding Farnham design," he choked up. Really. I never thought I'd see the CJ show any honest emotion of any kind. I could almost hear the sharp-tongued Mariam, lashing CJ over her humiliation, making it his.

"And it was a fake," I supplied, to help him out. He was a little pathetic, really. I wasn't used to him being so vulnerable. I thought of the CJ as a twit, but a powerful and controlling twit. At this point, he was just a pathetic victim of another con. The role fit him uncomfortably. What would he have done to restore his pride? Murder?

"Right," he said, morosely. "It was a fake. I was outraged, Mariam was mortified and Tiffany's wanted to report Otter to the authorities right then. I probably should have let them but I thought I could handle it myself." He took another large swallow of the scotch. "Dutch courage" they call it.

"What did you do?" George was interested in keeping this story moving along.

"I swore Mariam to silence, which she was only too willing to do. We came back to Tampa and confronted Otter. He acted surprised," CJ almost spat. "Said he thought I knew the necklace wasn't real. But he claimed it had still belonged to Carole Lombard and she'd worn it to the Academy Awards. That made it worth what I'd paid for it, he said. He offered to take it back and return my money. And he said if I took any action against him or told anyone, he'd sue me for defamation."

I felt the small hairs rise on the back of my neck.

I'd heard this story before.

Had Otter believed he could run this scam indefinitely?

"So why not let him take it back and wash your hands of the whole matter? Except for looking foolish, which isn't a crime and has never killed anyone that I know of, you wouldn't have been any worse off for the experience." I'd been right. CJ was a twit after all. Pride before the fall and all. Such an old story.

"I should have. Of course, I know that now. At the time, all Mariam and I could think of was what other people would think. Everybody we knew was aware of that necklace. We just couldn't act like we'd never owned it. We certainly didn't want to be named in a defamation suit." CJ said Mariam wore the necklace less frequently until, in the last few years, she hadn't even had it on. People seemed to have forgotten. And CJ got a good deal from Otter on anything else he ever bought. All of which CJ had appraised before paying, by the way.

"I think, over the years, he'd made it up to me in discounts on other pieces. And we just let it be our little secret." He finished his drink and set the glass down between us on the table.

"Why do I get the feeling we haven't heard the whole story?" I said, even though George kicked me under the table.

CJ grimaced as if he'd swallowed a sour lime. "It was the whole story. Until last week. Otter called me at home and told me about the Fitzgerald House case. He said it was just like my situation."

CJ sounded parched again, and I shook my head at the waitress to keep her from offering him another round.

"And he suggested he'd let people know about it unless you could make the Fitzgerald House case go away, is that it?" I suggested, as CJ nodded miserably.

"You didn't kill Otter over this, did you?" George asked CJ, straight out.

"No!" he blurted, then added more quietly, "But we argued about it. More than once. People might have heard us."

My heart sank, because I knew what was coming next. "When did you see him last, CJ?" I asked him.

"Saturday night. Late. In Ybor City after the Knight Parade."

"What happened?"

"We argued. I pushed him. And I left him there. Alive. I swear." CJ was trembling now, wanting another drink.

Now, I had the upper hand with the CJ and I didn't want it. It was one thing to play my little power games with him when I knew they weren't hurting anyone. But in this case, his wife's pride and his own ego got him way more than he bargained for.

"CJ, you really should tell all of this to your lawyer and see what you can work out with the Judicial Counsel. Because I won't complain, your call to me isn't something that should get you impeached. You'll get a slap on the wrist over it. That's all. You'll never be appointed to the Court of Appeals. But, no one needs to know. Resolve it confidentially. Do it now," I urged him, as sympathetically as I could, but he remained seated, not willing to give up yet.

He still thought he could persuade me to lie for him. Given his track record with trying to control me, his confidence was sorely misplaced. "Do it before they put me back on the witness stand and ask me about this entire conversation, which you know they will do," I told him.

That seemed to galvanize him to action. He said he needed to call his lawyer. Knowing who was defending him, I hoped the CJ would offer to let the lawyer keep his retainer to resolve the case. Otherwise, the lawyer wouldn't let the matter drop. None of us needed to let this get out of hand any more than it already was.

Before he left, I had one more question. "How did the Judicial Counsel find out about this, anyway?"

CJ seemed genuinely puzzled by this. "I don't know. Anonymous tip, I was told. Neither Mariam nor I told anyone, you can be sure of that. It makes no sense that Otter would have tipped them. But someone did."

THE NEXT MORNING, I was waiting on the couch in the lobby at the AmSouth building at 100 North Tampa Street for the bank to open. I didn't want to make the mistake of going to my office and being delayed again so that I missed the opportunity to get into Ron Wheaton's safety deposit box.

The gray marble Gothic building graced Tampa's skyline

with sufficient grandeur to win an award for Building of the
Year not long ago. Its interior lobby soars four stories and larger-
than-life murals painted on the walls soften the stark echo of the
unforgiving granite. Some days, a string quartet or a classical
flamenco guitarist play here during the lunch hour. This
morning, the lobby was filled with office workers traveling from
the parking garage on the north side of the building to the
elevator banks in each wing, beginning their workday.

The building's tenants included a more than ample supply of
lawyers and bankers, so I'd had to talk to quite a few people as
they arrived for work, even though I'd had my nose buried in the
Wall Street Journal, hoping that it would keep my privacy.
Instead, all it did was to give people a conversational opening.

"Morning, Judge. Anything good going on in the market?"

"Hello, Judge Carson. How about that NASDAQ?"

"Judge Carson, good to see you again. Hard to believe
Microsoft is merging, isn't it?"

In truth, I hadn't read a word in the paper. I was too
preoccupied. That didn't seem to matter to my colleagues as they
greeted me with enthusiasm and chattered on without regard to
my minimal responses.

A few minutes after ten o'clock, a woman opened the glass
door to the AmSouth branch office and I followed her inside,
asking where the safety deposit boxes were kept. I provided my
name and my key to the guardian, signed the register, and was
shown to a row of silver boxes along a narrow corridor inside a
locked gate.

The guardian, a burly security guard with a gun, put his key
in box number 372 and turned it. Then, he put my key in the
other keyhole and turned it. This caused a small door to pop
open, giving him a view of the black metal box inside. He slid

the long, narrow black box from its slot and showed me to a small room, placing the box on the plain metal table in front of a metal folding chair. With a nod, he closed the door and left me alone with the box that Ron Wheaton had wanted me to have.

I pulled a regulation length, eleven-inch legal pad and a blue Flair pen, my writing instrument of choice, out of my briefcase, laid them on the table and opened the box. Inside, I saw two regular, white number-ten business envelopes. Both were sealed. One had my name written on it. The other was addressed to Margaret.

I opened the envelope addressed to me and removed three sheets of letter-sized paper. One page was a list of assets. The other two contained a hand-written letter signed by Ron Wheaton. I glanced at the list of assets and was both surprised and chagrined at the value of Ron's estate. He'd left more than enough money to support a motive for murder, if the multi-million dollar life insurance policy was paid out.

I was happy and concerned for Margaret at the same time. Ben Hathaway would surely feel seven million dollars was an ample motive for murder, if Margaret knew about the money, which she probably did. I shook my head at the over-protectiveness Ron had demonstrated for Margaret, even in contemplation of death.

Ron Wheaton had earned a modest living, and both he and Margaret were comfortable with their chosen lifestyle. Ron had far over-insured himself long before he was diagnosed with ALS. Perhaps the insurance was cheaper because he'd bought it through the school system where he worked. Who knows? I just never figured Ron Wheaton for a guy with a desire to be wealthy. Yet, he'd apparently wanted Margaret to be well-heeled after he died. He surely never believed his attempted largess might cause Margaret more harm than good.

One of my former law partners, who was on his sixth wife, once told me that men don't leave a marriage unless they have somewhere to go. Chief Hathaway's theory must be the same for women, too. He believed Margaret was having an affair with Otter and killed her husband to be free of Ron so she and Otter could be together. Hathaway thought Otter had money, though. When he found out Margaret was the wealthy one, would Hathaway be more convinced that Margaret had killed her husband? Or less?

I set the asset list aside for the time being, and read the letter addressed to me.

"Dear Willa, Please forgive me for not discussing this with you personally," it began, in a way that made tears well up in my eyes. This was just like something Ron Wheaton would have said to me before he died. He was always polite and kind. He thought of everyone before himself.

Even in death, he was still Ron.

CHAPTER TWENTY-FIVE

Tampa, Florida
Wednesday 10:25 a.m.
February 21, 2001

HIS LETTER CONTINUED, "BUT I am truly hoping you will never need to know what I am about to tell you. If things change soon, I will have destroyed this letter before you've ever seen it. If not, I am dead now and you are the only one I can count on to take care of my Margaret."

Chills ran up my spine as I read these words.

Ron knew he was going to die before his ALS killed him. Would he name his killer? I read the rest of the letter.

"Margaret is having an affair. I don't begrudge her happiness and I would give her permission to love this man, if he was worthy of her. But he isn't. Armstrong Otter came to see me years ago, when he first moved to Pass-a-Grille. He knew Margaret before she married me. He wanted her back. But he had broken her heart. I found out what he'd done and I told him if he ever came around Margaret again, I'd kill him. So he waited until I was too weak to be a threat before he came back to hurt her. This is the next best thing. I've made a list of everything I have to leave to Margaret, and I've had Larry Davis create a trust for everything, including the life insurance. You are my trustee. Please look after it all. Don't give the money to Margaret, because he'll cheat her out of it and break her heart again."

Ron finished the letter simply. "Thank you, Willa, for being such a good friend to us. I know I can count on you. Sincerely, Ron Wheaton." The letter was dated two weeks before he died.

I put the letter to Margaret back into the box, along with the letter to me and the asset list. I knocked on the door and the guard came and returned the box to its place on the shelf, behind the little silver door. He gave me the key, which I put back in its envelope and returned to my purse. Then, I went on to my office, with much on my mind and no time to consider it.

I missed my journal. I needed to write down my chaotic thoughts. To set out the things I'd learned and the leaps of reasoning that had come to me. But, like the CJ, I, too, was a civil servant. There was no free time in my schedule today.

I took my troubled countenance into my courtroom and tried to focus on oral arguments I'd scheduled weeks before. I heard little and understood less. In my mind, Margaret and Ron Wheaton, CJ and Mariam Richardson, Gil and Sandra Kelley, and, finally, Armstrong Otter, elbowed each other around, fighting for my attention.

On the way home, I stopped off at Barnes & Noble on Dale Mabry Highway in South Tampa. I wanted to learn more about Paulding Farnham. From what I'd read in the *U.S. v. Otter* file, I felt certain there would be at least one biography of the man available in a good bookstore.

I made my way over to the information desk and spoke with

Connie Brown, the community relations manager. Connie had helped me out with inquiries about other matters in the past. It only took her a few minutes to find a beautiful coffee table book full of color pictures containing a history of Farnham's work. With a cup of Starbucks coffee, I sat in the café and looked at the pictures in *Paulding Farnham, Tiffany's Lost Genius*. The book described Farnham as "the pantheon of American jewelry design" and "the greatest native-born jewelry designer the United States has produced."

Well, if Otter was planning to impersonate someone's work, I supposed it made sense to choose a man of superior talent who was also surrounded by mystery. Farnham had left the public eye in 1908 and relatively little was known about him afterward. According to the legend, he left jewelry and silver for good when he left Tiffany's. But he was relatively young at the time, as well as extremely talented. It was plausible that he'd continued his work.

Otter had done his homework well in choosing Paulding Farnham to impersonate because Farnham's work was coveted by aficionados. I was beginning to see why so many presumably wealthy people were willing to believe Otter when he claimed the copies he sold them were originals.

The famous twenty-four karat gold and enamel orchid brooches, first shown at the Paris Exposition of 1889, were particularly coveted. I'd seen no evidence that Otter had attempted to pass off copies of the orchid brooches, but he did copy and sell Farnham's insect brooches, such as a cabochon beetle and a sapphire bee pin with ruby eyes.

When I looked down at my watch, I was alarmed to see I'd gotten so wrapped up in the beautiful pictures of Farnham's creations that the time had flown by. I pitched my now empty coffee cup, bought the book, and headed home.

CHAPTER TWENTY-SIX

Tampa, Florida
Saturday 7:00 a.m.
February 24, 2001

SATURDAY MORNING OF THE Gasparilla Distance Classic was cold and clear. I dressed as warmly as I dared and headed downtown. The race started at Morgan and Cumberland Streets and finished at Brorein and Tampa Streets. I was running in the 15k race, and I hoped to place in the top three.

I'm not a racer normally, and I don't take care of myself well enough to compete in serious races. I eat too much rich food, drink too much gin, and even the occasional smoking I do cuts down on my wind. Most good days, I run about an eight-to-nine minute mile. The Distance Classic isn't age adjusted, so I'd have to run my best times and then some to win.

Despite the odds, I was motivated to win more than the other runners. I still believed in the little engine that could, mind over matter, visualization, and all that. I've always had high aspirations and a finely-honed capacity for self-delusion.

I wanted to win the full $20,000 donation for Young Mothers' Second Chance. My mother had been a single mom for five years, from the time my biological father was killed while she was pregnant, until she'd married Jim Harper. She always told me how hard it had been to take care of a baby by herself.

I'd taken on the cause of single mothers several years ago, sat on the Second Chance board of directors, and raised money for the organization whenever I could to repay Mom. Not that she would approve of my motivation. Mothers do things for their children without thought of creating an interest-bearing receivable.

Even so, not being a mother myself was somewhat justified by my volunteer efforts to support single moms. Some of the young mothers we sponsored had been able to finish college and get good jobs. I'd been working with this organization for many years and this year's race money would be the largest contribution I'd ever managed.

On the theory that we should run before the day's temperatures rose above comfortable levels, the race was scheduled to take off at eight-fifteen. This was usually good planning, but this year, it was wishful thinking. Runners wore long pants, headbands and gloves on hands that held the warm water we were drinking as we waited for the gun, dancing around in the cold to keep our muscles warm. The 5k run was scheduled to begin immediately after ours and then the wheelchair race would roll. We were holding everyone up, but many of the 12,000 runners who had planned to come hadn't arrived and the organizers wanted to wait for them until the last minute. The longer we waited, the colder I became.

Eventually, the organizers told us to line up, and the starting gun gave us our cue to run like hell for just under ten miles. I quickly found myself in the middle of the pack, gasping heavily and watching my jerky, visible breath in the chilly air. Everyone around me was younger by ten years or more, so I guess I was doing well for my age group, which was beginning to feel like the "over 90" crowd.

There were older runners in the pack, but they were in the back and would be content just to finish. Before we started, I had had the conceit to believe I could win. Not just my class, but overall. Nothing like young bodies in top form to remind me of the mileage my body had already traveled. Now I realized I'd be lucky if I didn't die.

After about two miles, I began to get into the race and to warm up. I tried to put on a little speed and at least get nearer the front of the pack. The problem was that younger, faster runners were getting warmed up, too, and they stayed in front of me the whole way.

When I glanced to my left, I saw Sandra Kelley on the sidelines, cheering a young man who must have been one of the Kelley children. His resemblance to Gil Kelley was unmistakable; if he was about twenty years younger, they'd be twins. Which was curious in its own way, I remember thinking, since Sandra was more than twenty years younger than Gil. They had a three-generation family. And then I had to concentrate on the rest of the run.

Maybe the old girl still has it, but not enough of it. I managed to finish in the middle of the pack. I wasn't last, but I was nowhere near first. The promoters gave me my participatory tee-shirt and congratulatory approval for the pledges I'd obtained from corporate sponsors if I finished the race. I found myself walking around near the finish line, panting hard, sweating profusely, unable to talk and breathe at the same time.

Why did I do all that training if it wasn't going to make a bit of difference? Running alone and running in a race are not the same.

Maybe it helps to think you can, but I'm here to tell you, positive thoughts alone cannot make you a fast runner.

Walking around with my head down, looking at the ground, trying to catch my breath and keep my legs from cramping, I didn't see Sandra Kelley until I ran right into her and spilled most of the bottle of water I had in my hand all over her.

"I'm sorry, Sandra," I said, as I tried ineffectually to brush the water off of the bulky fur coat she wore.

I snagged my hand on the sharp edge of the large, elaborate pin she had on the lapel. I stuck my hand in my mouth, trying to make it feel better, without success, thinking it more than a little ridiculous for her to be wearing a mink coat.

It wasn't that cold. Only about forty-five degrees, not minus forty-five. She wore the coat just like she did everything else—to show off who she was and what she had.

If your husband owns the bank, you damn well better look the part, seemed to be her motto.

"Don't worry about it, Willa. It's not the only thing you've ruined lately," she said, sourly, as she tried to move past me, wiping my blood off her jewelry. But the crowd of runners, well wishers and fundraisers was too thick to let her go through. She was stuck next to me, unable to get away.

"I have (puff puff) no idea (puff puff) what you're (puff puff) talking about," I huffed and puffed and mumbled in her general direction, around the hand in my mouth. Really, I couldn't believe how out of breath I was. I had been running fifteen to sixteen miles a day for weeks. Could it possibly be just the cold? The stress? Too much food at dinner last night? What?

"Your kind never does," she snarled. "You go through life thinking you can just do whatever you want and damn the consequences." She turned her back to me.

This was just too much. I took her arm and pulled her around. Mustering all of my wind, I said in one complete sentence, "Exactly what the hell are you trying to say?"

She looked down at my bleeding hand clutching a big hunk of the fur on her coat along with her arm. The look could have dropped a flying quail at fifty yards. She made me feel even colder than I already was. People aren't often downright nasty to me. I'm not used to it.

"Do you think exposing thefts at Gil's bank is going to be a good thing for his depositors? For the city? Did you think for one minute that just the scandal of the investigation itself wouldn't harm us?"

I dropped her arm like it had singed my fingers.

Why had I thought she looked anything like Margaret Wheaton? Margaret would never, ever say anything so vicious.

Sandra looked feral. She frightened me. I'd never thought of Sandra as dangerous, but I'd underestimated her.

"I'm not investigating Gil or his bank, Sandra. I don't think anything about it."

"Did you think we'd just take that? From you?"

Was she threatening me?

"What are you saying?"

"Watch yourself, Willa Carson. You're not untouchable. I'd have thought you would've learned that by now." She moved off and the crowd quickly filled in the void behind her.

I was cold, sweating, tired, my hand was stinging, and I was more than a little shocked. I needed to go home, have a hot bath, a pot of hot tea and get out my journal.

Now was definitely the time for some serious thinking.

It seemed to me that all of South Tampa had completely taken leave of its senses.

CHAPTER TWENTY-SEVEN

Tampa, Florida
Saturday 1:30 p.m.
February 24, 2001

HOME ALONE, IN THE den, in my favorite chair with my feet
up, in front of a fire with hot *café con leche* and my journal, the
dogs lying at my feet, I felt calmer and more able to think
through the events of the last few days. I picked up journaling
where I had left off. I started to record everything that had
happened in chronological order as I knew it.

There were holes, things I wasn't aware of, things I was sure
I was forgetting. But all in all, it took me about two hours to
write everything down, with the bandage on the outside of my
right hand protecting the cut and, I hoped, keeping me from
needing stitches. When I'd finished, I had a clearer picture of
some things and more questions than answers.

I made a plan, as I always do. I could hear my mother
saying, "If you fail to plan, you plan to fail." Why do these old
tapes play in my head when I need guidance? I used to so rebel

against this piece of advice when Mom was alive. It was unfair of her to haunt me with it now.

In any event, I refilled my coffee cup and turned to a new page in my journal where I spent another hour. I wrote out my plan for helping Margaret Wheaton to avoid being arrested; Ben Hathaway to see that Ron Wheaton had either died by natural causes or Otter had killed him; Larry Davis to prove that Armstrong Otter either died accidentally or was killed by someone currently unknown to me; Dad to wrap up his investigation of Gil Kelley's bank and either file charges or go back to New York.

I paid little attention to the CJ, my continued testimony or his problems; George's concern over Aunt Minnie's jewelry or mine; Suzanne; or my work load. All of these issues dealt with my personal life. I rarely spent any time being concerned about my own problems. Which was a mistake, of course.

Kate tells me I spend too little time inside my circle of control and too much out there tilting at windmills on issues over which I have no influence. The problem with her advice, I thought with a smile, is that she doesn't realize just how influential I can be. For if there's anything my experience has taught me, it's how much one person with good will, positive effort, and the right attitude can do. Never mind that this approach doesn't help win races.

I closed my journal and put it aside. My stomach was rumbling to remind me that it was three o'clock and I hadn't eaten today. We had nothing edible in the kitchen and I didn't want microwaved popcorn, so I did a quick once-over of my appearance and went downstairs for lunch. The dining room was closed between lunch and dinner, but the Sunset Bar was always open and would serve me a sandwich or a salad or something.

Expecting the Sunset Bar to be nearly empty, I was surprised to see that Dad was there. Deep in conversation with, of all people, Sandra Kelley. They seemed to be arguing and, at first, even though I thought the curiosity might kill me, I wasn't going to join them. But Dad had seen me come in and motioned me over, without interrupting whatever Sandra was saying.

I stopped off at the bar, ordered a tuna salad sandwich on white, picked up an iced tea and took it over to Dad's table. Sandra sat on the bench across from him with a cup of hot tea.

"Sit down, Willa," Dad invited. "You know Sandra Kelley, of course, don't you?"

"Yes, of course. Hello, Sandra." I smiled weakly at the woman who would have killed me with her venom this morning. I was still considering a tetanus shot. Sandra gave me a curt and distinctly unfriendly nod.

"Sandra and I were talking about Tampa Bay Bank. She was telling me the unfortunate history of her deceased father-in-law, weren't you, Sandra?" Dad said, putting her on the spot and me into the conversation, despite Sandra's obvious wishes to the contrary. She said nothing, so he went on. "It turns out, Willa, that the late Mr. Gilbert Kelley, Senior, was a thief. Isn't that right, Sandra?"

Sandra looked decidedly uncomfortable discussing this with me. She had a string of pearls around her neck that was in danger of becoming a noose if she twisted them any tighter. Her left hand was gripping the table as if she would fall down without the support, even though she was seated.

"That's not what I said, Mr. Harper," she hissed.

"Call me Jim," he said, with all the concern of a Las Vegas Black Jack dealer watching a gambler bet the farm. "What did you say, then? I thought you were asking me not to investigate thefts from your husband's bank. Because, you said, it was really his father who had stolen millions of dollars from the other shareholders, the depositors and, ultimately, the Federal Government when we had to pay those insured accounts back. Depositors like Willa and George, here. Isn't that what you said?"

This was a side of Jim Harper I hadn't seen before. He was completely without compassion for her, even though Sandra Kelley was obviously in acute distress. She was dressed in a lavender wool St. John suit with a long-sleeved jacket. The temperatures had not warmed up outside, but Sandra was perspiring and fidgety. If she broke those pearls before they broke her neck, they'd scatter all over the floor, she was twisting them so ferociously now. Dad remained unmoved.

"No," she whispered, "that's not what I said. What I said was that Senior, as everyone called him, treated the bank's money as if it was his own because for many years, it was his. His wife had inherited the bank, but he became president when he married her. Senior ran the bank from then until he died. I said if there were any, um, improprieties, then, um, they must have happened when he was still, um, in charge." She seemed to stumble a little on this last part, when she'd been reasonably articulate before she tried to slander Senior.

"Let's just say I believed you, Mrs. Kelley," Dad started.

"Sandra," she said, automatically.

"Let's just say I believed you, Sandra," he began again. "How does that change anything? You and your husband are both officers of the bank. You're both responsible for what happens there. You didn't come to me and offer to pay the money back. You're only here because you're worried that I'll be able to prove that your husband is an embezzler and send him off to jail. Isn't that true?" He said this with a frightening calm. If she was trying to make Dad feel sorry for her, dressed to the nines in an outfit that, including jewelry, would set him back more than two month's salary, she'd come to the wrong place. Dad didn't begrudge the Kelleys of the world their silver spoons. He had accumulated a nice portfolio himself over the years. But he did begrudge them the theft of cheap stainless from the rest of the "little people," particularly little old people.

Sandra was so incensed, she actually sprayed spittle all the way over to Dad's face in the process of hissing her answer in four distinct words as if they were separated by exclamation points. "You Are A Horrid Man!"

Dad said nothing while she gathered up her dignity and stalked out.

"So much for Tampans never telling anyone exactly what they think of you," he said, bringing his iced tea up to his mouth.

"Yes," I smiled at him, and we both laughed out loud. Not at Sandra's distress, but at the irony of Dad's wit.

We talked a little while longer, and I became engrossed in Dad's day and his investigation of Tampa Bay Bank. He brought me up to date as we ate lunch.

"Are you planning to look into the father-in-law's culpability?" I asked him. "Sandra seemed pretty certain about it."

"I did a lot more than look at bank records in Miami," he said.

"What sent you down there in the first place?"

"It was that story your friend Marilee Aymes told you about Gil Kelley being banished to Miami in the fifties. It seemed like the money problems with the bank began about the time she said Gil Kelley was working in Miami. The story could have supported Sandra Kelley's version, which I'd already heard before today, of course."

"What do you mean?"

"Well, if the embezzlement started then, it could have been Senior who did it from Tampa, or it could have been Gil from Miami. I couldn't just walk into the Tampa office and ask, without tipping my hand, so I went to the Miami branch and looked at the books myself."

"They let you do that?"

"There's a clause in their insurance policy that requires them to let me look at their books whenever I want to," Dad said, a little wounded. "The bank has no choice but to let me investigate. I just wanted a little freedom from Kelley's personal oversight while I did it."

"I'd think Gil Kelley would have learned about your snooping pretty quickly, either way. But what did you find out?"

"That over three-hundred thousand dollars disappeared from the Miami branch office over a two-year period back in the late fifties—coinciding with Gil Kelley's period of expulsion from the family nest."

"But you knew that before you went there, based on Marilee's story."

"Ah, but what I didn't know before I went there was what had happened to the money and how it got paid back." Dad savored his own tuna sandwich as if he were dining on the finest smoked sturgeon, taking his time, forcing me to ask him the next question.

"Okay. What happened to the money and how did it get paid back?" I can be stubborn myself, but this wasn't one of those times. I was curious, and didn't mind showing my curiosity.

"Well, that's quite an interesting story. The money

disappeared in dribs and drabs. Just a few hundred at first, every couple of weeks. Then a few thousand. Then larger amounts. I was hoping to be able to pin that on Kelley, but it turned out to be a dead end. Literally."

I'd finished eating and we were now talking over freshened glasses of iced tea. "The thief was a low-level auditor named David Martin. Guess what happened to him?" Dad asked me.

"I give up."

"He died. Killed himself, And that's not all."

At this point, Dad looked a little like the remaining smile on the Cheshire cat. He waited for me to ask, but I didn't this time.

So he said, "It was the bonding company that paid off the debts after the guy died."

"So those early thefts didn't have anything to do with Gil Kelley?" I asked.

Dad sounded deeply disappointed. "Apparently not, unfortunately. It was a good lead. I'm just sorry it didn't pan out. If I could have tied those early thefts to Gil Kelley, it would have been a lot easier to tie the later ones to him, too."

"What a coincidence that there was a bonding company to pay. In those days, three-hundred thousand dollars was a lot of money."

I NEEDED A CHANGE of pace, somewhere else to go to think. I didn't tell anyone where I was going. When I left home Monday morning, instead of driving Greta toward downtown, I took Gandy to Westshore. Turning north, I reached Tampa International Airport in plenty of time for the nine o'clock flight to Miami.

Everything about this case seemed to point to Miami. Gil

Kelley, Margaret Wheaton and David Martin were in Miami from 1955 to 1957. What happened there? And how did it relate to what had gone on in Tampa the past few weeks? Was there a relationship between the three of them?

The commuter flight was just under an hour and I was on the ground, in my rental car, by eleven. Studying the map that Hertz had provided, I found my way to Coconut Grove. I drove to the Tampa Bay Bank branch where Gil Kelley and David Martin had worked.

The bank manager was a portly man, about sixty-five or so, who looked as if he'd never had a good hair day. I introduced myself, telling him I was the executor of Ron Wheaton's estate and I had come to look into some accounts Ron had held at the bank. It only took a little flirting and I had him in my pocket.

Once we had struck up a friendship, I said, "Mr. Wheaton asked me to look up a friend of his who works here. I think he left the man a little something in his will. I wonder if you could point me in the right direction to find him?" I broke my self-imposed rule against lying, but rationalized it as for a good cause. I promised myself a strong penance afterward.

"I'll surely try. What's his name?"

"David Martin," I told him, and watched his friendliness dry up like a slug exposed to salt.

CHAPTER TWENTY-EIGHT

Miami, Florida
Monday 12:20 p.m.
February 26, 2001

"MR. MARTIN DIED, QUITE some time ago. I'm afraid you won't be able to talk to him," he said curtly.

"Did he leave any family? I could give the gift to his wife," I coaxed.

"No. He had a young girlfriend, but when he died she left here. I don't know her name." The bank manager's easy manner was completely gone now, replaced by fidgeting with the papers on his desk to let me know he was ready to terminate this conversation. Now.

"Well, where did he live? I can see you're busy. Maybe I can trace the girlfriend through his last address."

"I'll get that for you, ma'am, if you'll wait just a minute," he said, decidedly cool in his tone, making it clear that I'd be dismissed after this last courtesy.

When he came back with the address, I asked him straight

up, "Is something wrong? You seem like you're not too happy that I'm asking about Mr. Martin."

"Not at all, ma'am," he said, not convincing me or himself, but offering nothing further. I put his reaction down to Martin's thefts from the bank. Men from the old school would have taken a dim view of bank theft, just as most of us do today. But a forty-year-old theft, paid back through a surety bond when the thief died, shouldn't engender such a long-held animosity. At least, I couldn't have held a grudge that long.

I stayed a while longer, talking to a couple of other employees who looked old enough to have been working at the bank while David Martin was there. Then I had to hustle to finish my investigation in time to catch my plane.

When I left the bank branch, I drove through McDonald's for a hamburger and fries on the run. I made my way over to the local library, gobbling the food out of the bag on the way, and rolling down the windows to get the smell out of the car. Once settled at the library machine with the microfilm of the local newspapers from 1956, I began to flip through the pages looking for references to David Martin. It didn't take me long to find the story of Martin's suicide by drowning in early 1957. Checking my watch and knowing I had one more stop to make, I copied the articles without reading them and paid for my copies at the desk. I jogged out to the rental car, remembering my vows after the distance classic to get in better shape. Of course, I should have remembered that before I ate a thousand-calorie, junk food lunch.

I traced Martin's address to a dreary rooming house close to the bank branch, where Martin had worked as an internal auditor. I parked the car at the curb, walked up to the house, and leaned on the button for the doorbell.

A woman as unkempt and unattractive as the house

answered the door. She identified herself as "Joan." Then she smiled, showing what was left of her teeth: cavities and broken pieces. Bad teeth arc usually a sign of someone who fears dentists and, in my experience, has other irrational fears as well.

"Hi, I'm Willa Carson. I'm looking for a man who used to live here. His name was David Martin. Did you know him?" Joan had started to nod before I finished the sentence.

"Yep. I did know him, before he died. My momma used to own this place then. David was pretty quiet. Good lookin', too. I was only about ten years old when he killed himself." She had pronounced it "kilt his-self," lisping through the "esses."

"Did he kill himself here? In your house?" I tried to sound properly horrified.

"God, no!" It sounded like "Gawd, nah." The accent was music to my ears. Amazingly, I'd found the only redneck left in Miami. "He went out fishin' and never came back. Curious thing was that he'd only taken up fishin' a few weeks earlier. But the night he died, he went out on the ocean by hisself. Everybody here found that odd at the time." The heavy Southern accent and the missing teeth made her difficult to understand. It gave me the feeling that my mind was processing the speech just a second or two behind, like the delay between dialogue and subtitles on a foreign film. Joan was speaking English, of sorts, even if I couldn't translate it in real time.

"Did Mr. Martin leave anything here that you might still have?" I asked her.

She was already shaking her head of lank, dirty brown hair before I got the question out. "Nope. That friend of his that he was always hanging around with took his car and everything after they found the body."

"Well, who was that? Maybe I can ask him."

"He was that big banker David worked for. What a flirt! I thought he was real handsome at the time, though," she laughed, showing her bad teeth to full effect.

Back at the airport just in time to catch my plane by running to the gate, I found myself cursing my junk food lunch and vowing to give up French fries forever. Once I was seated on the plane, I pulled out my journal and wrote down the day's conversations, as well as a few thoughts for investigation.

Joan had said that David Martin owned an old car, so he must have had a driver's license. I planned to contact the State to check it, maybe get a picture that I could then run through the Florida Department of Law Enforcement's facial recognition software. Martin had been fingerprinted for the bonding company, which would have filed his prints with the FBI. I would contact the FBI to run the prints to see if he had any kind of a criminal record. "Maybe all the leads won't be dead-ends," I wrote, smiling at my own bad pun.

When I got home, I searched until I found Dad in our den alone with the television tuned to a college basketball game. But work is always a more interesting topic to him. It was easy to convince him to compare notes on our respective trips to Miami.

"The newspaper accounts of his suicide described Martin as an internal auditor who stole money from the bank and then committed suicide when the bank examiners found out. He had been there for about two years before Gil Kelley arrived, but the money didn't start disappearing until Kelley got there," I told Dad.

He took a swallow of his iced tea. "That sounds promising."

"I thought so, too. Martin lived a quiet lifestyle until about the time Kelley arrived, though. I didn't see anything that would suggest he had lived large."

"Did you find anyone still at the bank in Miami who

remembered Martin?" I was already nodding my head before Dad had finished the question. "What did they tell you?" he asked.

"I talked to a couple of old-timers while I was there. They remembered Martin because of the theft. But not much else. They said he was a loner, kept to himself, and then struck up a friendship with Kelley because they were about the same age. They said Martin and Kelley got into some pretty wild living and there was even the idea that they'd gotten on the wrong side of the Mafia somehow, until Martin killed himself. Then, that idea went by the wayside. Other than that, they knew nothing."

Dad thought for a few minutes and then volunteered, "I can check the employment files, but it's probably too long ago. They've more than likely been destroyed. I already tried to pull up Martin's old IRS files, but even those have been archived somewhere. The IRS might find the files, but I'm not holding my breath until they do."

Dad had access to information not easily available to me. I asked him, "What about running the Social Security number?"

"I did that when I checked all this stuff before. David Martin was listed as deceased in 1957. I could contact the bonding company for you, if you want me to. I didn't look back that far when I called them originally. Since we're both in the insurance business, they would probably share their files with me," he said.

"I already asked them, actually. Since the investigation was so old, they didn't have much on it. But they faxed me what they had. I have their file here somewhere." I started rifling through the papers piled all over the table and onto the seat next to me. Then, in my briefcase on the floor. Finally, I came up with a thin green folder which, when I opened it, had a few sheets of photocopied microfilm. The pages were dark and blurry. "There's not much here. The complete file was destroyed long ago."

I showed him the bottom of the third page, which said "Disposition: Paid." The first two pages were the rest of the claim form and the comments by the investigator at the time. The claimant was listed as Tampa Bay Bank and the contact was Gilbert Kelley, Senior, now deceased. The description of the claim was "embezzled funds." The investigator's comments were equally terse. "Accounting irregularities beginning in 1955 and ending in 1957, equal to a loss of $300,000. Attributable to internal auditor, now deceased."

"What about the bond company investigator, can we interview him?" Dad was getting as frustrated about this as I was. Now I was shaking my head. "Let me guess," he said. "Deceased?"

"Yes. About ten years ago. Heart attack."

"So what you're saying is that you know the money began to disappear at the time Gil Kelley came to the Miami branch. You also know that he and Martin were friends. Then, the bank examiners found the money missing. Martin committed suicide and the bonding company paid off the debt. Case closed. Unless your other inquiries turn up something else."

"Except for one thing," I said.

"What's that?"

"The money kept disappearing from the bank. For years afterwards."

We both thought about the facts some more, trying to fit the pieces together to create a complete picture. But critical pieces of the puzzle were still missing and we couldn't even organize all the pieces of one section of the puzzle board on what we knew now. It was like those jigsaw puzzles where the finished picture is solid black. Only the shapes were important. There were no vivid pictures to match up.

"Did Martin have a wife? Kids? Other family?" Dad asked.

"Apparently not. He lived alone at the rooming house and as far as the old-timers at the bank knew, he had no family."

"Well, everyone has parents. What about that?" He raked a frustrated hand through his still thick head of salt-and-pepper hair.

"When I get the reports back that I'm looking for, I think I may be able to trace him. At this point, it's a brick wall. I don't know where he came from, don't even have a place and date of birth."

Dad looked at me quizzically. "I don't understand that, Willa. I checked his Social Security number. He had one. Didn't he have to provide a birth certificate to get the number in the first place?"

I shook my head again. "No. But not back when Martin applied. I'm hoping the fingerprints will check out and compare to some others somewhere. But in those days, people didn't get fingerprinted in the hospital or for most jobs. If Martin wasn't arrested somewhere or in some type of law enforcement, the fingerprints are likely to be a dead end, too." I ran my hands through my hair in frustration now, too. "Can a man just disappear without a trace in this country?"

Dad laughed out loud at this, got up and collected a couple of beers from the small fridge in the bar in our den. "Well, that's not exactly the question. We're not talking about him disappearing here."

"Sure we are. He's got no history. He just showed up at the Tampa Bay Bank in 1954 and they hired him, the bonding company accepted him, he embezzled money from the bank, and then killed himself. That's it? That's the whole story?"

I hadn't wanted a beer, I was about to say, as Dad twisted the caps off both bottles, clinked the neck of my bottle with his, handed me one and resumed his seat. Oh, what the hell, I thought, and took a big swig out of the longneck bottle. I just love Labatt Blue beer. We started drinking it when we lived in

Detroit. Now, George orders it in relatively small quantities because Canadian beer is not a big seller here. But, it's my beer of choice, when I drink beer. And it's best fresh, too. I was looking at the bottle, admiring the taste, when an idea occurred to me. "What about Canada?"

"For beer? Can't beat it." Dad gave me his biggest grin.

"No. I mean, what about Canada for tracing this guy? Could he have come from Canada? Florida gets thousands of tourists a year from Canada, if not millions. Miami must get them, too. Could he have come to the U.S. from Toronto or Windsor or something?"

"Maybe. But don't let yourself get distracted. It's probably unimportant where he came from. Once David Martin died, the link between Gil Kelley and the missing money was severed. And to answer your question, it's pretty easy to disappear in this country. Even today. Hundreds of people do it every year. All you do is to cut all your ties to your old self by telling no one about your plans, fabricate a new name and history, and pay for everything with cash. It's fairly easy if you just take on the identity of a dead person. What's hard is to stay away from your old life. Most people can't manage it. Even Mafia witnesses who have been granted witness protection and given new identities can't do it. And those guys are highly motivated."

Dad and I both laughed at the image of highly motivated Mafia witnesses.

"So, Martin came from somewhere. I think it's important to find out where that was," I insisted. "And why he left there. And how."

"I'll humor you on this one, Willa. I'll see what I can find out. But I honestly think it has nothing to do with what you're investigating. Which is, who killed Ron Wheaton and Armstrong Otter."

CHAPTER TWENTY-NINE

Tampa, Florida
Saturday 7:00 p.m.
March 3, 2001

GEORGE AND I WERE dressed and waiting for Dad and
Suzanne to join us for the Minaret Krewe Coronation Ball at the
Tampa Convention Center, where next year's King and Queen
would be crowned at the end of the night. I hadn't invited them
to join us but, apparently, George had. He didn't tell me because
he expected fireworks. I gave him none.

"It doesn't pay to become too predictable," Kate always
says. Takes the mystery out of marriage.

The ten-minute drive was spent with pleasantries, the only
conversation besides work Dad ever has with anyone. We pulled
up in front of the Tampa Convention Center to use the valet
service that Minaret Krewe had hired for the night. I was busy
getting my wrap around the bare-shouldered silver gown I had
foolishly decided to wear to this event about six weeks ago,
when it was still warm enough for it.

I'd chosen the dress because I planned to wear Aunt Minnie's jewelry. A spectacular emerald necklace set in platinum, with matching earrings. As I often did when using Aunt Minnie's things, I wondered what admirer had given her emeralds at a time when emeralds were not "manufactured," as most of them are now.

Aunt Minnie had lived a colorful life, and I was reaping all of her life's benefits while paying none of its costs. This was especially true in the case of her jewelry. George had had Aunt Minnie's pieces appraised. Thankfully, we learned they had not been stolen by Armstrong Otter when George had taken the pieces in for cleaning.

I turned around to speak to Suzanne, just as she shook her head, revealing diamond drop earrings that were hanging from her lobes.

They must have been five carats each. I couldn't imagine how strong her ears must have been to hold them up. Is it possible to do earlobe exercises?

"What beautiful earrings, Suzanne. They look positively fabulous on you."

And they did. Suzanne was a beautiful woman.

She looked so much like my mother I almost cried.

Suzanne beamed at Dad, who by now had made his way around the car. As she took his arm, she cooed, "Jimmy bought them for me from that Mr. Otter you introduced us to. Aren't they just perfect?"

Just perfect, I thought. Probably, just perfect fakes. But why spoil her night? With Otter dead, it wasn't likely Dad would get his money back. He must know now that the earrings weren't real.

I gave George a meaningful look as he took my hand. We all

walked over to the outdoor escalator and rode to the second floor where Minaret Krewe had rented one of the larger rooms for its *grande finale* of the season.

A few of the other Krewes were having their balls here at the convention center, too. For tonight, the Krewe members left their pirate costumes at home. All the rooms were filled with women in gowns and fine jewelry and men in tuxedos. Almost everyone we knew in Tampa would be here somewhere.

It was the longest night of the year for me, but the one I most looked forward to. Each of the Krewes would crown its Kings and Queens and then announce the results of its fundraising for the year. Except for the Gasparilla Festival of the Arts, which was thankfully not related to the Krewes in any way, this would be our last big night of the Gasparilla season.

Next week, we could enjoy the art festival like the rest of the more than 200,000 people who would be there. More importantly, as far as I was concerned, our lives would return to normal beginning tomorrow morning. I almost sighed, I was so happy with anticipation.

Suzanne and Dad were both mesmerized by the splendor of the whole thing. There was more jewelry here than you'd find at all the Tiffany stores in the country. More taffeta, silk, strappy sandals, fine cigars and expensive perfume.

Tonight, there seemed to be an equally large number of furs, something for which the center had hurriedly set up a coat check room to accommodate. Usually, there's no need to wear coats in Florida so there's no need to check them. Houses don't even have coat closets here. But tonight, the mercury promised to dip below the freezing point, and the Tampa ladies took the opportunity to show off what they had.

By midnight, I had been standing for five exhausting hours

on four-inch spike heels. We had dinner, but it was heavy hors d'oeuvres passed around by waiters in black tie and tails. We didn't sit, even when the King and Queen were crowned. I felt like I might soon collapse.

George was talking in a group that included Gilbert Kelley, which I found surprising since he knew as much about Dad's investigation as I did. I suppose George had no choice. Gil Kelley was the past Minaret Krewe king and George was the Krewe's main sponsor. They'd have to speak to each other occasionally. It might as well be in a public place.

I was standing there thinking about Gil when Ben Hathaway came up behind me and touched my elbow. "I know where there are a couple of seats out in the lobby. Are you interested?"

"Chief, you do know how to turn a girl's head," I told him, mocking the coquet, batting my eyelashes and lowering my gaze. I followed Ben out into the lobby and into a blissfully comfortable upholstered chair. Ben handed me a cup of coffee he'd snagged from the last of the circulating trays.

"You look mighty handsome in that tuxedo, Chief," I continued with the drawl.

"Thank 'ye, ma'am." If he'd had on a hat, he'd have tipped it. He smiled back at me as I drank the best coffee I'd had in weeks and actually groaned with pleasure. I was way too old to stand up all night in four-inch heels. What was I thinking?

"It was a good thing you hired Larry Davis for Margaret, Willa," Ben said, seriously now. "She's going to need a good lawyer and Larry's one of the best."

"What do you mean?"

"I'm going to arrest her tomorrow. For the murders of Ron Wheaton and Armstrong Otter."

I nearly spit out my coffee, which now tasted like old

grounds in my mouth. He'd picked this time and this place to tell me about Margaret's arrest so I couldn't protest about it as much as I would have anywhere else.

"I gather you think you've got a good reason to do that," I said, in a quiet but mean-spirited tone.

He had the grace to look troubled. "It isn't what I want to do, believe me. The evidence has left me no other choice."

"What evidence? What possible evidence could you have against a little old woman as sweet and gentle as Margaret? What?" I wasn't letting him off the hook. I set the coffee down and turned my full attention to him. I didn't want to be overheard any more than he did, but I wanted to know what Margaret was facing.

"I found a disinterested witness who saw Margaret push Armstrong Otter down in a quarrel at the Knight Parade. And, as you know, I got the autopsy and the full tox report back on Ron Wheaton. He died of an overdose of insulin. Margaret's an insulin-dependent diabetic. I'm sorry, Willa. I didn't want it to be Margaret, either." Hathaway looked so much like a basset hound after a bad meal that I believed him. I didn't like it, but I did believe him.

I was a little relieved. Dad had admitted to pushing Otter down, too. In front of witnesses. If Hathaway had focused on Margaret, he must have discounted Dad as a suspect. It seemed Otter had a knack for inspiring people to violence that ultimately got him killed. If Margaret pushed Otter down, which I doubted, it was because he had asked for it. That didn't mean I'd let Hathaway arrest Margaret. Because she didn't kill anyone. I knew it, even if he didn't.

I thought back to the evening of the Knight Parade. I, too, had seen Margaret on the float with Armstrong Otter. But they were so far toward the back that I never got around there to speak to them. Gil and Sandra Kelley were on the right side of the front of the float, opposite George and me. They could easily have gone back there and pushed Otter off. He could have hit his head then. But that's not when he died. It was later, on a dark street, off Seventh Avenue.

I remembered sweating and still being freezing cold while I waited for the shuttle bus to take us back to Minaret after the parade. We were standing at the end of the parade route, on 22nd Street. I didn't see Margaret and Otter there then. In fact, I'd seen Otter without Margaret. Then, I never saw either of them again. Nor did I see the Kelleys after that until we were all back at Minaret, later that night.

Someone must have argued with Otter, pushed him harder than intended, and Otter, being drunk, fell and hit his head. That's not really murder. But, leaving Otter alone on the street to die was at least negligence, if not depraved indifference to human life. He wouldn't have died right away. It would have taken a while for the bleeding inside his skull to kill him.

If the pusher had called for help, Otter might be alive today. Could Margaret have pushed Otter in anger, stalking off and leaving him there to die, not knowing the full extent of his injury? I now had to acknowledge that she could have done that. Anyone could have done that. It wasn't murder without an intent to kill. But, Otter was dead, just the same.

I continued to replay the scenes of that Saturday evening in my mind. Until I remembered the random thought I'd had when I first went down the stairs from our flat into George's restaurant lobby. When I saw Margaret standing next to Sandra Kelley.

They had been made up by the same artist, their black eyebrows, brightly rouged cheeks, and strong red mouths, applied with the same heavy hand. Their costumes had been the same colors and they both wore black wigs.

Maybe the "disinterested witness" Hathaway had interviewed didn't know both Margaret and Sandra. If not, an eyewitness easily could have confused them that night. Had Margaret pushed Armstrong Otter down to the sidewalk in anger? Or was it Sandra Kelley?

I finally got home and was able to change into jeans, leaving George sleeping in the flat. The drive to Margaret's house at two in the morning took only a few minutes. When I got there, the house was dark and not one small light was burning.

I rang the bell several times, each ring longer and more insistent. Margaret never came to answer it. In freezing frustration, I jogged quickly around to the back of the house where I'd found the door unlocked once before. It was unlocked again and I resolved to tell Margaret that she absolutely had to be more careful.

I opened the door quietly and went into the mudroom off the kitchen, just as I had the last time. I didn't want to startle Margaret, but I didn't want to kill myself walking around in the dark, either. I felt around the doorway for a light switch and found one, but it turned on the outside light over the door I'd just come through.

The porch light provided dim illumination as I walked into the kitchen and continued feeling around for another light switch. I found it on the opposite side of the doorway from the last one. When I flipped it, the hanging lamp over the kitchen table came on and illuminated the entire kitchen. A good thing, because the light kept me from tripping over the body in the middle of the floor.

CHAPTER THIRTY

Tampa, Florida
Sunday 12:07 a.m.
March 4, 2001

IT TOOK ME ABOUT two seconds to recognize Margaret lying there. She was fully dressed. I stooped down to check her pulse and found her breathing normally. Trying to wake her up took a few minutes, but eventually she did. I helped her to the living room couch. After giving her some water and finding her eyeglasses under the kitchen table, Margaret righted herself and was coherent enough to talk to me, but barely.

I spoke to her gently. "Honey, what happened? Why were you on the floor? Did you fall?" Elderly people were always falling down and breaking their hips. I feared this had happened to Margaret, although she didn't seem to be in any pain. She seemed bewildered and disoriented, but she knew who I was and where she was. As the doctors say, she was oriented to time and place.

After a little while Margaret was able to speak coherently. "I don't know what happened. I came out into the kitchen to get something and the next thing I remember is sitting here with you." As she exhaled, I got the slightly sweet smell of processed alcohol on her breath. I never thought of Margaret as a closet drinker. Maybe she'd gotten drunk and passed out. People have been driven to drink by lesser things than she had been dealing with lately.

"Well, come on, we're going to get you over to Tampa General and have them take a look at you." I started trying to get her up, but she was surprisingly resistant. She refused to budge.

"I'm not going to the hospital. I think I must have fainted or something. Nothing's broken. I don't hurt anywhere. I'll be fine in a few minutes." Margaret started feeling her hands, her arms, her feet and her legs.

She turned her head this way and that, feeling it with her hands as she did so. She straightened her shoulders and flexed them. Finally, she stood up, bent over at the waist, then stooped down by bending her knees and standing back up. All while I watched in silence. Her flexibility was remarkable. But then, I was learning how remarkable Margaret really was in many respects.

"You could have had a stroke or something, Margaret. Be reasonable. We should check it out, at least," I pleaded with her.

"I'm fine. Nothing's broken. I'll be okay," she told me, with firmness that meant I'd never get her to the hospital unless I called an ambulance and they sedated her, which I wasn't going to do. She patted me on the hand sitting in my lap. "Don't worry so much, Willa. I've been taking care of myself and Ron for a long time. I know when I need a doctor. I don't need one now."

We sat there in silence while she let me decide for myself that she wasn't going to any hospital with me voluntarily. Then she got up and went into the kitchen to put on the kettle for tea. I had no choice but to go after her.

"Why are you here, Willa?" she asked, her back to me while she worked at getting the tea put together.

"I came to tell you that Ben Hathaway is planning to arrest you for the murders of Ron and Armstrong Otter. Unless we can figure out a way to do something about that, he should be here bright and early."

Margaret's hands shook as she got the china cups and saucers out of the cabinet, but she said nothing.

"I need you to talk to me, Margaret. I can't help you if I don't know what's going on here. I tried asking Larry Davis, but he rightly feels he can't disclose your confidences to me." I got up from the table and walked up behind her, giving her a hug. She was so tiny, especially next to me. She felt so frail in my embrace. "Let me help you, Margaret. I really want to." And then she crumpled in my arms and started to cry. I held her for a while as the tears fell. When the teakettle began whistling insistently, I helped her over to the table and handed her the tissue box.

I finished up the tea while she composed herself. Then I sat down across the table from her and asked my question again.

"Tell me what's going on here. I have some influence with Ben Hathaway, but I don't know what to tell him. I need something to work with." Margaret nodded her head, not trusting herself to speak yet, lest tears begin afresh. I continued in her silence. "Okay. Here's what I've been told. I know that Ron was dying of ALS. I also know his death wasn't by natural causes. Hathaway believes you were having an affair with Armstrong Otter and that you killed Ron to be free of him so you could be with Otter. Then, he thinks you killed Otter in a quarrel, unintentionally. He says he has a witness who saw you two arguing and saw you push Otter after the parade Saturday night. I don't know what other evidence he thinks he has, but this is a big piece to start with." As I recited these facts, tears began to fall from her eyes again, but she was composed. Just sad. "Tell me about this, Margaret. Did you kill Ron?"

Her voice was quiet, but I could hear her. "No."

"Well, that's a relief. Do you know who did?"

"Yes."

"Tell me, Margaret. If you want to stay out of jail, I need to know."

"My first husband killed Ron."

If I hadn't been sitting down, I'd have fallen down.

"You were married before Ron? I had no idea. When was this?"

"Years ago. I was young. So was he. I thought he'd died, but he hadn't." Tears continued to pour out of her eyes and down her cheeks. "I'd never have done it if I'd known he was alive. Never."

I was confused. She told me she hadn't killed Ron. "Done what? What wouldn't you have done if you'd known your husband was alive?"

"I'd never have given our baby away." And she began to sob in loud gulps. Margaret put her head down on the table and cried with deep grief, for her lost child, her lost husband, and her lost life. There was nothing I could do but wait it out, feeling such sadness for her that tears appeared on my own cheeks.

By the time she stopped sobbing, Margaret was so exhausted she couldn't keep talking. It was after four o'clock in the morning. If I put her to bed, she'd sleep until Chief Hathaway came to arrest her in the morning.

No matter what else happened, it would do no good to put Margaret Wheaton in jail. I couldn't call Hathaway at this hour and ask him to put off the arrest another day, although I believed he would do so if I told him why.

If I called the police station and left a message, it would be recorded. I didn't want that. Besides, why did Hathaway tell me he was going to arrest Margaret tomorrow if he didn't expect me to do something about it?

So, what I did next wasn't obstruction of justice. Not exactly

I found Margaret's coat and helped her into it. I packed her a small bag, carried it out to the car, and then helped her into the car. As I drove back to Minaret in the deep darkness of early morning, I tried to plan how I would explain this to George, who would definitely understand. And how I would explain it to Hathaway, who might not. I avoided thinking about how I might have to explain my behavior the next time I was testifying under oath in the CJ's hearing.

It was too late, or too early, to go to bed after I had Margaret safely stowed in our guest room again. I made coffee and settled in the den with my journal. It was still quite cold, so I started another fire. While George, the dogs, Dad, Suzanne, and Margaret all slept, I picked up my journaling where I had left off, adding Margaret's revelations to what I knew already.

"Find Margaret's first husband and you'll find Ron Wheaton's murderer," I wrote.

Margaret had given me few clues before she'd completely broken down in her kitchen. But she said she'd been married a long time ago, for a very short time, and had a child. There must have been a record of the marriage somewhere. I logged onto my computer and entered the programs available to me through the contract the courts have with a public records search service.

If I wanted more information, I'd have to call one of my friends in the U.S. Marshal's office, and for now I wanted to avoid the questions that would raise. I found Margaret Rodriguez Wheaton's Social Security number and ran a check on it. I found the calculation of her benefits when she would turn sixty-five next month and her work history reflected in the list of deposits to her account through the years.

Margaret had been employed by the U.S. Government as long as I had. We'd started at the courthouse the same month and the same year, because I hired her right after my appointment had been confirmed. Before that, she'd worked in law offices around Tampa. Her last law firm secretarial position was with my old firm. I knew she'd been married to Ron Wheaton for over thirty years, so her earlier marriage must have been when she was less than thirty years old.

I scrolled back to the early deposit records, checking from her first employment in high school at the Colonnade, which was then a drive-in restaurant on Bayshore popular with the kids. Probably, she'd been a waitress. Her earnings were reported at less than a dollar an hour.

There were a few more entries in what looked like a series of waitress jobs in her teens and then a curious entry by an employer listed as "Mrs. Robert Prieto." The contributions continued each year for three years. There was a gap in the history then for about six months, and the next entry was another waitress job in Tampa. After that, all the entries were from Tampa law practices until she became employed as my secretary.

In the 1950s, a pregnant widow of very modest means with no family would have had a hard time taking care of herself and her child. My own mother was in the same situation, and she had told me many times how hard it had been for her. She said it was so difficult for her to manage even when Kate Austin had helped her by taking us in. We lived with the Austin family while Mom finished nursing school and got a job. If Margaret didn't have a Kate to help her, and I knew she had no family, being a young woman with a child and without a husband would have seemed impossible.

I looked at the records a little more closely. My eyes were so tired and the screen print was small. Even with my bifocals, I could barely read the tiny print.

Now, though, I focused on that six-month gap in Margaret's employment history. I calculated that in 1957, Margaret would have been twenty-one years old. Her work with Mrs. Prieto must have put her in a position to meet her husband. I looked closer at Mrs. Prieto's contribution history. The address listed was Coconut Grove, the same suburb of Miami that housed the branch of Tampa Bay Bank where Gil Kelley had worked.

So Margaret had left Tampa when she was eighteen, probably right after high school. She began living in Miami with Mrs. Prieto, doing some kind of domestic work, I imagined. She'd met and married, gotten pregnant, and then her husband had died. Margaret gave the baby up for adoption and then returned to Tampa, where no one would know she'd been married or pregnant. A few years later, she met and married Ron Wheaton.

Only Margaret's husband hadn't really died. Margaret must have found out at some point. How did she know? When did she know? Where was her husband now? And where was the child? I finished off my journaling with the questions that were puzzling me now. Maybe, my sleep-deprived brain said to my still awake and coffee-wired self, the answers would come to me if I could just close my eyes for a little catnap.

My head fell back against the chair and the next thing I knew, Harry and Bess had two feet each in my lap, licking my face with the vigor only well-trained Labradors can manage.

CHAPTER THIRTY-ONE

Tampa, Florida
Sunday 7:00 a.m.
March 4, 2001

JUDGING FROM THE WAY I felt, Margaret must have been at least as tired, so I let her sleep. It was seven o'clock Sunday morning, but I called Hathaway at home anyway. The last thing I wanted was for him to go to Margaret's to arrest her and find her gone. Then, I'd have hell to pay. It was going to be only slightly better when I told him myself that she wasn't at her home before he got there.

I held the cordless phone to my ear as I walked around the kitchen collecting coffee-making materials. I heard the telephone ring several times and then Hathaway's machine pick up. At least it was his home answering machine and not the office. Still, I was careful with my message.

"Ben, this is Willa Carson. Please call me first thing this morning. I have something important to tell you." That was urgent enough, I hoped, to keep him from making a fool of himself at Margaret's and then doing something equally stupid to save face.

After that, I argued with myself for a while over whether to call Larry Davis, going back and forth, with excellent arguments on both sides. A good lawyer can always argue both sides of any issue. Before I decided, George walked into the kitchen, gave me a hug and a morning-breath kiss. I held onto him much too long.

I was lucky to have him and feeling worse about Margaret's situation by the minute. She'd lost not one husband she loved, but two. Not to mention her child. How far would Margaret go when pushed beyond what a woman should be forced to endure?

Was she capable of murder?

We forget, sometimes, how fragile humans are. Maybe Margaret snapped.

It's happened before, under far less onerous circumstances.

"Hey," George said, as he gently pushed me away so he could look into my face. "Let a guy get a cup of Joe before you go mauling him in the morning so he can at least be awake enough to enjoy it, hmm?"

He gave me a kiss on the top of my head and then turned to pour himself some liquid fortification.

"The coffee's a good idea. I have a lot to tell you and not a lot of time to do it in."

I poured a cup for me and placed the cordless phone back in its cradle. I moved both of us into the den where we could close the door and talk undisturbed. I told him about my evening's adventure.

George is used to my nocturnal wanderings around the house and Plant Key, but he doesn't like it when I leave our island in the wee hours. Before he could get his protective bluster up, I gave him the short version. George is a quick study. It didn't take him long to grasp the implications of Margaret being in our guest room, both to Margaret and to me. But we've been married a long time. He knows better than to try to scold me into changing my mind. Especially over something I've already done.

"So, where are we?" he asked, when I'd finished.

"I'm not sure. Margaret said she didn't kill Ron and I believe her. She said her first husband did it. I still don't know why or how. I need to find that out."

"Aren't you a little confused here? Isn't that Ben Hathaway's job? Finding killers?"

When I started to say, "But, George," he cut me off at the B.

"It's one thing to rescue people you know and care about, Willa. I've accepted that I can't keep you from doing that. But you don't know anything about this character except that he's a killer. You've helped Margaret. Hearing the piece of news that we know who killed Ron Wheaton will be enough to get Ben Hathaway not to arrest Margaret until he checks it out, at least. Why not stop while you're ahead? Think about that while I refill my cup," he said, as he patted my knee and walked out of the room.

Before George came back for my answer, the telephone rang.

Ben Hathaway returning my call. I could tell he was up and dressed and ready to get to work, even if it was Sunday. He was wary of my tale, but knew me well enough to trust my word. At a minimum, he knew I believed Margaret's story. That was enough to make him want to investigate it.

Ben Hathaway has arrested the wrong person more than once when I told him not to. The State Attorney was getting a little sore about looking like a fool in public because Hathaway had done the wrong thing. Ben must have been "talked to," as they say downtown. He was a little more cautious than he's been in the past.

Ben agreed to meet here with Larry Davis, Margaret, George and me in three hours when I convinced him Margaret needed to sleep and I hadn't called Larry yet. At least now I knew I was going to do so. That was progress, of a sort.

Larry was home and answered the phone on the first ring. If you despise telephone tag and answering machines, early Sunday morning is a good time to call people in Tampa. Larry wasn't too keen on my interference with his client last night, but he agreed to come right over to Minaret and discuss it with me. "Then, I'll decide whether and what we tell Ben Hathaway, Willa. It's my job to represent Margaret. I'm not sure what it is you think you're doing."

A half hour later, I'd showered and changed into clean jeans and a long-sleeved tee-shirt. As an accommodation to the temperature, I'd put on socks with my Topsiders. I was forced to put some concealer on the dark circles under my eyes to keep from looking like a raccoon. Otherwise, I wore no makeup and no jewelry, the same as any other Sunday when I expected to stay home alone.

Larry Davis arrived on time. He and George and I repaired to the den and I told him everything I'd told George. Again, the short version, although he'd want more of the details later.

"So," Larry summarized at the end of my narrative, "what we need to do is to get Margaret to identify her first husband, to tell us how she knows he killed Ron Wheaton, and to give that information to Hathaway in exchange for his agreement not to further harass Margaret. Do you think he'll go for that?"

"I think he'll investigate it. If he confirms Margaret's story, no one need ever know that he was planning to arrest her today. Then the question is whether she can testify against the killer," I said.

Both men looked surprised at that. "Why couldn't she testify?" George was first to ask, which gave Larry a minute to think about it and reach his own conclusion.

Larry said, "Because Margaret was married. She never divorced him. We don't know whether he was ever declared legally dead. If he wasn't, the spousal privilege could keep her from testifying against him. On the other hand, she'll have to disclose whatever Ron Wheaton told her about wanting to die, because he wasn't really her husband."

I finished up, "And two marriages may also make Margaret a polygamist, technically. She could be prosecuted for that, although I doubt anyone would press charges, especially since she didn't intend to marry twice. But if she's not technically his wife, it may mean that Margaret won't collect Ron's life insurance or the rest of his estate. If anyone protests her claim to be Ron's sole beneficiary, it would be one unholy mess, that's for sure."

Larry said, "Trusts and estates are something I know about. It's highly unlikely that Margaret's first husband wasn't declared dead. Given that she believed he had died, surely there was a body, a death certificate and a funeral."

George seemed perplexed by all of this. "But, if he wasn't really dead, isn't all of that null and void?"

"Actually, no," Larry explained. "Once you've been declared dead, in the eyes of the law, you're dead. To change that, there's yet another legal procedure to go through."

"That figures," George said, with a wry smile. "You can't even be alive in this country without government intervention."

Larry laughed. "At least, not if you've been dead, first."

"Just one more thing I need to bring up," I said, finally deciding that now, if ever, was the time. They looked at me expectantly. "I have a piece of physical evidence to give Hathaway. I think it will help Margaret, but I'm not sure."

Larry was the first to jump in, "What kind of physical evidence?"

"I found a syringe in the bushes outside the veranda where Ron died. I suspect the syringe is the murder weapon. And that it'll have the killer's fingerprints on it. I want to give it to Hathaway."

As I thought, this piece of news didn't make George or Larry very happy. Before they had time to jump all over my frame about it, though, Dad showed Ben Hathaway into the room, saying, "I found this guy ringing the doorbell downstairs when I returned from my run. He says you're expecting him."

Another hour later, Larry and I had filled Ben in and secured his promise to investigate Margaret's claims that her first husband had killed Ron Wheaton. But to do that, he needed more information.

By now, it was going on eleven o'clock, so I thought I could awaken Margaret and have her come in to help us with this piece of the puzzle. I went down the hall to the guest room to find her while the others drank even more coffee.

I knocked on the guest room door, calling Margaret's name several times. When she didn't answer, I pushed the door open and looked into the room.

Margaret's bed was empty. The door to the bathroom was closed, so I went over and knocked there several times. Again, no response.

When I opened the bathroom door, it was empty, too.

Margaret had left sometime this morning, but when? Where did she go? And how did she get there?

The four of us discussed what to do about finding Margaret

and investigating her claims about the mysterious husband, divided up the job and went our separate ways. Larry fought with me over who got to go to Margaret's house, but in the end, agreed it was a job I could do best while he went to his office and began preparing to defend Margaret's arrest, if it came to that.

I gave Hathaway the syringe I'd been keeping in Greta's glove box. After sputtering at me about chain of custody and obstruction of justice for a relatively short time, he went off to investigate Margaret's claims. He had some ideas as to where he could look, and access to law enforcement files, he said. George, who was feeling a little left out, although he tried to describe it differently, came with me.

George drove us over to Margaret's house, which looked empty from the outside. I had him pull up in the driveway and we went to the back door, which had been unlocked the last two times I'd come here. It was unlocked again. George protested at just walking in without ringing the bell, but I was fairly sure Margaret wouldn't be here anyway, so I wasn't worried about catching her *in flagrante delicto* or anything.

George walked into the house calling Margaret's name. After we'd made a thorough check of all five small rooms, even he was convinced that Margaret wasn't here. I'd expected as much.

The reason I arm-wrestled Larry Davis for the right to come here was so that I could look around for evidence about the mysterious first husband, not because I really thought Margaret had gotten up this morning and taken a cab back home.

By now, I knew her agenda was something more complicated than that. There was more to Margaret Wheaton than I had initially suspected.

Hathaway was checking with the cab companies to see who picked Margaret up at Minaret this morning and where they took her. He had the manpower for that. I needed to investigate more cleverly.

After facing down George's protests, I began a systematic search of the places in Margaret's house where I thought she might have hidden something related to an earlier marriage and birth of a child that she'd wanted to keep from her husband for thirty years. It was pure assumption on my part that Ron Wheaton hadn't known about Margaret's first marriage, but it was based on knowing Ron as I had.

I believed that when they couldn't have children of their own, Ron would have suggested that they find and attempt to reclaim Margaret's first child, if he'd known about the child. Ron loved children and it had been a source of great sorrow to him that he and Margaret had never had any. They'd tried to adopt, I think, years ago.

Ron would definitely have taken Margaret's child, if not when he first met her, certainly in later years. I felt sure of it.

"I don't know, Willa. It's not right to snoop through Margaret's things. And, I have no idea what Ron would have done." George was getting in his usual mode of trying to do the "right thing," which I didn't have a lot of time for.

I let him keep talking, but I continued to search.

I tried under the bed, behind all the pictures, in her lingerie drawer.

What I was looking for would have been overlooked by Hathaway and his men when they searched because they weren't looking for old documents and pictures.

George kept up a steady stream of objections until I finally turned to him and said, "Just look in plain sight, then. Don't touch anything. Or wait out in the car. I'm going to finish here, one way or the other."

CHAPTER THIRTY-TWO

Tampa, Florida
Sunday 1:00 p.m.
March 4, 2001

GIVING ME THE "I know that voice" look, which is the way he deals with my stubborn refusals to listen to his good counsel, George left me to go back into the living room and wait. I kept looking through drawers, books, and other likely hiding places in Margaret's room.

The Wheaton house doesn't have a basement. Most houses in South Tampa don't. The water table is too high. But the small ranch style house does have an attic that I could reach by pulling down the stairs in the hallway between the two bedrooms. Despite the cold outside, the tiny crawl space was stifling. No air had circulated here for a long time.

The attic was filled primarily with dust, bugs, cobwebs and stale air. Ron Wheaton had probably never been up here. He was as tall as I am, if not taller, and quite a bit heavier before he got sick. Ron couldn't have maneuvered around the ceiling joists and the electrical wiring on his stomach. There wasn't enough room for him to walk around on his knees, if he'd been so inclined, even before he developed ALS. After ALS, such a maneuver would have been impossible.

No, this attic was Margaret's exclusive domain. She was so small, she could have stored things here that no one else would ever find. There was no lighting except for what came in through the vents on the side of the house.

Between sneezes caused by the dust, I cursed my lack of planning in not bringing a flashlight. I waited for my eyes to adjust to the dimness. After a while, I was able to make out boxes. They were just out of arms' reach from the opening where I stood, trying to figure out how to get to them.

I hoisted myself onto the floor and slithered out toward the boxes off to the left side. The dust continued to make me sneeze and I felt a couple of crawly things on my bare midriff when my tee-shirt bunched up. Was I out of my mind? Probably. George says I'm stubborn, but I like to think of it as tenacity. Whatever you call it, I thought as I sneezed again, it's not always a positive trait.

Slithering a few more inches, I was able to touch the boxes, grab their flaps with my fingers, and pull them toward me. There were five in all. I couldn't raise up enough to move them quickly. Eventually, I inched them all toward the pull-down stairs and lowered myself back out through the opening. I took all five boxes down the stairs and sat them on the floor. When George came around the corner, he burst out laughing.

"What?"

"You look like a fly caught in a giant spider's trap," he said, when he could contain his mirth.

"Thanks a lot. I sure appreciate your help," I said, with more than a little annoyance, as I started to brush the dust and dirt off my black jeans and black tee-shirt.

My hands and face felt positively grimy, so I didn't dare wipe one with the other. I folded the stairs back up and went into the bathroom to survey the damage and wash up. George was right.

I saw my ridiculously filthy visage in the mirror and did the best I could to repair myself.

When I got back into the hallway, I found George had taken the boxes and put them on the kitchen table. He'd apparently decided that he'd speed up the process by helping out. He'd already opened the first box.

I surveyed the boxes first. This was where Margaret's organizational skills, so important in a legal secretary, had spilled over into her home life. Each box was clearly marked. As I'd suspected, all pre-dated Margaret's life with Ron Wheaton. Maybe, she'd put them up in the attic crawl space and forgotten them.

In any event, they were labeled "High School," "Taxes 1952-1965," "Mother," "Miami," and "School." All the boxes were the same size and color, suggesting they had been bought and organized around the same time. They were also about the same weight.

"George, let's take these home and look through them. I want to finish up here while Margaret's not home." To his credit, he'd given up arguing with me. He re-closed the box he'd opened and began carrying them all out to the trunk of the Bentley.

I went back to Ron Wheaton's bedroom for a last look.

Ron's room had been thoroughly searched by the police and I had watched them do it. I didn't really think there would be anything here that would help me solve Margaret's life riddles. But I looked anyway. I checked the drawers of the nightstands, looked in the dresser drawers, under the bed and in the closet. I felt inside the pockets of all the jackets and shirts.

I used to hide things in clothes I hadn't worn in a long time. I'd once lost a pair of diamond earrings for over five years because I'd hidden them in a pair of snow boots left in our attic.

I didn't know what I was looking for, but apparently Margaret and Ron Wheaton either never had anything to hide or had better hiding places than I'd been able to find. There was nothing in any of Ron's pockets and I was about to give up.

Then, I decided to go ahead and check all the pockets in all the closets. There were only three closets, so it wouldn't take long.

Glancing down at my watch, I saw we'd been here over an hour and a half, and I was worried that Margaret would get home and keep me from taking the boxes from the attic. Yet, I felt pulled to try the pockets before I left.

In the guest bedroom, all of the clothes were packed in hanging garment bags. I started with the first bag and checked Margaret's clothes.

Judging from the number of outfits she had, she and Ron must have once been avid square dancers and party goers. The closet was filled with petticoats and western wear, evening clothes and party outfits, all from an earlier time. The closet was small, like the other two, and I found nothing remarkable in any of the clothes: a few tissues, a pen, some coins and one or two matchbooks.

Remembering how I'd lost my earrings, I bent down and opened the large plastic boxes on the floor that contained western boots and dress shoes, one for Ron's and one for

Margaret's. In Margaret's box there was a pair of red cowboy boots. I smiled at the younger, more vibrant Margaret that I imagined must have worn them. But I found nothing hidden in their depths.

A similarly thorough search of Margaret's closet revealed nothing but the matronly dresses and sturdy shoes she now wore to work. I dutifully, and with much less enthusiasm, felt each of the pockets in her sweaters and dresses.

Then I bent down to check the shoes. The only thing I found was a great deal of sand on the bottom of her sneakers. I'd wasted over thirty minutes on this project and I could feel time was running out. I closed the closet door, took one last look around the bedroom, living room and kitchen, and let myself out.

I left the back door unlocked, the way I'd found it.

GEORGE AND I HAD Margaret's boxes on our kitchen table. We both knew what we were looking for. I was tempted to start with the box labeled "Miami," but I thought it would reflect more general information about Margaret's work for Mrs. Prieto. Instead, I selected the box labeled "Mother" on the theory that what I was interested in happened long after "High School," and the "Mother" box might contain clues about Margaret's child. George had taken the "Taxes" box. I felt I already knew what it would contain, since I'd seen Margaret's Social Security records. Dad walked in just as we got started and for sheer speed, we gave him the box marked "High School."

"Mother" turned out to relate not to Margaret as a mother, but to Margaret's mother. She had died in 1954, the year Margaret graduated from Plant High School. There were neatly labeled manila folders with Margaret's mother's birth certificate, death certificate, and life insurance policies that had paid just enough to bury her.

The death certificate listed her as "widowed" and said she'd died of "heart failure." I recalled Margaret telling me her father had been killed in World War II and her mother had never remarried. The death certificate gave the age at death as forty-three, significantly younger than Margaret was now.

There were a few pictures of Margaret's parents and Margaret with her mother, who was a much larger woman than Margaret, although still small.

The rest of this box contained memorabilia and letters between Margaret's parents when her father was stationed overseas during the war. Although the letters probably would have told me a lot about their marriage and the young Margaret's life, reading them felt too intrusive, somehow. I might read them later, I thought, but not right now. I set the letters back in the box, put the dusty lid back on and set the box aside.

I stretched my back and got a glass of water before attacking the box labeled "School," thinking I could get through it quickly. I noticed that Dad was completely immersed in the box labeled "High School." He'd only removed about half its contents, and he'd made little progress with what he'd taken out. I could see yellowed newspapers poking out from more labeled manila folders.

Whatever he'd found, it was certainly capturing his imagination.

George was just as immersed in the "Taxes" box, which from my vantage point looked like old tax returns and back-up receipts. Of course, George is a numbers man. Just looking at the prices of goods and salaries from 1954 to 1965 would interest him.

I shook my head and smiled at the differences between us, stretching my arms above my head, getting the kinks out, on my way to the bathroom to empty the tank of the gallons of coffee I'd drunk today.

When I came back, both Dad and George were still engrossed in their boxes, so I pulled the "School" box toward me and opened the top. Again, the folders, labeled in Margaret's neat block printing, faded from years in the attic, filled the box.

This one was about Margaret's career at business school where she'd learned to be a legal secretary. I flipped through the folders containing transcripts, résumés, letters seeking employment, a few pieces of written work that had earned her top marks, and some old class notes. I guessed that Margaret had simply put this box in the attic when she moved to the little house on Coachman Street and never thought about it again. I moved through the box quickly because there was nothing in it I needed.

Not too hopefully, I opened the remaining box, the one labeled "Miami." I expected materials related to Margaret's job with Mrs. Prieto, and I wasn't too far off. Again, the neatly labeled folders. This box contained more folders than the other two boxes I'd already looked through. One folder contained a death certificate for Margaret's employer, Mrs. Prieto, which explained why Margaret stopped working for her. It gave Mrs. Prieto's date of death as 1957, and said she died of cancer. There was a letter and résumé from Margaret to Mrs. Prieto dated three years earlier, when Margaret was still in high school, applying for the job as "companion."

I was piecing together Margaret's early life.

Just she and her mother had lived together after her father died in the war. When her mother died the year Margaret graduated from high school, she must have been interested in getting away and seeing a little more of the world. She'd applied for the job with Mrs. Prieto and gotten it, moving to Miami. It must have been fun to be in Miami in those days, even if one was stuck being a companion to an elderly invalid. Still, Tampa was a pretty sleepy town in 1954. There would have been relatively little here for the young Margaret. Miami was a fairly sleepy town then, too, but it would have seemed ever so much more exciting.

The "Miami" box contained several old newspaper articles about Mrs. Prieto, who must have been something of a socialite at the time. The house where Margaret's employer had lived was shown in several pictures. It was a mansion of magnificent proportions. Eighteen-year-old Margaret the orphan must have felt she was in the middle of a real adventure when she arrived to take a job with the obviously wealthy Mrs. Prieto.

I marveled again at the fortunes that were amassed in this country. Even in 1956 Miami, the gap between the poor and the wealthy was a vast chasm.

The folders held stories from the society pages of parties at Mrs. Prieto's house and even a few pictures of her. She was a childless widow, the same as Margaret is now. I wondered whether Margaret ever thought about that. About how our lives progress in repetitious patterns.

One of the stories, dated 1956, had Margaret's name in it. Someone had underlined her name with a blue pen, which was now faded and faint. I read the short piece. It said Margaret was Mrs. Prieto's constant companion on frequent trips to Nassau, Bahamas, where Mrs. Prieto also had a home.

It was somewhat surprising to me that travel between Nassau and Miami appeared to be easy in 1956. A short boat ride from

Miami, Nassau was a paradise, complete with casinos, at a time when legalized gambling didn't exist in Florida.

Another article mentioning Margaret described her gown as "chic" and her dancing as "superb." A picture of Margaret, in a gown that Jackie Onassis might have worn at about the same time, showed her dancing with a middle-aged man.

Clearly, the orphan girl from Tampa had landed in a posh environment and seemed to be thriving there. If Mrs. Prieto had lived, I wondered whether Margaret would have ever returned to Tampa.

CHAPTER THIRTY-THREE

Tampa, Florida
Sunday 5:15 p.m.
March 4, 2001

THERE WERE SEVERAL OTHER articles of this sort and I started to move through them more quickly until another faded blue underline caught my eye. The names caused me to read the small article completely. It said:

> *Gilbert Kelley, Jr., son of the president of Tampa Bay Bank, and his friend, David Martin, of Coconut Grove, were among the many young professionals at Mrs. Prieto's Gasparilla Bash, given in honor of her guests from Tampa, to coincide with Tampa's annual Gasparilla Pirate Parade. More than one hundred members of Miami society attended the gala event, which was a charity ball held to support Young Mothers' Second Chance, a national organization providing financial support to the young widows of the Korean conflict.*

Why did it never occur to me that Margaret might have been in contact with Gil Kelley in Miami? Just because they travel in different social circles now didn't mean they always had.

I looked over at Dad, who had the "High School" box.

Asked, "Dad, do you have high school yearbooks there?"

He pointed inside the box and I looked to find four high-school yearbooks for the years 1950 through 1954. I didn't know how old Gil Kelley was, exactly, but he was older than Margaret. I picked up the 1950 yearbook first and turned to the index.

Bingo, on the first try.

Gilbert Allen Kelley, Junior, was listed several times. The first few pictures were group shots: Gil on the football team, the basketball team, the tennis team, the golf team. Gil on the homecoming court and being crowned "King," just as I'd seen him crowned as Minaret Krewe King last night. Gil had been a senior that year, so he was four years older than Margaret. His senior class picture carried the title: Most Likely to Succeed.

Gil Kelley was attractive, athletic and popular. Maybe his father's owning the bank had something to do with his popularity, but he must have had some athletic skill, too. Margaret easily could have fallen in love with him. Probably every girl in her freshman class would have been swooning over the "dreamy" Gil Kelley, as he was described in one of the yearbook pictures.

"Dad, when did Gil Kelley work at the bank in Miami?"

He was still distracted by something he was reading from the "High School" box.

He said, "1955, why?"

I didn't answer because I was looking for a piece of paper and a pen so that I could sketch out the dates.

If Gil Kelley was a senior in high school in 1950, that meant he would have finished college in 1954, at the same time Margaret was graduating from high school.

Gil would have returned to Tampa that summer to sow his wild oats, as Marilee Aymes had put it to us when she told the story.

Margaret could have been one of those "wild oats," or she just could have known Kelley or some of the girls he dated. Margaret could have known him, although he would have been ahead of her in school.

It would have been only natural for them to hook up again in 1956 when they were both in Miami.

Kelley could have been drafted into the armed services, but for some reason, he wasn't.

I considered that Gil Kelley could have been her first husband, but Margaret said she'd believed her first husband had died. Kelley had been living right here in Tampa for years and Margaret had to know it. Tampa Bay Bank was highly visible, as was its current and former president.

So, Kelley must not have been the one.

But this other guy mentioned in the faded newspaper article, David Martin, it could have been him.

I looked through the four high school yearbooks just in case the first husband had been a high school sweetheart. I found no evidence of the young Margaret even having a social life at the time. There was one picture of her in each yearbook, the one taken with her class, and her senior picture in the 1954 book. Margaret was voted The Sweetest Girl.

Maybe we never surpass where we were in high school. I wrinkled my nose at the thought. I'd been voted the most likely to grow taller.

On my list, my doodles said something like this: 1950 Gil

Kelley graduates h.s.; 1954 college; 1955 moves to Miami. 1954 Margaret graduates h.s.; 1956 moves to Miami.

Coincidence? I don't believe in coincidences, but I didn't know what it meant, either.

Then I wrote: David Martin, 1953 Miami. Margaret married, 1956? Husband died? Margaret's baby born 1957?

I turned my attention back to the "Miami" box and now felt I knew what I was looking for.

I pulled out the folder labeled "Young Mothers' Second Chance."

And there it was.

The birth certificate. The adoption papers. The father's name and "deceased" following it. Baby's sex was listed as female. And at the very bottom of the folder was an obituary. For David Martin, who died in 1957 by accidental drowning.

The obituary had a picture of Martin on the top. The picture was over forty years old, yellowed and grainy. The hair was darker and the eyes more vibrant.

But I recognized him, and Margaret must have, too. The first time she laid eyes on him. The man who held the key to all her dreams and heartaches.

David Martin, a/k/a Armstrong Otter.

I'd taken the final folder, my coffee, and my cryptic notes back to the den to work it all through in my journal. An hour later, George and Dad both wandered in, with their most interesting pieces of the puzzle from Margaret's boxes. I'd switched to gin halfway through my scribbles. George poured himself and Dad a Scotch. We sat and watched the fire for a while.

"You were pretty engrossed in that 'High School' box. What did you find?" I asked Dad first.

"What you'd think might interest me. Quite a bit about Tampa during Margaret's high school years. She's kept some old newspaper accounts of events going on here in the early fifties, including some stories about Gil Kelley, Senior, and the hijinks of Gil Kelley, Junior."

"Anything you can use in your bank fraud case?" George asked him.

Dad said, "Maybe. Nothing conclusive, but it did seem the Kelleys lived pretty far above what I would think a 1950 banker's means would have been."

"Meaning?" I asked.

"Meaning Sandra Kelley may have been telling the truth. Maybe Senior did embezzle from the bank. And maybe that's where Gil, Junior, learned it. Doesn't excuse the thefts. Just gives me an explanation for them. One story was interesting, though. It was about Gil, Junior, being caught at an illegal poker game over in Ybor City on a Saturday night during his senior year. Charges were dropped because of who his parents were."

"I'd heard Kelley had a gambling problem. Being in Miami all those years must have made that worse," George offered.

"How so?" Dad asked.

"Well, Miami is a short hop over to Nassau, where gambling has always been legal. Of course, the casinos are all owned by the Mafia, or they were then. A young fellow with ready cash could easily and quickly get himself into a lot of trouble. Especially if he had a wild streak already," George told Dad, as another little piece of the puzzle clicked into place for me.

"I wonder..." Dad said aloud, letting his voice trail off as he stared into space.

"What?" I asked him.

"George, when you were in banking, did you have any

dealings with Caribbean offshore banks?" Dad asked, turning his attention to us.

George replied, "We were leery of the whole process, so we kept away from it."

"What are you two talking about?" I asked.

"Well," George explained, "when a large and reputable American bank like ours was queried about accepting millions of dollars from what amounted to little more than a laptop computer on a Caribbean island, we were more than just a little curious about the origin of the money. So we wouldn't take it."

"Not all of your competitors are so conscientious, though," Dad replied. "Some bankers are so happy to have the deposits that they don't question those accounts. They end up abetting money launderers. It's been going on for years, but recently the Feds have been poking into the practice. The offshore banking process is under investigation right now in the Senate investigations subcommittee. It seems American banks have facilitated quite a bit of money laundering through their so-called correspondent accounts for high-risk foreign banks."

"How much money are we talking about here?" I asked.

Dad said, "Well, I got an executive summary of the hearings the other day. The summary claimed a dozen offshore banks have moved billions of dollars through certain American banks in the last few years."

George whistled. "That's a lot of motivation."

"What are you thinking?" My brain was too mushy at the moment to grasp Dad's idea.

"He's suggesting that Gil Kelley may be embezzling even more than we first thought," George responded.

Dad, excited now, eyes twinkling, stood to pace and picked up the thread. "If Gil was laundering money from a Nassau rogue bank, he could have been taking even more than appeared on the legitimate books that I've looked at. He could be taking a cut off the top before the money is ever deposited."

"Which would give Kelley more than enough to share with Armstrong Otter. So why kill him?" I asked.

"True." Dad admitted, a bit deflated. "And the deals typically pay a finder's fee on the front end, too. That kind of a fee would usually be paid off the books. There would be no way to trace it. But, if they've been dealing in offshore banking, the Kelleys should be extraordinarily wealthy by now."

The Kelleys should be "wealthier than God," as the kids say. But they aren't.

Or at least, not obviously so. I filed away this piece of the puzzle in my weary brain. It fit somewhere.

George stood at the fireplace, trying to warm up, if the chill I was feeling was any indication. I asked him to throw another log on the blaze. We were all lost in our individual thoughts for a while.

Later, I looked down at my watch and noticed the rapidly fleeting time. "How about you, George, what did you learn? You looked pretty involved in your files, too."

"Clever of you to give me the box that you knew fit my interests, hmm?" he smiled. "Margaret's tax returns from 1952, before she graduated from high school, until 1965, when she married Ron Wheaton, were full of the names of old Tampa lions. People whose names I've read and heard, but never met. Or friends of ours long before we met them."

Promising.

Dad asked, "Like who?"

"Well, Margaret worked at several law offices from the time she came back from that Miami business school. One of them was the CJ's office, did you know that?" As I shook my head, George continued, "She's also been on the board of Young Mothers' Second Chance since 1958. She's given them a bundle of money over the years."

And I knew why, if they didn't yet.

He said, "There's also a gap in her work history for about six months. Even when she was in business school, she held down a few part-time jobs. But for six months in 1957, she had no income at all. I wonder how she lived? And why she didn't work?"

Of course, I already knew the answer to that one, too.

We continued comparing notes and working out the back story, but I was convinced that Margaret had met, fallen in love with and married David Martin in 1955 or 1956. She'd become pregnant, which I doubt that he or anyone else knew. Martin and Gil Kelley were embezzling from the bank. They must have been having a wonderful time over at the Nassau casinos, where they had no doubt met Margaret while she was working as Mrs. Prieto's companion there. I made a note to check the Miami marriage licenses, but I suspected we'd find the license, if at all, recorded in a Nassau, Bahamas, clerk's office.

When the bank examiners got close to uncovering Gil Kelley and David Martin's early embezzlement, they must have come up with the suicide scheme to get the bonding company to pay back their debts. When David Martin "died," Margaret gave birth to her daughter and gave her up for adoption. She had no support to raise a child. Margaret returned to Tampa heartbroken and didn't marry again for nine years. Then, she married Ron Wheaton.

Did Ron know? The whole story?

It would have been like Margaret to tell him before she

married him. And it would have been like Ron to have married her anyway.

On the last day I saw him, Ron was as in love with Margaret as ever. I believed he would have done anything for her, always.

How Kelley convinced Martin to go along with the suicide scheme, I still didn't know. Whose body did they bury?

There was only one person left alive to tell me that now, and I intended to ask him. I didn't have the strength to do it tonight. I needed sleep. To work out a few of the loose ends first in my office in the morning.

CHAPTER THIRTY-FOUR

Tampa, Florida
Monday 8:30 a.m.
March 5, 2001

THE *U.S. V. AIELO* CASE was begging for my attention. My
clerks had read the briefs and prepared a three-page order for my
review. I read it through quickly. I was about to sign the order
transferring the case to Philadelphia for trial, when the short
statement of relevant facts at the beginning caught my attention.

Mr. Aielo reinvented himself in Miami. He opened a club in
1992 that was destroyed by fire, providing the insurance money
to start his more trendy and lucrative clubs believed to be
money-laundering operations.

Something about the statement tickled my brain.

I chased it around in my head for a while, but couldn't catch
it. I re-read the passage several times and finally put it aside,
knowing that I'd remember if I thought about something else,
and let the thought peek around the corner like a kitten.

Only in this case, it was a lion.

About thirty minutes later, it fairly pounced on my thinking with claws fully extended and a deafening roar.

I checked the computer once again. In just a few minutes, I found the death certificate I was looking for.

Death records for Miami going back fifty years had recently been updated in the Dade County database, but not integrated into the search service database.

Which explained why I didn't find it when I had looked the first time.

I PULLED OUT THE tattered article George had given me from the *Tribune* the Sunday after Gasparilla and read it one more time. The article related the story of a former IRS agent who had made a living in much the same way as Dad did, by pursuing white-collar criminals. The agent compiled the more legal methods of changing your life and wrote a book about it. The article reflected the agent's advice about how to hide your assets and disappear.

The most difficult aspects of changing one's identity were not the initial strategies, such as acquiring foreign passports under assumed names. Instead, the hardest thing to do, the agent said, was to cut all ties to your old self. Most people can't manage it and eventually return to their old lives in some fashion.

The article talked about well-known, admitted former Mafia criminals who became government informants, but have abandoned the federal Witness Protection Program. The fear of Mafia retribution has disappeared and was probably overstated anyway, the agent claimed.

But the big problem is that once one creates a certain

lifestyle, it's nearly impossible to abandon all of the past. Friends, family and co-workers are our firmly tethered human anchors. They drag us back when we float too far away. Some secrets never leave us alone. Eastern mystics say that no karmic debt ever remains unpaid. Scientists claim the human body replaces itself once every seven years. The problem is, the new body is exactly like the old one. It's got the same scars, the same colors and a few more aches and pains.

We think the past is past, but it's the foundation for all that comes after. The past seeps into our very sinews and remains in our cells, just like the genes we're born with.

It doesn't mean that humans can't change. But it does mean we don't change much at the fundamental level.

Those cells just keep reproducing themselves, over and over and over.

Americans attempt to reinvent themselves all the time, without hiding their assets and disappearing. How ironic that the Fitzgerald House case had found its way to my docket, obscuring my first clue to Otter's identity.

After all, F. Scott Fitzgerald's myth of reinvention when James Gatz became Jay Gatsby, was the very reason for Fitzgerald House's existence as a charitable organization.

Like many clues, this one was right in front of me all the time, and I didn't see it.

Without Gatsby, Fitzgerald House would have had no historical significance. Without Fitzgerald House, Martin's becoming Otter might never have been discovered.

Yet, James Gatz did no more than get a fresh start by attempting to leave his past in the past. I thought of everyone I knew who has done the same thing.

Jim Harper has become a good husband and father. Suzanne

302 | DIANE CAPRI

Harper has become a wife and soon-to-be mother.

Mariam Richardson became a well-respected matron and wife of the Chief Judge.

Sandra Kelley, an abandoned and adopted child, was now a wealthy socialite.

Even George and I changed our lives from a staid banker and Detroit attorney to a Tampa restaurateur and judge.

To David Martin and Gilbert Kelley, young men who were looking for fun and fortune gambling in Nassau and wound up on the wrong side of the Mafia-owned casinos, re-inventing the obscure David Martin must have seemed the logical answer.

The readily accessible money from Kelley's bank was an overwhelming temptation to solve their problems. They met the young, unchaperoned Margaret, another American, and added her to their youthful exuberance.

In 1956, when the bank examiners arrived, Martin and Kelley must have panicked to learn that their actions had serious potential consequences.

The suicide plot they concocted had the added benefits of stopping the investigation and forcing the bonding company to pay off their debt to the bank. They must have also found a source of living money for Martin "after death."

Exactly how they managed that, I couldn't guess.

Maybe that was when they got hooked up with the offshore banks. The entire scheme would only have worked if Martin had no ties to anyone.

Either Kelley didn't know that Martin and Margaret had married, or he didn't care. Or maybe they just saw no way out.

It was the kind of youthful solution that didn't plan for all the consequences. Like maybe there was a child on the way.

I had no way of knowing how long Martin had managed to

stay away from Kelley. But, at some point, whatever money they had managed to get Martin for his fresh start must have run out.

Martin/Otter seemed to have an insatiable appetite for spending that could only have been a problem from the very beginning.

So Martin resurfaced as Armstrong Otter, and Kelley had been helping to feed Otter's voracious demands for cash from the vaults of the Tampa Bay Bank, via offshore banking deposits.

When did Ron Wheaton find out that Margaret's one true love was not dead? That he was, instead, alive and well and living just over the bay in Pass-a-Grille?

It was likely a long while ago. The Wheatons didn't socialize with the Kelleys and their set, but it was unlikely that Martin/Otter would have been able to stay away from Margaret. Or maybe he saw Margaret by accident.

In any event, Ron definitely knew about Otter and planned to protect Margaret in death as he always had in life.

There were just a few loose ends yet for me to tie up, and I would have it all resolved.

I picked up the phone and called the CJ's chambers, dialing the number for his secretary instead of himself. I confirmed that CJ was in his office, grabbed my purse, and walked the short block between my building and his. It took me only about ten minutes from the time I'd made the call.

When I arrived, unannounced, CJ consented to see me. He wasn't in a position to antagonize me today, since I still hadn't completed my testimony in his ethics hearing. I tried to keep the envy from putting an unnecessary edge in my tone as I sat in his palatial chambers, admiring the rich mahogany and beautiful upholstery.

He offered me coffee. I declined. I didn't want to get too comfortable—with him or in these surroundings.

I said, "I came to ask you some questions about Armstrong Otter."

CJ looked down at his desk, then back up at me, with resignation. "I was afraid that was why you're here."

I came right out with it. "Why was Otter asking you for money outside Minaret Friday before the Knight Parade?"

He jerked back, startled. "How do you know about that?"

"I was the one who walked past the two of you. Didn't you recognize me?"

Shaking his head, he said, "I didn't want to recognize you. I was hoping you were a misplaced tourist."

"But, I wasn't. Tell me what you were arguing about."

For a few seconds, CJ looked like he would refuse. Or, at least, come up with an excuse not to answer the question.

He spent some time rearranging the pens on his desk, fidgeting in his chair. He looked past me to the Picasso on his wall that his wife had given him when he was elected Chief Judge. Then, he sighed with resignation, and told me what I'd come to find out.

CJ said, "Otter had been in trouble for a long time, but I didn't know about it. I swear, I didn't. I didn't even know that he was involved in a criminal case until after I'd tried to get you to dismiss Fitzgerald House."

CJ sounded insistent, because he was. He needed me to believe he hadn't known that Otter was being prosecuted for a massive fraud that could have put Otter in prison for much longer than the rest of his life.

The curious thing was that I believed CJ hadn't known. Because I hadn't known.

Just because we're judges, doesn't mean we're any better informed than most other citizens on a lot of issues. There's no way I could know all the cases pending on my docket. There were just too many of them to keep track, except on the computers.

I nodded my understanding and CJ continued, "Well, in the past, Otter resolved complaints against him by offering restitution of some kind, counting on people like me and Mariam to keep quiet because of shame and pride. Or, if that didn't work, he'd deny the validity of the complaint and threaten to counter-sue. He told me later that the complaints that got the U.S. Attorney's attention were started by that restaurant guy in Michigan. Otter said the guy had bought millions of dollars worth of gems, intending to re-sell them for billions. When the guy wasn't able to make the profit he wanted, he collected a bunch of other claims and filed a criminal complaint."

Otter's version of the facts wasn't too far from the allegations made by the U.S. Attorney. It was easy to believe that Otter probably would have been convicted. There didn't seem to be much of a defense building there.

I asked, "How does that relate to Otter trying to get money from you?"

"He was shaking down everyone he knew. He thought if he could get enough money together to pay off the restaurant guy, he could get the criminal complaint dismissed and then avoid going to jail."

"Sounds like a plan," I said, with some sarcasm. "At least, it would have been better than getting himself killed to stay out of prison."

CJ gave me a grimace. "I'm sure Otter didn't plan on his arm-twisting scheme getting him killed. He'd had good luck with it in the past."

306 | DIANE CAPRI

Yes, I thought, he certainly had. For years, he'd been collecting money from every available source.

I was sure now that Otter had killed Ron Wheaton because he'd found out that Ron had life insurance and other assets worth over $7 million.

That was probably why he'd contacted Margaret again after all the years he had been living in the Bay area, too. He could have found her at any time. His buddy, Gil Kelley, certainly would have told Otter where to find Margaret.

And Otter's desire to stay out of prison explained, to a certain extent, Gil Kelley's continued embezzlement from Tampa Bay Bank.

Otter was probably using their past crimes to support his ongoing ones.

I didn't doubt that Kelley also had a gambling problem. That's one addiction that can easily take over your life. Gambling, plus Otter's voracious and insatiable appetite for luxurious living, gave Kelley a powerful motive for murder, too.

Otter had been bleeding Kelley for decades. And who knows? If they were both involved in Mafia money laundering, they might have wanted to stop. The Mafia has a low tolerance for quitters. The sky was literally the limit to their need for money.

But as I sat there working it through, I knew Gilbert Kelley wasn't Otter's only source of cash. Otter never would have thought Kelley could give him enough to satisfy all of the creditors listed in the *U.S. v. Otter* criminal indictment.

"One last thing, CJ," I said. "Did you give Otter any money?"

His defeat was now complete. He shrunk before my very eyes. The man who had seen fit to lecture me on appropriate judicial conduct had let himself down. He couldn't meet his own high standards, to say nothing of the lower standards set by the law for the behavior of judges. Paying a blackmailer was more than the appearance of impropriety.

There was no way his behavior, and the reason for it, wouldn't become public.

The voice was barely recognizable to me when he said, "What else could I do? Mariam couldn't be humiliated again."

So, I added two more names to the list of possible suspects in Otter's death, although I continued to believe whoever had killed him hadn't intended to do so.

Lack of intent could keep the killer off death row, anyway.

I had to make one phone call and then I could do the final interview.

CHAPTER THIRTY-FIVE

Tampa, Florida
Monday 4:30 p.m.
March 5, 2001

GILBERT AND SANDRA KELLEY lived in a new house in the gated community at the foot of Gandy Boulevard. Technically they had a Bayshore address, although their house was on a cul-de-sac that served six homes. All were three-storied, peach-colored structures built to have a waterfront address without Bayshore Boulevard running between them and the water.

The Kelleys had moved here from their home near the Tampa Yacht Club a couple of years ago. We'd attended the housewarming party, but we hadn't been back since. Even though Gil Kelley is a charter member of Minaret Krewe, the Kelleys are not in our social circle. Avoiding the Kelleys was mostly my doing, but George didn't protest.

The gate wasn't guarded, but it did have a system that required a numerical code to open. I knew another couple with a home in this development, so I rang them on the intercom and asked their maid to let me in. Like many communities in Tampa, if you know the staff, you can expect quite a bit better treatment than if you don't. I make it a point to cultivate the domestic help of my friends and acquaintances, just as I cultivate my friends' office staffs. You never know when you might need a favor.

I'd had enough experience confronting killers to know that I needed backup. I'd called Chief Hathaway from my car and asked him to meet me here in half an hour. He wouldn't be able to wait that long. I expected him sooner. I only had about fifteen minutes to speak to Gil Kelley alone. What surprised me when the maid let me into the front hall were the loud, angry voices from the sitting room on the right. One of those voices belonged to Margaret Wheaton.

The maid tried to keep me waiting, but I pushed past her and went into the room where Gil and Margaret were arguing. I caught the tail end of Margaret's accusation.

"You didn't have to kill him!"

"No, Gil," I said as I entered the fray, "You didn't. So why did you?"

They were both startled into silence when I appeared. Margaret had been crying. Kelley seemed as cool and collected as ever. It was an act to keep Margaret from going completely wild.

He asked, "Why did I what?"

"Why did you kill David Martin?" Again, both were shocked by my statement.

Margaret jerked her head over in my direction. Demanded, "How did you know about him?"

"You told me, Margaret. Don't you remember? You said you had been married before and you believed your husband had died. But he hadn't. It didn't take a lot for me to connect him to Armstrong Otter."

That was true, but some people would call breaking, entering and burglarizing Margaret's home of her most personal possessions quite a lot.

I tried not to add up the list of my own crimes. I was fairly sure Margaret would never file a complaint against me, and my intentions were good.

I wish I had remembered the saying about "good intentions" and the road to hell.

I asked, "Has he told you why he and David Martin faked Martin's death?" I looked over at Gil Kelley and could see he was getting a little rattled now. He probably felt he could subdue and control Margaret Wheaton, but he knew dealing with me was another matter altogether.

"They did it to cover up Kelley's crimes," I continued. "They'd been embezzling from the bank to cover those trips to Nassau where you met them."

Margaret drew a sharp breath.

I pressed on. "When the time came to pay the piper, they needed the money from the bonding company to cover the debt. Killing David Martin was an easy way to get it, wasn't it Gil? You didn't care about Margaret or her husband, did you? You gave no thought to the child."

When I mentioned the child, out of the corner of my eye I saw Margaret lift her right arm.

Watching Kelley, I didn't turn fast enough to catch Margaret before she pulled the trigger. The sound was deafening.

Gil slumped against the wall, holding his chest, while Margaret crumpled to the floor at the same time.

I didn't know who to help first, but the noise brought Sandra Kelley and the maid running into the room. I left them to attend to Gil while I checked on Margaret.

She was in shock, holding tight to the gun, which was still radiating heat where she held it out to her right side. I left it in her hand.

I heard the siren of Chief Hathaway's car as it pulled into the driveway, followed by his loud pounding on the front door.

He was just in time to arrest Sandra Kelley for the death of Armstrong Otter.

CHAPTER THIRTY-SIX

Tampa, Florida
Saturday 10:30 a.m.
March 10, 2001

THE GASPARILLA FESTIVAL OF the Arts began on
Saturday. For the first time during Gasparilla month, daylight
brought a bright, warm Tampa morning. I looked forward to
spending the entire day at the festival.

George and I planned to walk around downtown on Ashley
Drive and in Curtis Hixon Park with Dad and Suzanne, enjoying
the many fine art pieces on display for the two-day festival. The
live entertainment promised groups from schools in both
Hillsborough and Pinellas Counties during the daytime. Jazz
vocalists and Latin bands would round out the music in the
evening.

All of us were interested in the jewelry exhibits and the fate
of Armstrong Otter's "Gasparilla Gold" pin.

We were looking forward to a day of relaxation, beauty and
music.

Margaret was going to the festival with us. I went to collect her while everyone else was still getting ready. When I pulled into the driveway of her small home, I saw that she already had a "For Sale" sign on the front lawn. I parked in the driveway and went to the front door.

Fully intending to put my breaking and entering days behind me, I rang the bell.

Margaret came to the door and ushered me inside to wait while she collected her fanny pack. She sat on the sofa across from my chair and tied on her red walking shoes. Today, she was dressed in a snazzy red silk slacks outfit that would have been more suitable for Suzanne. If I'd ever thought of Margaret as "grandmotherly," she was so only in the thoroughly current sense that grandmothers can be so young and vibrant, too.

I watched Margaret with recognition that, once again, life is often not what it appears. I had thought Margaret was an elderly, happily married woman, utterly content with the quiet life. Nothing could have been further from the truth. Instead, she was a lively woman with a life and a mind of her own. I would miss the Margaret I had created in my mind, but I felt more confident that this Margaret would get the most out of the rest of her life.

"Margaret, it's time for you to tell me some things, now that Chief Hathaway has decided not to prosecute you for shooting Gil."

Gil Kelley didn't die. Margaret had wounded him in the shoulder and he spent time at Tampa General Hospital before being arrested for theft and fraud. He's hired a well-known defense attorney to try to get him off, and he probably will.

Maybe Kelley had some kind of conscience, after all. He couldn't be held to account for ruining Margaret's life. Perhaps he accepted that pressing criminal charges against her would be more than he should, in all decency, do.

"Like what?" she asked me, bent over at the waist, tying the red shoelaces.

"Several unanswered questions have been bothering me. For instance, why did you faint when you saw Armstrong Otter in our courtroom on the day of the Fitzgerald House motions?"

She could have told me to mind my own business, I guess. But as much as I had underestimated Margaret, she wouldn't be rude to me. I might not have given her enough credit for having a full life, but she had spent every day with me for eons. I did understand some things about her character.

Margaret dusted off her hands, reached into her pocket and pulled out a lace handkerchief, the kind my grandmother once carried. I hadn't seen a woman with a lace handkerchief in years. Somehow, it didn't seem odd.

Margaret shrugged and smiled slightly as she answered my question. "My life hasn't turned out like I thought it would. When I graduated from Plant High School, I was the first person in my family to have gone that far in school. My mother was so proud of me. I felt I had the world by the tail. I was going to go great places, do great things."

She sounded as excited as that long-ago school girl.

"Like what?"

"Oh, I don't know that I knew exactly what I would do, even then. But I didn't expect to wind up a sixty-five-year-old adulteress. I suppose, if I had grandchildren, they'd be appalled," she smiled, with a little wickedness and no regret.

"So you were having an affair with Armstrong Otter?"

"I wasn't having an affair with Armstrong Otter. At least, I didn't know that I was. I'd never met Armstrong Otter in my life before that day in the courtroom."

"I don't understand," I said.

"No, I don't suppose you do. Your life has been so different from mine, Willa. You've never been on your own. You've never been completely free, with no one to answer to and only your whims to guide you. You wouldn't know what it's like to fall madly in love with a dashing young man who loved you back, and have no chaperone to tell you 'No.' You have no idea how quickly and completely a young girl with a little spirit can lose her heart. And her head."

As much as I hated to admit it, even to myself, Margaret was right.

I had never been so footloose, so free with myself.

I've always felt a keen sense of responsibility, a need to work hard, to keep my nose to the grindstone.

I didn't know what a carefree life would be like, but I was more than a little envious of those who had lived one.

"So you were in love with Otter?"

"Not exactly. I fell in love with David Martin in Nassau. He was friends with Gil Kelley, a boy from home. Although Gil and I certainly were never social equals. David was handsome, kind, fun. I ran into the two of them one day in the straw market and we started doing things together. Exciting things. Like drinking and gambling and riding in fast cars. Things I'd never done before. I loved it. And pretty soon, I loved David, too. It was a short step from there to an affair and a secret marriage a few months later." She shook her head at her own folly.

"You must have been thrilled, then?" I imagined a younger, carefree Margaret, in love and happy with the man of her dreams.

"For a short while, I was. Exceedingly happy. Happier than I'd ever been before or have ever been since. But then David died and I was devastated. We'd kept our marriage a secret, so I couldn't tell anyone I was a widow," she said.

Margaret went to the funeral, where they had a closed casket. No one came except Martin's co-workers from the bank. She never saw his body or knew who identified it.

"For a long time, I thought David really hadn't died," she told me. "The kind of wishful thinking young girls engage in when they want to avoid the truth."

"But you were right. He hadn't died," I reminded her.

"Yes, but I didn't know that. I didn't know it for forty years," she sighed.

A moment later, she explained, "Right after David died, I found out I was pregnant. There was no way I could have raised a child alone in those days. So I gave the baby up for adoption, came back to Tampa. Eventually, I met and married Ron Wheaton and started a new life. I thought Ron would be my life forever. Until I saw David Martin again, quite by accident. I was over at St. Pete Beach, just thinking, one day. I went into the Hurricane restaurant for lunch. Ron was dying, my life was changing before my eyes. The man I had always loved more than any other was truly alive. I had no choice but to keep loving him. I counted on Ron to understand that." She blinked back tears at the memory.

Another piece of the puzzle fit into place. Margaret's reaction to Otter when she saw him in the courtroom had bothered me. What had caused her to faint? There was nothing particularly shocking about his appearance as far as I could tell. Otter was dressed a little better for court, but otherwise, looked much the same as I had seen him the day Ron Wheaton died.

But Margaret hadn't known "David Martin" was "Armstrong Otter."

It was hearing her lover called by the name of a man she knew to be accused of countless crimes in *U.S. v. Otter*, the case on my docket that she was familiar with, that crushed her.

Margaret's dreams of a return to an idyllic life were extinguished by that chance encounter; Otter could have continued to lie to her for a long time if she hadn't seen him in the courtroom.

"How did you know Otter had killed Ron?" My gut had been right on this one. Chief Hathaway had confirmed the syringe I'd found in Minaret's azalea bushes was Ron Wheaton's murder weapon. And he'd confirmed Otter's fingerprints on it.

Otter had easily overpowered Ron and injected him in the stomach. The medical examiner found the puncture.

Margaret shrugged. "Just a feeling. Ron and I had been arguing about Otter, whom I still thought was David Martin at the time. Ron knew all about my marriage to Martin and our daughter, of course. But he also knew about Otter living in Pass-a-Grille. Ron wanted Otter to stop seeing me. They quarreled the day of the Parade of Pirates at Minaret. At first, I really thought Ron had had a heart attack. But when the suggestion was made that he'd been murdered, I just felt Otter had killed him. It made sense. No one else would want to hurt Ron."

"Now, let me ask you something," she said to me. I nodded. "How did you know it was Sandra who had killed Otter?"

Margaret managed to say the name clearly, without choking up, which I saw as another sign she was healing.

What should I tell her, though?

I didn't know Sandra had killed Otter. Not for sure.

But when Hathaway told me he'd found a witness who saw Margaret push Otter to the ground on Eighteenth Street and leave him there, I remembered how much alike Sandra and Margaret had looked that night.

I suspected Sandra but couldn't figure her motive.

Until Dad told me about the offshore bank deals.

Sandra was an officer of Tampa Bay Bank, too. She easily could have set up the offshore deals and taken the finder's fee. I figured Gil didn't know Sandra was taking the finder's fee. Nor did she know Gil was embezzling funds from the bank after the deposits had been made. Somehow, Otter had found out and was bleeding them both.

I made the connection when I remembered cutting my hand on the sharp sword point of Sandra's lapel pin on the day of the Distance Classic. The pin that was a perfect copy of Otter's Gasparilla Gold.

As nasty as Sandra had been to me and to Dad, it was no small bet that she was as vicious as a female tiger when protecting her children and her way of life.

Otter must have threatened to expose her thefts when he tried to squeeze her for more money. Sandra probably hadn't meant to kill him when she shoved him down. But we'd never know.

"Just a lucky guess," I said, in response to Margaret's question. "Let's go."

I pulled Margaret up off the couch, helped her lock the door, and we fairly sauntered out to Greta, who already had her top down, basking in the Florida sunshine.

Today, Margaret and Willa would have a carefree, frivolous adventure. And, I vowed, more such days to come.

It was long past time for me to lighten up.

EPILOGUE

USING WHAT WE HAD learned from Margaret's old boxes and what she told us afterward, Dad filed a federal complaint against Gil and Sandra Kelley. Dad hopes the Kelleys will be convicted and go to prison. The insurance company will pay off some of the money they embezzled. On Dad's recommendation, the company sued Gil and Sandra for restitution. The legal wrangling will go on for years, but at least Dad stopped the bleeding from Tampa Bay Bank.

Margaret has retired. She was eligible to retire anyway and she wants to spend time looking for her daughter. Adoption laws in Florida have changed in the last forty years. With the help of a good investigator, Margaret should be able to find her only child.

Ron Wheaton's estate went to Margaret. He had no other heirs and since no one objected, the life insurance company paid the death benefits to Margaret. She was lucky, but she also was helped along by a certain United States District Court judge.

Not me.

The CJ.

He had not only employed Margaret at one time, but he thought very highly of her work at the court. CJ made a couple of telephone calls and actually did influence someone to do the right thing.

Not that he thought of it all on his own.

The CJ's investigation was settled quietly when he admitted guilt. He was able to arrange a confidential agreement allowing him to remain on the bench in an administrative capacity until retirement. His opportunities for advancement to the Eleventh Circuit Court of Appeals are ruined now. This is unfortunate for me, since the only hope I had of getting rid of him was the Peter Principle—to have him kicked upstairs to Atlanta. I thought maybe this experience might make him more humble.

But, of course, it did nothing of the kind.

Dad and Suzanne returned to New York after the Gasparilla Festival of the Arts. Dad was tempted to buy a few more of Otter's "Jewels of the World." Since Otter had died, Dad thought they'd increase in value because of the notoriety of the case. We talked him out of it for the time being. We can only hope that he forgets about the gems until after Otter's estate is settled.

Otter left Margaret everything in his will, except that his debts so far exceeded his assets that she'll be unlikely to inherit anything.

Margaret did want the Gasparilla Gold pin that Otter had entered in the Festival of the Arts. She had to pay fair value for it, which was considerably higher because it won the Raymond James Financial Best of Show award.

What she inherited from Ron Wheaton's estate, after I gave it all over to her, made Margaret a wealthy woman.

She hopes to spend the money spoiling her grandchildren.

EARLY IN MARCH, AFTER all the Gasparilla hoopla had finally ended and everyone had left, George and I were sitting at our favorite booth in the Sunset Bar, enjoying the quiet. My soul-mother, Kate Austin, walked in unannounced, two days early from her month-long trip to Italy.

I jumped up from the booth and hugged her like I hadn't seen her in thirty years, not just thirty days. I was telling her how much I missed her and how happy I was to have her home, when I noticed, finally, that she wasn't alone.

A young man stood behind her.

He looked to be very Italian and about twenty-five years old. He had dark, curly hair and fabulously blue eyes that reminded me of the Aegean. Kate was always bringing someone by the restaurant asking George to give them work.

Oh, no, I thought. Not another chef. The last one she'd offered us was Japanese.

I could see George preparing to tell the young fellow that George's restaurant didn't need any more chefs at the moment, when Kate pulled back from me a little and gave George a hug, too.

Then, holding both our hands, she said, "Willa, George, darlings, I'd like you to meet Leonardo Columbo. My husband."

THE END

ABOUT THE AUTHOR

Diane Capri is a *New York Times*, *USA Today*, and worldwide bestselling author.

She's a recovering lawyer and snowbird who divides her time between Florida and Michigan. An active member of Mystery Writers of America, Author's Guild, International Thriller Writers, Alliance of Independent Authors, and Sisters in Crime, she loves to hear from readers and is hard at work on her next novel.

Please connect with her online:

Website: http://www.DianeCapri.com
Twitter: http://twitter.com/@DianeCapri
Facebook: http://www.facebook.com/Diane.Capri1
http://www.facebook.com/DianeCapriBooks

If you would like to be kept up to date with infrequent email including release dates for Diane Capri books, free offers, gifts, and general information for members only, please sign up for our Diane Capri Crowd mailing list. We don't want to leave you out! Sign up here:

http://dianecapri.com/contact

Made in the USA
Middletown, DE
17 December 2023

46036147R00194